Suzanne's place was watering daisies, not skulking after druggies.

Logan understood why she wanted to do this. She'd lost someone. But she didn't know what revenge could do to you—what it could turn you into.

He'd once vowed vengeance against the entire criminal element. And he'd gotten lost in his own twisted maze of paybacks.

He understood revenge, all right. It was an empty exercise in emotions that would destroy you if you weren't careful.

And that was why Suzanne Stewart would not fit into this scheme. She would bring raw emotion into the operation. And he didn't want that.

He wanted her out.

Dear Reader,

We've got a book this month that every romance reader will want to add to her personal collection, the conclusion of *New York Times* bestselling author Nora Roberts's *Night Tales*. It's called *Nightshade*, and it's also our American Hero title this month. And once you know those three facts, what else is there to say? Except—of course—don't miss it!

We've got lots more great reading for you, too. Diana Whitney's back with *Midnight Stranger*, the sequel to her popular *Still Married*, her first book for the Intimate Moments line. Carla Cassidy, a popular writer in several of our other lines— including spooky newcomer Shadows—debuts with *One of the Good Guys*. Marilyn Tracy is back with *Extreme Justice*, Elley Crain returns with *New Year's Resolution*, and new author Suzette Vann makes a promising first appearance with *His Other Mother*.

Once again, Intimate Moments is the place to be if you're looking for some of the best romantic reading to be found anywhere.

As always, enjoy!

Yours,

Leslie Wainger
Senior Editor and Editorial Coordinator

NEW YEAR'S RESOLUTION

Elley Crain

Published by Silhouette Books

America's Publisher of Contemporary Romance

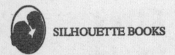

SILHOUETTE BOOKS

ISBN 0-373-07533-2

NEW YEAR'S RESOLUTION

Books by Elley Crain

Silhouette Intimate Moments

Deep in the Heart #478
New Year's Resolution #533

ELLEY CRAIN

is the pseudonym used by the writing team of Carol Mendenhall and Elyse Allen. Elyse grew up one of six children on three hundred acres of South Texas brushland. When she isn't busy writing, she's busy teaching high school English and watching her two daughters at athletic events. Romance has always been a part of Elyse's life—from her honeymoon in Jamaica to candlelight dinners—and she views writing romances as a natural extension of the things she loves.

Carol is married, with two very active sons who think it's great that Mom is finally getting her "love books" published. Outside of reading and writing romances, she enjoys scuba diving. Carol confesses that she writes romances because "I fell in love on a blind date and still feel those special tingles when my husband looks at me."

To Ruth, Helen, Ruth Dean and Elaine—
strong, warm, independent women who taught us to
go for it.

Chapter 1

Nothing to wear to a drug bust. Absolutely nothing.

Standing in front of her open closet, Suzanne Stewart wiped her sweaty palms on her jeans, and launched another search. None of her swingy skirts and silky pastel blouses looked right, especially not the ones with lace around the big collars. Her dresses had too many flowers on them. Maybe leggings and a tunic?

Suzanne checked her watch. She'd given herself exactly one hour to drive into Austin, and even with the excellent highway system in Texas, she'd be cutting it close. She had only ten more minutes to make her choice. She decided that since she wasn't really going to a drug bust this morning, but was only meeting with the police, it would be all right to wear a skirt and blouse.

Today she was going to meet the man who would help her fulfill her New Year's resolution to put Natalie's killers in jail. Keep them from ever killing anyone else with their drugs that promised dreams but delivered death. Fighting back the tears, she remembered the pledge she'd made to herself at Natalie's grave site six weeks ago that she'd do whatever it took to stop them.

"I'm not going to do it." Logan Davis threw the manila folder onto his boss's desk, turned around and headed for the door.

"Stop right there," Dan Rider boomed. "What are you talking about?"

"I'm not going to take a Girl Scout and put her under-cover." Logan faced his old friend, pointing at the material on the desk. "It's too dangerous."

Dan picked up the folder and glanced at the name in the corner. Suzanne Stewart. He sighed. "I know this is un-usual, but—"

"Unusual! Hell, this is one for the books. Have you looked in here?" Logan yanked the file away from Dan. As he was leafing through the information, he continued talk-ing. "This girl—"

"She's twenty-eight years old."

"I don't care if she's fifty-five—she's still a *girl*. Look at her life. She's never been more than one hundred miles from home. She teaches Sunday school, was a Girl Scout until she was seventeen, works in some flower shop. Just look at her picture." He hurled the eight-by-ten glossy at Dan.

"I've seen it," Dan said, but glanced down anyway to see the heart-shaped face, the open, clear emerald eyes and the welcoming smile. Raising his head, his eyes met Logan's evenly.

"And you still think she's suitable? Well, then, you're closer to retirement than you think." Logan began pacing in front of the desk. As he came to the wall at the far end of the office, he swung around and launched another volley. "You want this sweet, naive girl—" he looked at the raised eyebrow of the chief "—excuse me, *woman*, to help me ferret out and stop the drug business in that little town she lives in, Gruenville?"

"Yes," Dan said quietly but firmly.

Logan swore loudly and started pacing again, searching for the right words to hurl at his stubborn boss to make him understand how ludicrous this whole idea was. He knew they needed to get into the tight network in Gruenville, the safe haven where more and more drug deals were being made. But he also knew, sensed with his unfailing gut instinct, that this Suzanne was not the one to help them.

He looked again at the picture on the desk. Drawn to the open naive look in her eyes, he knew this woman could never tell a lie and make it stick.

Hell, he was opposed to ever using civilians in these deals. Carla Carmody came quickly to his mind's eye, but it was too painful to think of her so he pushed her memory out and thought instead of himself. He didn't count himself in the category of a civilian. He'd spent eight years on the beat, and now was attached to a special task force of the Austin Police Department that worked undercover drug operations.

Times had certainly changed in the narcotics business. Now a lot of the drug operations were moving out of the big cities and hiding themselves in small towns. They lured one or two top citizens into the business by promising outrageous sums of money and were, in turn, sheltered by the very nature of small towns—distrust of strangers. The operations weren't huge or vicious in terms of what one read in the newspapers about the Colombian cartels and such, but they destroyed people nonetheless and therefore were just as deadly.

If you really wanted to infiltrate these networks, you had to do more than wear dirty clothes and talk like a junkie. You had to become a member of the town or become attached to someone everyone knew, liked and trusted.

Suzanne Stewart was that!

From what Logan had read in her file, everyone, even the town grouch and gossip adored sweet Sue. No one would ever suspect her of anything sneaky. No, she was too squeaky-clean, this woman who grew flowers, baked bread and enjoyed long walks in the woods. He'd almost choked when he'd read that in her letter to Dan, as if those things qualified her for this job!

"I can't believe she wants to do this, no matter what her dossier says. How did you talk her into this?" Logan pinned his superior with a demanding gaze. "Prey on her natural goodness? Tell her she'd be doing something for her country?"

Dan Rider relaxed his stance. "I didn't recruit her. She's a gift from the Gruenville police. She walked in there two days ago and told them she wanted to volunteer for undercover work. They sent her here and she begged me for the opportunity to help."

Logan's eyes widened with surprise. "And you just said yes?" He sat in one of the chairs facing the cluttered desk. "It doesn't matter. I won't work with her."

"Logan, you know I let my field bosses make their own decisions." Dan sat in his chair but leaned forward for emphasis. "But this time I'm thinking about pulling rank. I want you to meet this woman before you decide."

Logan squinted at Dan. "Would you look at me and tell me what you see, old man?"

Dan leaned back in his chair, as if he were enjoying this part. His eyes narrowed. "I see an okay-looking guy who's about thirty-five, needs a shave and haircut."

"That's not what I mean and you know it." Logan pushed the chair back. "Do I look like the type of guy who walks around on eggshells, mutters polite phrases like, 'Can I get you a drink?' or 'Let me get that door for you'?"

Dan scoffed. "No, you don't."

"You see?" Logan said, a grim frown wrinkling his brow. "I can't be your man. This Suzanne—" he pointed to the picture "—definitely needs someone like that."

"No! She needs someone who'll protect her with his life, someone who's worked with civilians before." Dan pointed an index finger at Logan. "Someone exactly like you."

"You son of a bitch." Logan stared at Dan. "You really want this bad, don't you? To use *her* as a bargaining chip." He got up and leaned over the desk, grinding out his next words. "Have you forgotten about Carla? She died with me protecting her." He closed his eyes, trying to stop the memory.

"Yes, this case needs you that bad." Dan softened his voice. "And I've forgotten nothing. You need to let it go. It wasn't your fault. Carla put herself in that final situation without backup."

"Tell that to her family." Logan walked again over to the window, pretending to look out at the day.

"Look, Logan, you can't blame yourself forever that she was working with you and got killed."

"Don't you get it, Dan?" Logan turned back to face his superior, unable to keep the haunted look out of his eyes. "I put her through only a minimum of training. I thought I had the situation in control. You know me, Logan Davis, sure of every angle. Hell, I'm known as the king of precision in the field." He slammed his right fist into his left hand, the sound reverberating like a gunshot in the small room.

"Logan—"

"But she wasn't prepared. She went off on a buy without me. She got herself killed and *it was my fault.*" With each phrase, his voice had grown progressively louder until he shouted the last in Dan's face. Then he whirled and stalked back over to stare again out the plate-glass window. From Dan's fifth floor office in the Austin police station, he could see the tower at the University of Texas, flanked by the other buildings of academia. His peripheral senses noticed the spring green that decorated the city, heralding the season of hope, rebirth.

But he didn't really see the sights below or the bright sunshine or any of the people hurrying below him. Instead, he saw the blue-white face of Carla Carmody in its grisly death mask. She'd been smothered, then stuffed into the trunk of his car. As a warning.

He'd never forget the cold rage that had settled within him on that blistering hot day in August. He could never forget that a good, caring human being had died on his watch. Their investigation had unraveled with her death. The drug cartel had closed shop and run for cover. But Logan, with cold, deliberate police work, had tracked them to Gruenville. He had a score to settle, and he didn't need this woman to complicate his operation.

God, the world was crazier than usual today.

He turned back to Dan, his voice calmer when he spoke. He held up his hand to keep Dan from talking. "Don't try amateur psychology on me. Intellectually I know I'm not to blame for Carla's death, but emotionally it will always burn a hole in my gut." He took a deep breath, letting his words sink through to Dan, he hoped. "Think about it. Carla had some training in police work, and she'd gone into the assignment with some skill." Again he looked at Suzanne's picture as if he wanted to burn the image into his memory. "This young thing has no idea what she's asking for."

Dan shrugged his shoulders. "I think you'll be surprised when you meet her."

"You haven't been paying attention. I'm not *going* to meet her. You're going to explain to her that she can't help. Tell her thanks, but no thanks." Logan moved to leave.

A soft knock sounded on the door. Logan stopped as a clear female voice called, "Mr. Rider." Another knock and the door opened. "Can I come in?"

Dan Rider stood up and rushed around his desk, throwing Logan a warning look as he went by. "Come in, Ms. Stewart. You're right on time."

Logan stiffened, mentally going through every curse word he knew. What a disaster! He'd hoped to talk Dan out of this idiotic idea without having to face Suzanne Stewart at all, but she was here now. It was just as well, he told himself. He would tell her what a stupid, insane idea this was. He watched her smile guilelessly at Dan before she noticed him.

"Oh, I'm sorry." She nodded politely and backed away. "I didn't know you were in a conference, Mr. Rider. The man at the front desk said I could come in. I'll wait until you're finished."

"No, that's okay." Dan smiled at her. "In fact, it's good you're here. We were just talking about you."

She looked from one man to the other, her green eyes wide. "Really?"

Logan purposefully leaned slightly toward her, hoping his six-two frame would intimidate her slight form. The whole five feet of it. What kind of police action could *she* hope to handle?

"Yes, we were discussing the pros and cons of your proposal to help us infiltrate the drug business in Gruenville." Dan motioned toward Logan. "Suzanne Stewart, this is Logan Davis, the agent who will be working with you. Logan, this is Ms. Stewart."

Logan took the hand she offered. "I can see that. She looks just like her picture."

"Yes, she does," Dan said quickly. The two men exchanged glances, and Logan's deep frown confirmed that he was not impressed with Ms. Stewart in the flesh.

"Sit down, Ms. Stewart." Dan glowered at Logan. "You, too."

Logan sat in the chair closest to Suzanne, forcing her to walk in front of him to get to the other one. He ignored Dan's scowl and spent the time looking her over. She did look exactly like her picture. Huge green eyes, curly russet hair. *Pixie.* That was the word that sprang to his mind.

Dressed in an ivory skirt and blouse with brown polka dots all over it, she looked like a bowl of vanilla ice cream with chocolate sprinkles.

Delicious.

Summer.

Totally wrong for this assignment.

Suzanne Stewart was all of these things, and she sat next to him with such an expectant look on her face, he groaned inwardly. The only thing marring the perfection of her image was the shadow of pain he detected buried deep within her green eyes.

Dan cleared his throat. "Mr. Davis was so...er... so...interested in your dossier, that he came here earlier than I'd expected."

"Oh?" Suzanne looked at Logan.

Logan raised an eyebrow at his boss, but said nothing. At that moment, he remembered why Dan Rider was in charge of the whole operation and he wasn't. Dan Rider could tell a lie and make it the truth better than anyone, and in this business, that was an enviable skill.

"I did come in here as soon as I'd read your file—" he sat forward in his chair and leaned toward her "—because I don't think you should get involved in a drug sting."

She leaned back, tightly clasping her hands.

Logan continued, his voice revving up a notch or two. "I'm here to tell you and Dan that this won't work. You're not right for this job, and I won't be your partner."

Suzanne straightened against the back of her chair and eyed him, her pert chin set at a defiant angle. "I don't care what *you* do. I'm in."

"Ms. Stewart—" Logan began before she cut him off with more nerve than he'd thought she would be able to muster.

"I'm usually not this rude, but this assignment is important to me."

She looked him straight in the eyes. "And it doesn't matter about working with you, because *I will* make this work if I have to be partners with the devil himself."

"Is that so?" Logan challenged.

She'd said that as if she thought he were the devil himself. "You, the epitome of law enforcement, are going to make this work?"

Her features relaxed somewhat as she nodded. "Yes, I am." She turned her attention to Dan. "Mr. Rider, since Mr. Davis doesn't want to do this, and since you told me we were under a time crunch, shouldn't we be looking for someone else?"

"Honey," Logan exploded, "you're missing the point. But I'm not surprised. I'm not the one who's not going to work on this case. *You* are not going to work on this case."

"Logan, I don't think—" Dan tried to interrupt.

"No, it's time to tell the truth." Feeling too confined by the chair, Logan stood to deliver his lecture. "We've been working on Gruenville for almost six months. I can assure you we're going to get these guys. And we're going to do that without your help."

"You can't do it without my help." Her voice was even, calm, putting him smoothly in his place.

"Really? Why not?" He crossed his arms and rested them on his chest.

"If you could, you already would have."

"She's right, Logan," Dan said, interrupting the verbal sparring.

Logan narrowed his eyes and studied Suzanne Stewart. He knew all the facts about the case the Austin Police Department and the DEA were building. His part of the operation was to get the hard evidence, and they *were* stalled right now.

"We've tried to infiltrate and gotten nowhere. The community's too insulated, too suspicious of anyone new." Dan glanced at Suzanne. "We have a list of suspects but not much in the way of evidence—evidence that will stick in court.''

Logan turned to Dan, ignoring the woman. "I know that. But I think we should wait until we find someone more...suitable for the job.''

"And how long will that take?'' Dan rubbed the back of his neck. "We can't wait. We've lined up the suspects. Suzanne is a perfect 'in' for us in the community so we can get that hard evidence. Then we can go in for the collar.''

Suzanne drew Logan's attention with the biting tone of her voice. "If *you'd* done your job better, I wouldn't be here today.''

"What the hell does that mean?''

"I'm here because you didn't move fast enough and my sister died of an overdose.'' Her eyes challenged him for a moment, then closed as she composed herself.

Logan sat down with a thud. He rifled his fingers through his hair, flexed them, then balled them into fists. He grimaced before looking at Dan for support, giving him an I-told-you-so look. She was worse than he'd imagined. There was nothing more dangerous to an undercover operation than a civilian with a mission, a quest, a damn score to settle.

And Suzanne Stewart had "martyr" written all over her.

"I...didn't know.'' He looked accusingly at Dan. "I'm sorry. I must not have seen it in your file.''

"It wasn't in her file. I was going to tell you just before Ms. Stewart came in,'' Dan informed him.

"I'm sorry about your sister.'' Logan gentled his voice. "But that only multiplies the reasons you shouldn't do this.''

Suzanne stared at him. "What do you mean?''

"Too much emotion is a dangerous thing in these assignments. You have to be calm, stable, to pull this off.''

"But that's exactly why I'm perfect. I'm one of the most stable people in the entire town and everyone knows it.'' She settled back in her chair and crossed her arms confidently, turning her attention to Dan Rider. "Are we ready to start talking about how this is going to work now?"

Dan glanced at Logan. "I'm ready, if Logan is."

Logan, feeling as if he were moving underwater, unable to move quickly or surely, kept his eyes focused on Suzanne Stewart's face. Guileless. The woman was actually guileless. Her eyes were clear of deception; no lies were lurking in them. He hadn't thought there were women left in the world like that, at least not twenty-eight-year-olds. She actually believed everything had been cleared up with just one little statement from her. He needed to snap her back to reality.

"No."

"Why not?" Suzanne turned to him.

"Because you haven't been paying attention. I really am sorry about your sister, but that doesn't change anything. You are not going undercover in this case."

Suzanne gave an exasperated sigh and then tried explaining again, although she couldn't keep the shade of doubt out of her voice. "Mr. Davis, I'm already *on* the case. Mr. Rider put me on it yesterday. This meeting is just to finalize the deal." She looked to Dan for confirmation, but got none.

Instead, Logan told her, "You misunderstood Mr. Rider. I'm the one who will decide if you work with us. I'm in charge of the field operation. I'm the one you'll have to convince."

He emphasized his last words by making them soft, deadly. "And so far, I'm not satisfied."

She hoped her face betrayed none of her misgivings. This man was nothing like what she'd pictured. Her image of her would-be partner had been of an older, more mature man. One who could become a friend, an uncle figure. She considered it one of her strengths, making friends with men. She'd counted on the friendly type for her partner.

Instead, she was confronted with this man who reminded her of a powerful mountain cat, caged and dangerous. He even prowled when he walked. And she sensed the controlled energy he kept leashed when he looked at her.

Hooded eyes.

Wide shoulders.

Totally wrong for her partner image.

"I understand why you might have some reservations about me doing this." She tried to be reassuring. "But Mr. Rider explained all of the dangers to me. I want to do this." She pleaded with him. "I *need* to do this. I can't let my sister become a statistic in a tired policeman's file."

Logan turned on Dan Rider. "You're a piece of work, you know that? You've explained the dangers to her?" he snarled, jerking his head in Suzanne's direction.

Dan nodded and Logan pushed both hands through his hair. "I bet."

He sprang from his chair again and began pacing, mimicking the movements of a caged animal. "Did Mr. Rider tell you that you could get killed doing this? Or that I could get killed if you screwed up? Or that we both could get killed?" He whirled to face her. *"Did he?"*

Suzanne scooted back in the chair and looked up at him as he towered over her. This man scared her. But she would see her vow through, even if it meant dealing with this wild animal turned policeman.

So she looked him dead in the chest. "Yes, he did."

Logan swore out loud.

With a clenched jaw, Dan Rider directed his words to Logan. "You and I can talk about this at another time, Logan. Please sit down. Right now you need to explain to Ms. Stewart how you envision her role in this case."

Logan knew Dan was just as stubborn as he was, so he finally slouched into his chair as Dan added, "I want you to listen to Suzanne's story. After that, we'll figure out exactly how to proceed from here."

Both men turned to her.

Knowing Logan disapproved of her, Suzanne had a sudden urge to leave, to go anywhere that he wasn't. But she hadn't come this far to turn back. She drew in a steadying breath. She'd told her story once. It had been hard then, with only Dan Rider in the room. Now there was *him*. The room felt too small all of a sudden. Air seemed to be missing. She wanted to excuse herself and get a drink of water, but she didn't. Even that reeked of running.

Instead, she said, "I had a sister, Natalie, who enrolled in Gruenville Community College two years ago. Everything seemed fine for a while. Then she started acting funny." She stopped, gathering her thoughts, trying to remember only the necessary pieces.

"Acting funny?" Logan prompted.

"Natalie had always been sweet, helpful. Even when she was a teenager, she liked staying around home, taking care of younger kids."

"Must run in the family," Logan muttered.

"Yes, it does," Suzanne confirmed and gave a small smile as she explained the eccentricities of her family. "My gran says we get it from our father. She says he was the first vegetarian in Gruenville, couldn't stand to eat something that had been killed.

"Anyway... After Natalie's freshman year, she began staying out late, sneaking away and running around with people we didn't know. When we asked her about it, she told us to leave her alone and let her have a life."

"She was taking drugs," Logan said.

"Probably, but we didn't know that." Suzanne straightened her skirt and looked up at Logan. "It's not that I'm naive about drugs." She ignored his blatant smirk. "I know they've been around. I even know people who've played around with them. They've just never been a part of my life."

"I believe that. Get on with Natalie."

"She began lying. Finally we caught her with some pills and cocaine." Suzanne looked at Dan Rider. "We tried to get her into a clinic, but she refused to go. After that, it got worse. She would disappear for days, and come back looking awful. We kept trying to get her help. Finally she broke down and agreed to stop using the drugs. She moved in with me."

"What were you supposed to do?" Logan asked.

"Keep an eye on her. Try to talk her into going to the clinic."

"You were supposed to be her savior?"

Suzanne started. How did he know that was exactly what her family had said? *If anyone can bring her around, it's you, Suzanne.* Instead, she'd killed Natalie.

She answered quietly, "They thought I could help—yes." She tried to avoid Logan's gaze, feeling trapped by his stare. He was sensing her guilt; she could tell by the way his eyes narrowed and his nostrils flared.

"And what happened?"

"She seemed to get better for a while. Even helped me a little down at the nursery." Suzanne smiled, remembering how Natalie had complained about how awful her fingernails had looked after working all day. "She had a boyfriend, though, who seemed to bring out the worst in her."

Logan nodded. "Yeah, there's usually a boyfriend or a girlfriend mixed up in this kind of racket."

Suzanne chose to ignore his comment, although he couldn't know how she had already decided that certainly was the case. She continued, "One night she came to me and asked if she could go out with some friends. She'd been like her old self that day, so I told her it was all right."

Suzanne stopped in her litany. She stared over the top of Logan's head. Should she tell them that not only had she given Natalie permission to go out, but that she had also supplied the money that had enabled her sister to buy the drugs? No, that was her private hell. She had been the one most responsible for Natalie's death. She couldn't share it with anyone, most especially this man. He would never understand.

"And then?" Logan forced her to continue.

He had, Suzanne noticed, shuffled his chair so that he was facing her at right angles, crowding her space. She thought again that he reminded her of a predator closing in for the kill. She kept herself from scooting away from him.

"Then I got the call from the police." She lowered her eyes, unable to meet the penetrating hardness of his.

"You're lucky."

Her eyes flew to his face. "Lucky? What do you mean?"

"Most drug addicts will steal, prostitute themselves—anything for their habit. It sounds like you saved her from that."

Suzanne gasped. "But Natalie wouldn't do any of that." She saw Logan's eyes flash with sympathy for an instant, before they returned to their cynical glare. She realized how silly she sounded, but she refused to believe Natalie would prostitute herself. Some things you just knew in your heart.

"So the police called?" Logan prompted.

Emotion colored Suzanne's voice, causing it to rise an octave. "They'd found her in an abandoned house at the edge of town. She was only five miles from where I lived."

She stopped talking, reliving those horrible hours. The phone call. Identifying the body. Being paralyzed by guilt. If only she hadn't given Natalie the money! She took a deep breath and continued in a more subdued voice. "She was dead. From an overdose."

Silence shrouded the room. Dan broke it by explaining, "Ms. Stewart went to the Gruenville police and offered her story. They sent her here. I listened, checked her out and asked her to meet with us. And that's where we stand right now."

"It won't work," Logan stated flatly, glad he'd found a loophole in this mess. "If everybody in the town knows your sister died of an overdose, the sellers won't touch you. They're too smart for this setup."

"But the town doesn't know," Suzanne told him. "Cause of death was listed as alcohol poisoning. People thought it was a drinking party accident. Only my family and the police know the truth."

Logan looked at his boss, then at the woman with the haunting sadness in her eyes. Damn, this too-good-to-be-true woman was ready to sacrifice everything to see justice done, putting him between the proverbial rock and a hard place. She'd gotten to him with her story, but he still knew she could never handle being undercover in her hometown. Wanting to was one thing. Reality, another.

And his reality was, he had to figure out a way to get Tinkerbell out of the Gruenville drug scene. Finally he decided he'd have to talk to her away from Dan.

"Well—" he shrugged "—it looks like we'll be partners." He held out his hand.

Suzanne's smile made him wince with its hopefulness. "I promise to try to do everything you tell me to. I'm very good at following directions."

"Good." He leaned forward. "My first order is for you to go home. Now."

"What? Why?"

Logan sighed. "I thought you were going to do what I told you? If this is an example of how you follow orders, we've already got a problem."

"But I thought we were going to talk strategy—you were going to tell me all the ins and outs of the case."

"And I will. I'll tell you what I think you need to know. I'll tell you about how dirty this work can be." Logan looked over at Rider, daring him with his glance. "I'll come out to your place tomorrow and we'll start then."

"What do you mean what I 'need to know'?" Suzanne's eyes snapped green fire. "Don't think you can keep me in the background. I'm going to be an integral part of this."

Logan was taken off guard by her feistiness. She reminded him of a small terrier snapping at the heels of a giant.

"You need me," she continued. "I can get you into the homes of everyone in the town. My business—flowers, landscaping and catering—puts me in almost every house in Gruenville. So don't patronize me, Mr. Davis."

"I wouldn't dream of it," Logan said sarcastically. "I'll see you tomorrow."

Suzanne stared at him as if she were deciding whether to believe him or not. "You'll come tomorrow? And we'll really start?"

"Yes."

When Logan said nothing else, Suzanne looked expectantly at Dan Rider. He shrugged his shoulders and nodded.

"Okay." She stood. "But come in the morning. I'll be on a job site in the afternoon."

Logan opened the door for her. "Done. I'll see you in the morning."

After Suzanne's exit, Logan turned to Dan Rider, ready to launch an attack. He was stalled when Dan said, "You handled that very smoothly. Didn't I tell you she would be a surprise?"

"She didn't surprise me. But *you* do. Letting a civilian in on this who looks like a strong breeze would blow her away." Logan leaned on the front of the desk. "Maybe you've caved in to that sweet smile, but I haven't given up yet."

"Just what does that mean?" Dan's eyebrows lowered, a speculative gleam in his eyes.

"I'm going to do my damnedest to get her out of this case."

"You and I have been friends for a long time, Logan, but listen to me. You're not being objective about this. Think about this before you try running her off." He softened his voice as he continued. "She's a gift we can't afford to throw away. As much as it grates, you need her to speed this case up." He jabbed a finger at Logan's chest. "Don't make me order you to take her."

"Dan—"

"And I don't want to hear anymore about Carla Carmody. You've been on this case from the beginning and know about small-town operations, you can identify drugs and we've already worked out a cover for you. Suzanne Stewart will get you into the places we need to be in Gruenville."

Logan narrowed his eyes and studied Dan. He knew he was the right person for the job, but he'd be damned if he'd work with the Girl Scout.

"All right, you've convinced me. But let me try to get Ms. Stewart to quit. I need to see if she can really withstand some pressure."

"Don't threaten her." Dan's voice snapped as he warned Logan. "She's been through enough. Think about it. We've got the list of who we think are the main dealers. She can get us into their homes, you can test the drugs and protect her. You know the Gruenville police aren't equipped to handle this. We're lucky they covered up Natalie's death. She's got to work with us."

"Save your speeches for the captain. I'm not going to threaten her." Logan grabbed the doorknob. "But I'll tell you this. You owe me, Dan. If you want me to continue on this, you're going to swear to me that if Little Miss Sunshine comes in here and resigns, you're going to accept it."

Dan's voice was calm but forceful. "Okay, but if she stays on, you'll work with her."

"Yes, sir." Logan spun on his heel and slammed out of the room, vowing to himself he would find a way to send Suzanne running for safety.

Chapter 2

Suzanne smiled at her customer as she wrapped the dozen long-stemmed yellow roses. "If this doesn't get you out of the doghouse, nothing will. Don't forget to put this packet of plant nourisher in the water."

"Thanks."

"And don't forget your special croissants." Suzanne motioned toward the front of the store. "Sara bagged them for you."

She watched as the man picked up his other purchases before she began cleaning up the plant counter. This combination nursery, bakery and natural-foods store was her dream child.

Five years ago it had been difficult to get the financing to open the place. The banker hadn't thought a twenty-three-year-old woman was worth the risk, especially with the soft Texas economy. But her cousin—sad, sardonic Brandon—had stepped in and put up a parcel of one of his ranches for collateral.

Her business had skyrocketed and each year she'd added a new speciality. Initially the store was going to be a bakery; then she'd added the natural foods and vegetables. For some reason, it had seemed logical to add the plant nursery when she'd discovered that she had a talent for growing things. Nurturing had always come easily to her, whether it meant people, a stubborn soufflé or pesky petunias. That was why Natalie's death had gouged such a hole in her soul.

She had been given the charge of helping her sister; instead, her actions had led to her death. Suzanne swatted the counter, showering potting soil on the floor. Natalie would never come through those doors swinging her purse and singing off-key again. Just that thought made Suzanne resolve again to punish those responsible for Natalie's death. Her pledge had become so real to her, it was a rock that had settled into the pit of her soul. And only revenging Natalie's death could destroy it.

She thought about her meeting with Logan Davis yesterday. He wasn't exactly what she'd been expecting. She'd hoped her partner would be a little more friendly, more open. But if he wanted to be the strong, silent type—she shook her head and corrected herself, the strong, *loud* type—then she'd let him.

Although her experience with men was limited, the one lesson she'd learned was that most men did what they wanted anyway. The one man in college, John, who had shown a fleeting interest in her, had deceived her. He'd only wanted to make her a notch on his bedpost, and when she'd resisted, he'd practically raped her and then tried ruining her reputation. Since then, she'd had a healthy distrust of men. She'd managed to deflect interested male attention and had taken refuge in her store The Good Earth.

But there was something different about Logan Davis. Those tawny eyes of his had issued a warning to her, but they'd also created an excitement in her that she couldn't label. His stalking mountain lion demeanor scared her. And the way his eyes had looked into her soul, the way he'd cocked his head when she'd talked about Natalie, as if he knew her secret about the money, made her realize that she couldn't cope with an attraction to him at this point.

She wiped her hands on her jeans, effectively wiping the negative thoughts from her head. She reminded herself she would tolerate anything as long as Natalie's killers were found and brought to justice. Needing to check on a shipment of pear trees, she wandered into the large hothouse at the back of her shop.

Logan eased into a parking space in front of Suzanne Stewart's store. He shook his head as he looked at the sign: The Good Earth. Pictures of fruit, bread and flowers decorated the sign. It oozed normal, traditional, environmentally sound charm. He was surprised it didn't have a halo over the logo as a finishing touch.

He levered himself out of his Jeep and walked toward the door.

"Can you help me?" a masculine voice called to him.

Logan stopped and looked around, but didn't see anyone. He continued walking.

"Please," the voice persisted, "I can't get this bush out of here on my own."

Logan finally spied a head through the windshield of a Chevy Suburban.

"Come over and give me a hand."

Walking over to the back of the vehicle, he watched as an elderly man tried to tug a gigantic bush out of his truck. He rushed to help.

"What are you doing with this thing?"

"Bringing it in for Suzanne to look at." The elderly gentleman stepped back and let Logan do the work. "A little to the left. There." He gave directions as he whipped a handkerchief out of the breast pocket of his shirt and mopped sweat from his forehead.

Logan listed back from the weight of the bush. "You're bringing this in for a house call?" He gasped, righting himself.

"Yeah. Didn't want to make Suzanne come all the way out to my place." He opened the door for Logan and at the same time seemed to cling to the door handle as if to steady himself. "It's a good hour from here."

Logan grunted. It was almost too much. She inspired such reactions from people. Bringing in a *bush* for a house call, from sixty miles away.

He struggled with his bundle as he wove his way around vegetable stands and made for a big opening at the back of the store. He figured it was the right one because he saw plants and trees beyond it. Just as he was ready to drop the bush, the old man, who was still perspiring profusely and whose complexion was a waxy white, said, "Leave it here."

Logan plopped it down, brushed off his hands and looked around. The inside of The Good Earth was as homey as the sign promised. Bright, fresh flowers dotted the place, perched next to pineapples, oranges and kiwis. Flowers also dotted the top of a bakery counter and hung from hooks, creating colorful clouds over customers' heads. He stood in what appeared to be some sort of neutral ground—not bakery, not food store, but not the real part of the nursery, either.

The old man mumbled his thanks and went off, as if looking for something or someone. Logan figured he was scouting for Suzanne.

Forgetting the old man and his bush, Logan forced himself to focus on why he was even in this place at all. His foolproof plan. He was going to make Suzanne Stewart give up the idea of going undercover. If meeting her in the office hadn't already convinced him of her unsuitability, this trip to her natural habitat clinched it.

He looked around again to confirm his earlier impression and then shook his head. The owner of this place could never, and he meant *never*, do anything to intentionally hurt anyone. Now he just had to convince her of that, had to make her see that her place was here watering the daisies, not skulking after druggies.

It wasn't that he didn't understand why she wanted to do this. She'd lost someone, and she wanted to take away a little of the pain by hurting the people responsible. But she didn't know what revenge could do to a person—what it could turn one into.

After Carla's death, he'd vowed vengeance against the entire criminal element of Texas. He'd been so busy chasing bad guys, that the good guys at home, Debby and Ryan—his wife and son—had gotten lost in his twisted maze of paybacks. After their divorce, Debby had taken Ryan and moved to Seattle. Since then he'd only been able to squeeze in a few visits to his son whenever work would allow. Debby refused to let Ryan fly alone so Logan was limited in his ability to see him.

Oh, he understood revenge, all right. It was an empty exercise in emotions. One that would destroy you if you weren't careful. Suzanne Stewart needed to just get on with her life.

As he had. After the failure of his marriage, Logan had also made a vow: never to get involved in anything he couldn't control. That was why he loved being the field director of this task force. He controlled who worked with him and what his agents did, making sure everything was neat and clean. And that was why he knew Suzanne wouldn't fit into his scheme. She would bring raw emotion into this operation, and he didn't want it. He didn't need this woman cluttering up his job, his life. He wanted her out of this whole deal.

Mentally rehearsing his attack, he went over his plan. He would make Suzanne see, regardless of what it took, that her going undercover just wouldn't work. If she wouldn't buckle, then he'd tighten the notches a little. He had an ace in the hole that would make her run for cover, literally and figuratively. Convinced that he was doing it for her own good, Logan walked in the direction the old man had gone.

He noticed little plaques all over the walls and on bronze markers in the plants. He picked one up and noticed it had a saying about keeping the earth green for future generations. But just because she had seemingly dedicated her life to cleaning up the earth for the next generation, didn't mean she could clean up an illegal drug operation.

It was one thing to replace the world's ozone layer, quite another to put away a narcotics boss. After all, the ozone layer didn't shoot bullets. Suzanne was out of her element.

Logan straightened his shoulders. He knew what he was doing. She would only be in the way, he rationalized. She only thought she wanted to do this. He would try to promise her justice in her sister's death, and maybe that would appease her. Suddenly he noticed the place looked deserted. Where had the old man gone?

He continued winding through the plant-laden nursery until he came to the entrance of a large greenhouse. Opening the door, he stepped inside. Immediately he was overwhelmed with the smell of earth, plants and flowers. His skin became slick from the moisture in the room. He heard a firm, scolding voice and moved cautiously toward it. Near a forest of evergreens he spotted Suzanne, having a heated discussion with a pot of marigolds.

"Do you usually win these arguments?" Logan asked as he walked toward her. "Or do the plants get the better of you?"

Suzanne jerked, almost knocking over a tray of the marigolds.

"Whoa." Logan leapt to the rescue and steadied the tray. "You scare easy, don't you?" He shook his head. "That's not good for this assignment."

"I'm not usually under attack here," she told him. "But now I'll know to be careful whenever I know you're around. And, to answer your question, it's a toss-up."

Logan, still balancing the plant tray, arched his eyebrows. "What?"

"The arguments. Sometimes I win and they flourish." The sweeping gesture of her hand encompassed the greenhouse. "And other times, they win and just wilt."

Logan nodded and put the marigolds back in their place. He hadn't come here to talk about plants. He had come here to get rid of her, not to find her charming and engaging, which was exactly what he was doing. Meeting her on her home turf was *not* turning out to be such a good idea.

"Can I give you a tour of the place?" Suzanne walked past rows of lush greenery. "You'll probably be seeing a lot of it now that we're partners."

Logan focused on the word *partners. What was the matter with him?* He had to get his plan in action. For a man with a mission, he was being easily distracted. So far, all he'd done was bring in a sick bush and rescue a row of marigolds. He needed to get back on track. But it was hard to think tough when in front of him was a woman who looked beautiful even talking to plants, especially with the wispy curls framing her pixielike face.

"No. I didn't come here for a tour." Logan stopped her by taking her elbow. "Can we go somewhere and talk?" He pulled the collar away from his neck. "Somewhere cool."

"Sorry. I'm used to it." Suzanne turned toward the greenhouse entrance. "We can go to my office."

Logan followed her as she maneuvered through the nursery to a corner of the place. She opened the door and let him go in first. He stopped short just inside the door. She ran into his back and grabbed his waist to steady herself.

"My fault." Logan moved aside, giving her room to come in. "I've never seen this many plants in such a small space before."

"These are some of my favorites. I keep them here because they give the place resonance, energy—don't you think?" Suzanne asked as she sat behind a small, cluttered desk.

"I've never thought about it. Personally, I get my energy from making sure criminals spend time in jail." Logan eased himself into the only other chair in the office. He immediately felt cloistered. All around him and dripping on him were the tendrils of hanging plants, everything from ivy to what he thought must be hanging orchids. He could barely see Suzanne through the green curtain of vines.

"Could I get you some tea? I have some interesting herbal mixtures."

Logan parted a few of the leaves, raised his eyebrows and shook his head.

Herbal tea. Figures, he thought. Probably made from some of these buddies hanging around my shoulders. He unwound an ivy clump to make a peephole.

Suzanne shrugged and smiled. "I'll just make myself some, then." She turned behind her to a pot and poured hot water into a cup.

Finally, after unsuccessfully trying to find a slot large enough to see Suzanne through, Logan grumbled under his breath and stood. He took down three of the plants and set them on the floor.

He sat back down and intercepted Suzanne's questioning look. "I'll put them back when I leave."

"That's okay. I should have realized. It's just that they don't bother me." She pushed a shiny lock of hair behind her ear.

Logan noticed her automatic gesture. Staring at her hair, he found himself thinking that it looked like rust-colored satin. She belonged here, surrounded by this lush life; it complemented her grace and naturalness. The only anomaly to the scene were the lines of pain etched around her eyes. Lines even her smile couldn't camouflage. Those cobwebs of grief told him he was doing the right thing. She wasn't tough enough for this job. Inwardly he rehearsed the speech he'd prepared. Show time.

"Ms. Stewart, I think it's time we get down to specifics about your assignment."

"I agree." She dipped a tea bag in the steaming liquid.

Good start, thought Logan. "Going undercover isn't the way it's portrayed on television or in the movies. Especially in drug cases."

"Okay, what is going undercover really like?" Expertly, she wrapped the string of the tea bag around her spoon and pulled.

"It's lying to your neighbors, suspecting your best friend and watching someone you know go to jail." Logan watched her face as he pounded out the words. She'll never be able to do this, he thought. She doesn't have a suspicious bone in her body.

But like everything else about his plan so far, this backfired, too. She sipped her herbal brew and eyed him levelly over the rim of the yellow cup. Finally she surprised him with her answer. "I'm prepared to do that. Whoever is doing this in Gruenville might be neighbors, but they are definitely not my friends, and they should go to jail."

Logan started. Her voice was clear and harsh and for an instant her eyes had been an unyielding, agate green. Yet, just as quickly, with a smile, she'd changed back into the innocent plant lady.

His lips formed a grim line as she rushed on. "Is that what you came all the way out here to tell me? I thought you were going to explain how we're going to work as a team." She took another sip of her tea. "Are you going to work in the nursery so we can be close?"

"No. I'm putting my expensive education to use." Logan flashed back to lugging in the bush, glad he didn't have to do that for a cover. "I'm going to teach at Gruenville Community College. Chemistry."

"Really? Can you do that?" she asked.

Logan shifted in the chair, trying to control his patience. "I don't know what you think I am, Ms. Stewart, but I'm not some two-bit flunky who doesn't know which way is up."

She blushed. "I didn't mean that. It's just...I don't know...I thought you had to have a degree in chemistry to teach it."

"You do, and I have." Logan gritted out his answer. He hadn't intended to give her his official cover story. Why couldn't she just listen and do what he wanted?

"I'll be teaching three classes. Since I'll be a member of the faculty at the college, I'll be able to blend into the community. It's a perfect cover for me, and it will also give me access to the college's labs." Logan saw her mouth open and rushed to stop her. "Before you ask, I'm a chemist. That's what makes me so effective in this job. I can not only capture the evidence, I can analyze what it is and where it came from. Another part of my job is to discover what new drugs are being sold and how they're being made."

"You mean you're really not a policeman?" Suzanne set her cup down and grabbed the edge of her desk. Her eyes, large and innocent, were a vibrant green against her rapidly paling complexion.

Instinctively Logan knew if he made her believe he really wasn't a policeman, she might, from fear, refuse to work with him. He almost played into her illusion but then realized she would just ask that a "real" policeman be assigned to the case. And for some inexplicable reason, the thought of someone else working with her, protecting her, kept him from pressing his advantage.

"I was a chemistry major in college, but during my senior year I took an elective class in law enforcement. I discovered I had a talent for that, too.

"The Austin Police Department recruited me to work for them. My chemistry background made me a natural to be diverted to drug undercover work.'' Carla's blue-tinged face rose in his mind, but he quickly shuffled it to a back corner of his consciousness. ''The department even paid for me to get my master's degree in chemistry.''

He moved another drooping vine out of his way. ''You don't have to worry, though. I was a cop on the beat for eight years. But I can do more good helping on the task force, both undercover and in the lab, making sure evidence is solid and criminals don't get off through fancy lawyer work. The street cops like knowing I'm on their side and can help make their busts stick.'' Logan stopped for breath, amazed that he'd felt the need to justify himself. He raked his fingers through his hair.

He continued. ''And I've done a lot of work in small towns, so I understand how small drug rings work. I'm as close to an expert in small-narcotics trafficking as the department has. Have I satisfied you?''

''Yes. But I do have one more question. What will *I* do?'' Suzanne asked. She still held on to the desk, but her body looked less tense.

''You'll do what you've always done. Just listen more, ask some different kinds of questions,'' Logan explained. ''You'll have to become a convincing snoop and then rat on your friends.'' He decided to wait and play his ace later.

''I can do that.'' Suzanne released the desk and moved her fingers to clutch the mug of tea instead.

''You'll tell me what you hear, and I'll start piecing together the drug operation. I'll also be verifying some of the information we already have. Remember, we've been on this case for a while. I'll be the contact with the Gruenville police. We don't want anyone suspecting you, so I'll be your sole intermediary.''

''That's all I have to do?''

''For now. But as soon as we're sure who we're dealing with, the scenario will change.'' Logan leaned forward. This was his ace. He knew with one sentence he could make this virginal female fold her hand. "You're going to have to my—"

A loud crash outside the office brought both Suzanne a Logan out of their seats and scrambling into the nurse before he'd finished his sentence.

"Suzanne, Mr. Brown has fainted," a young female e ployee shouted. "I'm calling EMS."

Logan ran toward the front of the store, and there, t tween the tomato bin and the lettuce cart, lay Mr. Brow the old man whose bush he had dragged in. Logan kn beside him and felt for a pulse in his neck. Nothing. He h ripped open the man's shirt, ready to begin CPR, when heard a raspy breath come from Mr. Brown's mouth.

"He's breathing." Suzanne's voice came from behind h shoulder. "Will he be all right?"

Logan sat back on his haunches and let some of the te sion leave his body. Color was coming back into M Brown's face, and his eyelids were fluttering. "I'm no do tor, but he looks like he'll be okay. But he should go to th hospital for observation."

He looked at the woman who rushed up to them. Appa ently she was the one who'd called EMS. "Did you see wha happened?"

"No. I saw him come in with you. I thought you wer with him or something. Then I noticed him wanderin around alone."

"And you didn't ask to help him?" Logan's voice wa brisk, censure in his tone.

Suzanne intervened. "Mr. Brown is a regular. He come in here about once a month, talks to everyone, buys a plan or two and leaves. His wandering around is nothing unusu al. He's lonely since his wife left him. I think the bakery smells remind him of her."

She knelt down beside Logan and picked up Mr. Brown's hand. "He was probably looking for me. Sometimes w have a cup of tea together."

Logan stared at Suzanne. There was such a cordial, friendly quality about her. She exuded genuineness. Nothing phony about Suzanne Stewart. She would give time out of her day to have tea with a lonely old man. Or a bad-tempered policeman.

"You're probably right. He brought you a bush to look at." Logan pointed to it, in the exact spot where he'd dropped it.

Suzanne smiled. "Oh. Probably just an excuse to come and visit me."

Logan looked sharply at her. From anyone else, this sweet, innocent routine would have made him suspicious. But this woman had the opposite effect on him. The warm, open look in her eyes and the soft sensuousness of her smile sent Logan's mind spinning out into dangerous territory.

He stared at her fingers rubbing Mr. Brown's hand and imagined them moving on him. He wondered how sweet her mouth would feel under his. The sirens announcing the arrival of the ambulance forced his wandering thoughts to the back of his mind.

Within seconds the attendants had taken vital signs, strapped Mr. Brown to a stretcher, radioed ahead and wheeled him out of the store. One of the technicians asked, "Anyone know who we can call to let them know about him?"

Suzanne's assistant answered. "I know his neighbor. They probably know how to get in touch with his son. I can go with Mr. Brown and call from the hospital."

"You don't have to, Sara. I can go," Suzanne said.

"No, I want to." Sara pointed to Logan. "He was right, I should have been paying more attention."

Suzanne hesitated for a minute, then looked at Logan. "Okay. You go with the ambulance. But call me from the hospital when they know what happened."

"I will," Sara promised as she followed the stretcher out.

When the ambulance drove away, Suzanne turned to Logan. "We're going to have to finish our talk in here. I can't leave the front unattended."

Logan looked around and didn't see any customers, but he shrugged and agreed. "Fine."

Suzanne strolled over to the bush. "I'd better put this in a tub and feed it some plant food so it doesn't die." She leaned over to pick it up. Logan stopped her by laying a hand on her arm.

"That thing is heavy. I oughta know—I carried it in. Let me get it. I'll follow you." He knelt and scooped up the bush. Cocking his head to the side, he managed to keep Suzanne in sight as she walked to the rear of the nursery. All of a sudden, from the corner of his eye, he saw what looked like a black-and-white cat. As it got closer, Logan realized it wasn't a cat—it was a skunk. And it was headed straight for Suzanne. Instantly he set the bush down and lunged for Suzanne, shielding her with his body as they both fell into a pile of peat-moss sacks.

Suzanne, startled by the sudden fall and the pressure of Logan's body on top of hers, screamed. She pushed against his chest, trying to get him to move.

"Stop it," Logan whispered. "He's still around here somewhere and I don't want him spraying us."

Suzanne pulled back and looked into Logan's face. What was the matter with him? He looked at her and put his fingers over her mouth to keep her quiet. As she lay there trying to figure out what was going on, she became aware of Logan's body pressed against her. The total feel of him.

Her heart began beating double time, then triple time, and she felt a sheen of perspiration on her top lip. A small gasp escaped her lips as she realized that their bodies were perfectly fitted together.

"Suzanne, *what* are you doing?" A stern voice interrupted Suzanne's thoughts.

She looked over to see her grandmother and cousin standing not three feet away, their mouths open. "Gram. Christine. What are you two doing here?" She pushed Logan off and jumped up, avoiding looking at him as he got up, too.

"We were coming to the store today anyway, but the ambulance outside made us rush in. Henry Johnson was outside and said Sara went with Will Brown to the hospital because he fainted in here," Gram answered. "Now that explains what *we're* doing here, but it doesn't explain what you two were doing."

Suzanne stammered. "We were just, we were—"

"I pushed Suzanne over because a skunk had gotten in here and was making its way right at her."

Suzanne gasped. "A skunk?" She looked at the two other women. When she saw they were about to start laughing, she laughed herself.

Logan shook his head. "I don't get what's so funny. I've been sprayed by a skunk, and it's not a laughing matter."

"Oh, we know." Suzanne straightened and looked at his serious expression. She burst out laughing all over again. After several minutes of giggling, when she'd gotten her breath back, she explained. "That skunk can't spray you. He's a pet—Sweet Thing. We had his 'stink sac' removed."

"A pet?" Logan echoed. "That *thing* is a pet?"

Christine nodded. "He's been a pet here ever since Suzanne's owned the place. We consider him a good-luck charm."

Logan shook his head and then tossed a reluctant smile in Suzanne's direction. "Then I guess I owe you an apology for throwing you into the dirt that way."

Suzanne smiled. "No, you don't. You did the logical thing. In fact, it was a very knightly thing to do." She curtsied. "Thank you."

Logan grunted his "You're welcome." Damn, he thought. I've got to extricate myself from this never-never land before it's too late. This pixie's magic dust of honesty, charm and laughter was threatening to turn him into a man who wore tights and tried to fly. It was time to get back to his plan to discourage her.

Suzanne turned to Gram and Christine. Just as she was about to make introductions, Logan took her hand and began to rub it gently at the wrist. Suzanne stilled and out of the corner of her eye noticed Gram and Christine exchanging glances.

Suzanne, flustered, tried to yank her hand away, but Logan held on and even pulled her into the curve of his arm, securing her by his side.

"My name is Logan Davis. I'm a—" Logan waited a carefully calculated beat before finishing his sentence "—a friend of Suzanne's."

Suzanne's face felt on fire. She again tried, unsuccessfully, to disengage herself.

Logan held out his hand. "You must be relatives."

Christine came forward and said, "Yes, I'm Christine, Suzanne's cousin, and this is our grandmother, Rosemary Stewart."

Looking into the younger woman's face, Logan was startled by the pain shadowing Christine's cloudy gray eyes. They reminded him of the sky before a lightning storm. It was the same sadness he'd seen mirrored in Suzanne's, only magnified a hundred times. Did all the women in this family have such tragedy? Somehow he sensed that more than Natalie's death had caused the intense suffering he witnessed in the depths of Christine's eyes.

His gaze switched to the grandmother. She was short, like Suzanne, but looked as feisty as a bantam hen. Her seamed face radiated spirit and common sense. Instinctively, he knew she didn't miss anything, and right now she was regarding him with a suspicious gleam in those eyes of hers. Logan liked her immediately.

Everyone exchanged handshakes as Logan continued. "I feel like I know you already. Suzanne has told me so much about you."

Suzanne started to stammer something, but stopped by the pressure of Logan's arm, smiled weakly instead.

"Really," Gram said. "Then you have the advantage, because we haven't heard anything about you. But we can fix that. You'll have to come out for Sunday dinner tomorrow."

"We'd love to," Logan said quickly.

"Good." Gram looked them over suspiciously before she asked, "Just how did the two of you meet? In Gruenville everyone knows everyone else, and I haven't heard about you." Her raised eyebrows almost camouflaged the wink she gave Logan. "And I know I would've heard about you."

An uncomfortable silence filled the air. Several seconds and several erratic heartbeats later, Suzanne fumbled through an explanation. "Logan was the professor of the last college course I took in Austin. He's accepted a part-time position teaching at the community college here. We've been getting reacquainted in the last week since he's moved here."

Nervously, she walked toward a plant stand and started trimming an overgrown honeysuckle vine. "In fact, he's here picking out some plants for his house."

Logan smiled and went over to Suzanne. He placed his hand on her shoulder and gave it a companionable squeeze. "Yes. Suzanne promised me something that wouldn't need a lot of care."

Gram studied them. "Interesting. I'm sure whatever Suzanne picks out for you will flourish. She's good at matching plants with people." She turned to Christine. "Why don't you stay and give Suzanne a hand this afternoon since Sara is at the hospital? Suzanne, you can run her home this evening." Gram turned to go. "Nice to have met you, Mr. Davis."

"Same here." Amused, Logan watched her eye Suzanne one more time, then turn and leave, apparently saving all her questions for Sunday.

"I'll work in the front of the store. There were a few people milling around when we came in," Christine said. She disappeared into the store, but not before her eyes sent a piercing look to Suzanne.

Suzanne waited until Christine was out of earshot before she whirled on Logan. "Have you lost your mind? What was that all about?"

Logan, smiling, took both her hands and brought them to his lips for a caressing kiss. "That, Ms. Stewart, is police undercover work. Like it?"

Suzanne stopped and looked at the self-satisfied expression on Logan's face, itching to wipe it off. "Undercover work? Looked more like a sneak attack to me."

"Get used to it. Because, as I was about to explain in your office, before the bush man got sick, while we're on this case, you're going to play the part of my woman, my mistress, my one and only," Logan finished with a quick kiss on her mouth. "And if you can't do that, you'll just have to quit the case." He strolled by her, leaving her openmouthed.

"Think it over and let me know." He winked at her. "Soon, Sweet Thing." He walked out the door.

Chapter 3

Logan snapped his fingers in time to his humming as he sauntered to his Jeep. He climbed in, started the engine and began backing out of the parking lot. A loud slapping noise crashed on the hood of his vehicle. Startled, he slammed on the brakes and jerked his head around to see what had hit his vehicle. Standing in front of him, hands on hips, eyes flashing, was Suzanne Stewart.

He glared right back at her, cut the engine and leapt out the door. "What do you think you're doing? You're lucky I wasn't carrying a gun. I could've—"

"Don't you dare threaten to shoot me after what you just did to me." Suzanne marched to within one foot of him. "I didn't want you to get away before I gave you my answer."

Logan smiled, mentally congratulating himself on his easily won victory. Confident in his success, he acknowledged to himself he was actually going to miss working with this exasperating mixture of nymph and Girl Scout. But now, because of his cunning, he wouldn't have to partner her. He leaned against the Jeep, his smug thoughts on the speech he was going to give Dan when he crowed about this.

Suzanne edged closer, trapping him against the fender.

"I do want to thank you this time. You made my decision especially easy." She feathered his arms with her fingers. He felt her trembling touch but that didn't make their impact on his nerves any less shattering.

Logan's smile faltered when he saw the calculating gleam in her eyes, and looked at her fingers that could become claws at any minute. She didn't look like someone who was about to cash in her chips. In fact, she had that enigmatic smile that women get right before they're about to announce something that will change your life forever.

"Suzanne, you'll be glad you decided to let us handle the ca—" Logan's sentence was cut off when Suzanne stood on her toes, took a big gulp of air, pressed herself against him and pulled his head down to kiss his lips.

A sweet, potent kiss.

Before he could fully register what was happening, she stepped back. His eyes narrowed as she coyly sucked in her bottom lip. Damn her. She was trying some of his own medicine on him . . . and it was working. One kiss from this girl-woman and he felt as if he were a human explosive device and she were the firing pin.

Quick to recover his equilibrium, but still astounded at the change in her, he asserted, "Suzanne, I know you're angry—"

"Angry?" She arched her brows. "What makes you think I'm angry?"

"I came on to you in front of your relatives to show you just what undercover work would be like. It's not the movies or television. It's real."

"I understand. I just wish you would've warned me." Suzanne smiled sweetly. "But, now that I know, I'll play along." She leaned in to kiss him again, but he sidestepped her. She considered him with determination shining in her green eyes. "How am I doing so far?"

Logan studied her for a second through half-closed eyes. She was in way over her head, and he intended to *show* her how well she was doing. The last image he saw before he claimed her mouth was her eyes widening in surprise and alarm.

His kiss wasn't sweet; it demanded, consumed her lips. He registered the soft warmth of her mouth when his tongue pressed into hers. She tasted like honey—rich and warm. When he heard the slight catch deep in her throat, he eased away from her. He steadied himself by steadying her, watching her as she fought for control of her shallow breathing. His own breathing was abnormally rapid, and he chastised himself for getting carried away by a simple kiss.

Suzanne's emotions whirled inside her. If she hadn't been so determined to show Logan she could handle police work instead of just telling him, she never would've kissed him. But something about his arrogance had pricked her anger and her courage so that she'd acted out of character. He was an exasperating man and she had wanted to prove her mettle.

But his kiss!

Never in her limited experience had a man's touch ignited such a quivering, burning fever in her. Again she had to remind herself that now wasn't the time to get caught up in romantic complications with anyone, especially not her police partner. She didn't want to end up being at the beck and call of a man who might use her and then throw her away. The image of John's leering smile as he'd tried ripping off her blouse flashed before her. She shuddered.

When she finally took a deep breath, Logan said, "The answer to your question? You're doing just fine."

He waited for the explosion that never came. Instead she merely backed away and said calmly, "Logan, you need to pick me up at ten-thirty tomorrow morning if you want to get to Gram's on time for dinner.''

"What!" Logan shouted. "Pick you up! I thought you were going to tell me to forget it.''

Shaking her head, Suzanne said, "No. I've already told you. I'll do whatever it takes to get the people responsible for Natalie's death.'' She took his head between her hands. "Even if it means kissing an arrogant, two-bit snake like you.'' She kissed him and landed on his instep at the same time.

"Ouch.'' Logan jumped back.

"See you at ten-thirty.'' Suzanne turned and headed for The Good Earth.

Logan heard her chuckle and bellowed after her, "Suzanne, get back out here.''

Suzanne stopped, but only to call back, "I don't think so, Logan. By the way, dress is always casual at Gram's.'' She let the door slam closed behind her as she left him standing, raging, by his Jeep.

"Are you going to sulk the entire way to Gram's?'' Suzanne asked, after fifteen minutes of obvious I'm-ignoring-you silence from Logan.

"I don't sulk.''

"Then what do you call this silent treatment?''

"Thinking. Something you might consider doing before you try besting me again,'' Logan bit out.

Suzanne looked at him with wide eyes. "Are you talking about our discussion in front of The Good Earth?''

Logan glanced her way. "Yes. Don't try anything like that again. Save all the playacting for your relatives. The next time you come on to me like that when we're alone, I'm going to take you up on your offer.''

Suzanne gasped. "I wasn't offering you anything.''

"Save your games for the locals. I'm not playing.'' With that comment, Logan effectively silenced Suzanne. She stared at him, waiting for him to finish his earlier thought. After several minutes, she asked, "Still thinking?"

"I like to think when I'm driving. Besides, I need to pay attention. I don't know the way. I need to get all the landmarks internalized."

"Why?"

"Because we're going to be sweethearts, and we'll be coming here a lot. I want to be sure I can put my brain on automatic pilot and the car will get there."

He spared a second glance at her and raised one eyebrow leeringly. Suzanne wished she'd just let him brood in silence. But for some reason she couldn't seem to leave this man alone. She couldn't seem to treat him either as a brother or a bother—like she did all other men. Imagining him as a brother was out of the question after his kiss. Imagining him as a bother was an easier assignment, only he bothered her in ways she'd never experienced before. No man had ever made her stomach tighten like that—or caused her breath to leave her body and float somewhere above her.

She didn't want to think about what she *could* imagine him as. A lover? She'd never thought of herself as ever having a lover. She'd thought of herself as a wife, a mother, but never as a lover. Never. She knew that made her odd, a throwback to the Victorian era. But, then again, she'd never met a man whose presence filled and heated a space the way Logan's did. No, she wouldn't concentrate on that. Instead, she turned to stare at the scenery flying by.

"Well, you wanted to talk, now talk, sweetheart."

He spoke calmly, emphasizing no word in particular, but Suzanne's attention focused on the word *sweetheart*. What an old-fashioned word for him to use. After his sleazy behavior in front of Gram and Christine, she'd expected him to call her doll face, or toots, or—anything but sweetheart. It almost had a romantic sound to it. She stopped herself. Romance wasn't in this man's repertoire, and she had to stop thinking about him that way.

Logan reached over and touched her leg to get her attention. Suzanne flinched in surprise and drew away from him. He cursed under his breath, eased on the brakes and pulled the car to the side of the road. Suzanne stared at him, trying to make herself disappear into the door.

"Why are you stopping?"

"Because we've got a few things to straighten out before we show up at your relatives." He grabbed her shoulders and tried pulling her toward him. She resisted his efforts.

"What are you doing?"

"Getting you straight. Stop jumping every time I touch you." He pulled her gently toward him. She yielded, but still remained stiff in his arms.

"Look at yourself." She obediently looked down at her lap. "You're as stiff as that oak tree over there." He pointed toward a live oak in the middle of a field. Her eyes followed his motion.

"So?"

Logan sighed. "We're supposed to be a couple, an item. Get it? But no one's going to believe our story if you keep flinching every time I touch you." Logan continued to ease her over to his side of the car. "Think of me as your last boyfriend, and relax."

Suzanne lowered her eyes. "I've never really had a boyfriend."

Seconds ticked off with the only sound being an occasional car whizzing by them on the highway.

"Perfect. I've got a partner who really can't do anything required for the job." Logan took a deep breath before he continued. "You've never had a boyfriend because . . . ?"

Suzanne bristled. "Because it's never been convenient, and I've been too busy with The Good Earth. And just to clear the record, I can do whatever it takes. I've told you that."

"Prove it. Let me touch you without you shrinking away." Logan reached up and cradled her face in his hands, then smoothed his thumb over her bottom lip. Suzanne trembled, then closed her eyes. He then traced her eyebrows with the pads of his index fingers. She parted her lips. Though it hadn't been his intention, he couldn't resist. He leaned in to kiss her, but then a horn from a passing truck made her jump. Suzanne's eyes snapped open. Logan backed away.

Heat. Raw, steamy heat boiled in Suzanne's body. Suddenly the enormity of what she'd have to do, *how* she'd have to pretend, bubbled like a hot spring inside her. She fought down images of John Randolph, forcing herself to remember her promise to catch Natalie's killers. If this is what it would take, could she do it?

Logan—the man and his touch—brought out emotions she hadn't known she possessed, and she surely didn't want to explore right now. She had to focus on Natalie, cleaning away the guilt of giving her the money. Logan didn't fit into her plan of revenge. She didn't need a man, especially a bullying man like Logan Davis, in her life. She stared into his eyes and tried to telegraph that message to him.

He tilted his head, then tucked a stray wisp of hair behind her ear. "Okay, you passed." He turned on the engine. "Just remember to react like that around your family."

Suzanne sat quietly for about three miles before she told him, "You're a bully. You know that?"

Logan looked over at her. "You can always quit."

"No. No, I can't," Suzanne said softly, almost to herself. She drifted into silence for a minute.

Logan broke the silence. "What usually happens at these Sunday barbecues?"

"The whole clan gathers, trades gossip, eats way too much and then grumbles about who's going to do the dishes and who's going to watch all the kids."

"Sounds like I can handle it. Are you sure that's the usual fare?"

Suzanne thought for a minute, and then said in a quieter voice, "Usually, my sister Natalie would have been here."

That thought conjured up the image of Natalie as she had last seen her. Lying lifeless on a cheap linoleum floor, reaching out, her mouth open as if she was calling for help. She would never forget that picture. It was that scene that fortified her resolve, made her determined to succeed.

Another silence gripped the car, only this time it was a warmer, more comforting kind. Suzanne gave herself another minute to think about Natalie. About how unfair it was she wouldn't ever be with the family again. Then she compartmentalized those feelings and decided to get down to the business of trying to fulfill her New Year's resolution, getting Natalie's killers.

Suzanne wasn't naive enough to believe that Logan was all wrong about her qualifications for this job. Nothing in her background had prepared her for this job, for this man. But she had loved Natalie, and she needed to redeem herself. She would succeed.

Suzanne figured a real police officer would brief his partner, so she adopted what she hoped was a professional, brisk tone. "I guess I should fill you in on the family."

"I know a little about your family from your file, but you can flesh them out for me if you want. I wouldn't want to start some family feud by saying the wrong thing to Aunt Polly."

"I don't have an Aunt Polly."

"Really? You come from such a storybook world, I was sure you had an Aunt Polly somewhere."

Ready to launch at him for being patronizing, Suzanne stopped short when she realized he was testing her. The glint in his eyes was unmistakable. "Well, you're wrong again. You need to stop trying to figure me out, and just deal with the facts."

Logan grunted. "I would if you'd give me some. Tell me about the woman who was with Gram at your store. Christine, wasn't it?"

"Yes. That's my cousin, Christine Abbott." Suzanne wondered for a minute if she should try to skirt around all her family's idiosyncrasies, or just plunge in. Her honest nature prevailed.

"Christine's staying with Gram now, since her husband and unborn baby were killed in a traffic accident." She didn't go on to explain just how unhappy Christine's marriage had been.

"That's what I saw in her eyes in the store." Logan said half under his breath.

Suzanne turned to look at him to see if the understanding she'd heard in his voice was also on his face. She willed him to look at her and when he did, she saw the light of sympathy in his eyes. What a paradox this man could be— one minute a callous, controlled policeman, and the next an earnest, sympathetic listener. She wondered if this was a "good cop, bad cop" routine. Regardless of what it was, Suzanne wanted to make sure she never put herself in the same position with a man that Christine had—where she couldn't break free of a destructive cycle.

She pointed at a sign that signaled ten miles to their destination. Logan acknowledged her directions with a nod.

She continued with Christine's story. "When she's ready, she'll go out on her own again. But right now she helps me in the store when I'm in a bind.

"It's ironic, really. Christine was always the one who wanted to escape. She thought the world away from here was going to be one big picnic."

"You never felt that way?" Logan turned down the road she indicated.

"No, I always wanted to nest here. It was so *real* to me. Compared to Houston."

"Houston?"

"Yeah, I was just a sometime-cousin. I only came to Gruenville in the summers when school was out. The rest of the time I lived in Houston with my parents and Natalie. It wasn't until I graduated from high school that I moved here. Natalie joined me at Gram's after she graduated." Suzanne leaned forward and pointed. "Turn at the tree up there."

A minute later Logan turned onto a dirt road and began wondering just how far away from civilization this place was.

"What about your parents? Are they still in Houston?" He frowned and glanced at her. "Have they recovered from Natalie's death?"

Suzanne sighed. "I don't think any of us will ever fully recover. My parents are in Pakistan, working with an international group to help the children over there. It's their way of dealing with it."

Logan heard the strained tone in Suzanne's voice. "What's here that you can't find in Houston?"

Suzanne seemed to gather her thoughts before answering. "A backyard. Time moves slower here, people care about each other. The world isn't a maze of concrete and glass. It's a simple, uncomplicated reality."

"Nothing's ever simple," Logan said flatly.

Suzanne barely heard him. Her thoughts had turned inward. How could she tell Logan that her parents had gone overseas to help less fortunate children because her father had blamed one of his children for killing the other? Daddy had never said anything outright, of course, but Suzanne had felt a coldness, a censure toward her because she had given Natalie the money to buy the narcotics that had taken her life. As for her mother, she had always done whatever George Stewart asked of her, so she had gone along with the trip to Pakistan.

Suzanne loved her parents, but she considered her mother weak, and it hurt to think that she hadn't defended her daughter to her husband. Of course, Suzanne *was* responsible, but she could never tell someone as sure of himself and cocky as Logan Davis what had really sent her parents so far away. He wouldn't understand. Nor would he understand the deep searing pain her role in Natalie's death had burned into her soul. A little thing like guilt would never overwhelm him.

Logan made no comment. He sensed something was missing here. She wasn't telling him the whole story. People didn't run from such a perfect home to find a backyard. Then he realized that she'd given him just enough details to make him think she'd told him all of it. He'd played the same game, so he recognized a fellow evader. He was ready to tell her just that when he rounded a curve and saw a stone-and-wood ranch house. The house itself was nothing unusual, but the setting, the landscaping around it, was magnificent.

He felt like stopping the car just to get a real look at the place from a distance. Nestled in its natural setting, the house was surrounded by oaks, and under these trees a ground cover flourished, dotting the area with white and purple shots of color.

A wide porch fronted the house. Purple sage and other native shrubs formed a boundary around it. Plants, purple and white, hung across the front porch. He felt as though he were driving into the scene on a cover of *House and Garden*. As the car came to a stop, the front door of the house burst open and out poured three children, yelling Suzanne's name.

"Get ready. Here come the wild Indians," Suzanne said as she opened her door and held out her arms. The three children, two girls and a boy, scrambled into the car, blocking her way out.

"Hey, let me out and we can all have a big hug together."

"Great," the boy shouted. They backed away and when she stepped down, hurled themselves at her.

"Suzanne, guess what?"

"What?"

"We found some new babies," the blond girl announced.

"Gram says we each can have one," the boy said.

"But we have to wait until their mama doesn't have to feed them anymore," declared the brunette, who was hopping from one foot to the other.

"Jennifer, do you have to go to the bathroom?"

"Yeah, but I had to tell you the news first." Jennifer sped back into the house.

"Elizabeth and Josh, I want you to meet a friend of mine." Suzanne motioned for Logan to come around the car. "This is Logan Davis. These two, and Jennifer, the one who ran back inside, are my cousins."

"Once removed," said Josh importantly.

"It's good to meet you." Logan stretched out his hand. Elizabeth giggled and took it shyly. But when his turn came, Josh shook it, pumping vigorously while he grinned and nodded his head. "Gotta go," Josh announced, and both children then ran back to the house.

"What kind of babies did they find?"

"Oh, probably some kittens." Suzanne looked toward the house and then at Logan. "Well, we'd better go inside. They'll all be wondering about you."

He took her hand and placed it securely in the crook of his arm. When he felt her stiffen, he gave her a warning glance, then leaned close and whispered, "Remember, today is a test for you. We're lovers." He kissed her softly on the neck to accentuate his point.

They both walked toward the house. He wished he didn't feel as if he were marching into a battle without any weapons. His family had consisted of himself and a sister ten years older. His father was a cold man and his mother, an alcoholic, had died when he was fourteen. He'd always been comfortable with only a few people around him. He never figured he'd have to fit into the Waltons.

He remembered to smile when the door opened.

"Brandon." Suzanne broke away from Logan and threw her arms around a tall, lean, scowling man. "I didn't know you were going to be here." She kissed him briefly on the lips. "What a wonderful surprise."

"Hi." He hugged her and kissed the top of her head.

"I'm Logan Davis." Logan stepped up to Suzanne and put a protective arm around her before he held out his hand. His policeman's eyes took in the man's features in a millisecond. Logan knew women would find Brandon's dark, rugged looks attractive and most men would find them intimidating. "And you're . . . ?"

"Brandon Stewart." He took Logan's hand.

"Brandon's another cousin," Suzanne explained. "A first cousin, just like Christine."

"How many other cousins are there out here?" Logan asked.

"Too many for you to learn in one day," Suzanne told him. Stepping between the two of them, she hooked her arms around their waists, and pulled them with her as she announced to the occupants of the house, "Everybody, come meet Logan."

Out of the other rooms of the house came more people than Logan had seen in months. Most looked genuinely happy for Suzanne. Logan chose to ignore the questioning glances from some of the women.

He lasted through the introductions, trying to memorize as many names as he could, but gave up after the fifteenth person whose last name was Stewart. He decided he'd ask Suzanne for a directory so he could keep her clan straight.

He was impressed with the warmth and caring he felt from the group, especially when he got the distinct impression that Suzanne had never brought a man here before. For a minute, he found he liked that. Then, before those thoughts could follow their natural course, he shut them down, reminding himself exactly why he was there. To set the stage, the cover, to get people used to seeing them together.

He was still determined to get her off this job, but just in case, he needed the cover set. She could get him into the places he needed to go, and Logan knew he would use her for that if he had to. Even though exposing this woman to the seamier side of life bothered him, he would do it. This was the part of his job he hated, but if it meant jail time for drug traffickers, his sensibilities be damned.

Gram was calling her. "Suzanne, how about peeling potatoes for us? We can visit in the kitchen."

"Yes, ma'am." Suzanne smiled at her grandmother, glad to break out of Logan's embrace. His touch, even though she knew it was only for show, did funny things to her equilibrium.

She followed Gram into the kitchen, only to find Logan dogging her footsteps. Gram introduced him to several female relatives who were assembling dishes of food. Suzanne watched him joke and charm the women unmercifully. How easy this charade is for him, she thought.

As she began peeling the potatoes at the sink, Logan came up behind her and slid his arms around her waist, his hands stopping dangerously close to her breasts. Her breath flew out the open window. She leaned toward the window, chasing it. Logan pressed closer. His body was solid and warm. He was going too far.

"Logan," she whispered violently. He didn't move. Face beet red, she turned in his arms and glanced quickly at Gram before looking up into Logan's tawny eyes. "I can't concentrate on what I'm doing." Her voice, breathy, pleaded with him. He eased away.

"Shoo." She flicked her hands in his face. "Go watch television with the other men. We're old-fashioned here. This is the woman's domain."

Logan's eyes narrowed briefly, but he dropped his arms and stepped back.

"Join me when you're through here," he said before grinning at the other ladies and retreating from the room.

Suzanne whirled around and furiously peeled the potatoes, ignoring the pointed silence in the room. She was so tense, she thought she'd explode. Why did she respond to Logan's make-believe touches? He managed to stay cool, so why did she melt when he was near her? She had to remember to remain emotionally calm and stable. Catching Natalie's killers depended on it.

Having been thrown out of the kitchen, Logan found himself in the den, watching basketball on TV. He glanced around at the occupants of the room. All normal-looking men, relaxing in front of the television. All except Brandon. He studied Brandon covertly for several minutes. Even though Suzanne's cousin was watching the game, Logan could sense his restlessness, his agitation. His withdrawn, brooding attitude contrasted with the open friendliness of the rest of the Stewart clan. What was his story?

Logan's attention was drawn back to the televised basketball game by a spectacular jump shot. It was sometime later before he realized that Suzanne hadn't joined him yet. How were they going to convince these people they were a couple if she kept avoiding him?

He poked his head into the kitchen quickly, noticing that there seemed to be more women in there than he could remember meeting. Of course, he recognized Gram and Christine, but the others were a blur. They were busy mixing, stirring and just generally getting a feast together. Gram saw him and stopped patting out her biscuits.

"Looking for something to eat?"

Logan shook his head. "No, I'm looking for Suzanne. I've lost her."

Gram toweled off her hands and walked over to him. "I'll show you where she is." She took him out the back door and stopped on the second step. "You can probably find her at the lightning tree out back."

"The lightning tree?"

Gram explained, "Lightning struck it during a storm years ago. It really was a small miracle it survived. It's one of Suzanne's favorite places."

Logan nodded.

Gram softly touched his arm, stopping him from immediately going in search of Suzanne. "I want to know more about you and Suzanne. She never mentioned you, and that's not like her."

"I don't know why she didn't tell you. Maybe she was embarrassed because I was her professor." Logan looked her in the eyes and continued to lie smoothly. "But you know now. And isn't that what's important?"

Gram narrowed her eyes and met his wide-open stare. "I don't know. Is it?"

"I think you should ask Suzanne that," Logan said gently but firmly. His conscience twinging uncomfortably, he started down the steps.

"I'll just do that," Gram told him as she walked back into the house.

As he approached the trees, he stopped for an instant and sucked in his breath. If the front of the house looked like a magazine cover, then the back looked like the setting for a movie—a movie about family, about love, about beauty.

In the middle of the yard was the lightning tree, a giant oak with a large limb split right down the middle, making a natural hammock. But around it were living, or play areas. Off to the right there was a place where children could run, with few shrubs to break their path. To the left was another gathering place, with a tiered flowered area as a backdrop and lawn chairs and recliners facing the lush scenery.

Then, on a raised platform off the porch, sat the barbe-cue pit, again surrounded by shrubs and plants, another cozy hideaway. He spotted the pink of Suzanne's blouse amid the foliage and as he got closer saw she was reclining on the branches of the lightning tree, staring at him.

He headed toward her, drawn by the relaxed look in her eyes and the supple way her body fit into the tree. Her hair, windblown and tousled, made her look more sexy than any woman he'd ever seen. His stomach clenched as he watched her blink slowly at his approach. She continued lying there, waiting for him.

"I was looking for you. You know we're here to do a job. Stop running away from me."

"I needed some time alone. You may be able to lie without thinking, but I'm not a pro at it . . . yet."

"I warned you in Dan's office and during the ride here. This isn't easy and it isn't going to get any easier. If you can't take it, resign. Tell me you've had enough." His voice was hard.

She shook her head stubbornly.

"You're going to be lying to your family and friends. Do you think you're going to be able to carry this charade through?"

She didn't say anything for so long, Logan thought she wasn't going to answer, but finally she raised her head and pierced him with the look of unhappiness in her green gaze.

"This is the most difficult thing I've ever done." Her voice was soft and trembled with conviction. "I've never knowingly deceived anyone before. Gram trusts me and so does Christine. It's hard for me to fool them into thinking we're lovers, that we're happy together."

"I just had a little chat with Gram about our previous re-lationship. She sounded suspicious. You're going to have to answer her questions, Suzanne. No dodging."

She took a deep breath. The dappled light filtering through the tree branches turned her hair a deep copper.

"I'm doing this so other families in Gruenville won't have to suffer through the death of a loved one from drugs. That's the only reason I can lie to Gram and my family." It was a reaffirmation of her resolve.

Logan studied her for a moment. "You really think you can do this?"

Suzanne looked at him and nodded. "Yes, I can. I just needed some space, so I came out here. This is where I come to *think*," she pronounced.

Logan ignored her barb and looked around, noticing they were shielded on all sides by weeping vines. It was like a natural gazebo. In the middle of a very public area, there was an intimacy, a closeness to this place.

"This yard is really something." He motioned with his hand.

Her smile widened. "Do you really like it?"

Logan nodded. "I've never seen anything like it. It's almost like a movie set or something."

"Thanks."

"*You* did this?"

"Don't sound so surprised. It's my business."

"Well, you did a hell of a job."

"Gram says I did a heavenly job."

Logan chuckled. "She's right."

They stared into each other's eyes for a long second before Suzanne said, "This was my favorite place from when I was a child. It was here I got the idea to be a landscape artist. In fact, it was in this very tree that I developed my philosophy about it."

Logan watched her become animated as she spoke. He was again struck by her innocence and also with the unconscious sensuality that laced all of her movements. Her sex appeal was as natural as these surroundings. "What's your philosophy?"

"That your yard—this earth—is the setting for your life. And you should make that setting as beautiful as you can."

Logan frowned as he reflected on her statement. He'd never in his life thought of bushes and trees as anything but... well, bushes and trees. Now, as he looked at her sitting in this tree, surrounded by the lacy canopy of leaves and fresh smell of flowers, he almost wished he could see what she saw. Almost.

But he couldn't keep his eyes off her, and compared to her beauty, the natural setting wilted. Her sweet spirit glowed through every pore of her satiny skin, literally stealing the show from the leaves and flowers. The lure of her eyes, of her lips, forced him toward her. Damn, she was sexy—and beautiful. He walked over to the giant oak and sat down beside her.

Since they'd gotten to Gram's, Suzanne had been having trouble coping with pretending affection for Logan. She was scared to death because she was discovering a very natural inclination to touching him and being close to him, but it went against her plans of remaining aloof from men until she had all the problems in her life worked out.

Logan affected her as no other man ever had. His lonely mountain lion demeanor drew her attention. Worse yet, she found she wanted more than to nurture him and replace that somber expression with a more cheerful one. She wanted to feel his lips moving against hers again. She wanted to feel the weight of his big body on hers as she'd felt it when he'd hurled himself on top of her when he'd seen Sweet Thing. And she wanted to trace the hard planes and rugged muscles that were evident under the knit shirt he wore today, with her fingers, her mouth.

What was the matter with her? She hadn't been ready to handle the feelings he generated in her, so she'd sought solace in her lightning tree. But even here she was drawn to him.

She rose slowly from her languorous position on the branch, as if pulled by invisible strings, and glanced at him.

His gaze fused with hers and it was a mistake. Logan was unable to control the jab of desire that plunged through him. This was stupid, he tried to tell himself. She was a wood sprite and he a hard-bitten cop. But reason lost the battle that raged within him and he pulled her into the V of his spread thighs.

"Well, you've done it," he said.

Framing her face with his fingers, he brushed her lips. With only that touch, a jolt of electricity charged through him.

"Done what?" Suzanne's breath mixed with his.

"Made this setting beautiful." He kissed her softly. "Like you."

Her brows knitted in surprise. "No one ever mistook me for beautiful."

"Well, all these local yokels are blind," Logan said forcefully. "You're beautiful." As if to punctuate his declaration, he pulled her into his arms and kissed her. Really kissed her. Her lips, soft and lush as the surrounding flora, made him groan deep in his throat. Her small surrendering sigh gave him permission to deepen the kiss. He slid his tongue between her teeth and plundered. His gut wrenched in pleasure-pain when she tentatively touched her tongue to his—hesitant, innocent. He stroked it with his own, and she opened her mouth wide, inviting him to take more, give more. Slanting his head to enjoy every morsel of nectar her kiss offered, he plumbed the secrets behind her lips. It was a shattering kiss. It rolled through him like a tidal wave.

It scared the hell out of him.

It scared the hell out of Suzanne, too. This man had entered her sanctuary and suddenly it was no longer a safe place. Logan's touch ignited feelings John had extinguished that fateful night when he'd mauled her.

For a fleeting moment, John Randolph's face rose before her, leering. But just as quickly, Logan's warm touch and sweet breath washed free her images of the other man.

Now she was letting Logan touch her in ways she'd forgotten existed. Her mind whirled with turmoil and confusion. Would her life ever shift back to being calm and safe again? Did she really want that?

Logan felt her leaning into him, unconsciously asking for more, and he groaned, pushing himself away from her. He'd promised her he would take what she offered the next time, but he couldn't. She was too innocent and he wasn't.

Her eyes opened and he found himself staring into a green sea of awakening passion. He groaned again. She was too fresh and too easily lured into something he knew she'd regret later. And he was far too old and cynical to cope with virginal puppy love. He forced himself to look at the facts.

From the look in those green eyes, he knew she was seeing visions of romantic dreams, creating castles, knights and damsels in distress aching for rescue. He had to destroy those images. Which meant he'd have to force himself back into his role of an undercover cop, a man who traveled in the dark places of the world and worked intimately with its slimy inhabitants.

"That was great, Suzanne." He purposely hardened his voice.

"What?" Suzanne's breathless whisper wafted through his mind and made his insides tighten reflexively.

Gritting his teeth against the tears he knew would sparkle in Suzanne's eyes, he delivered his next crushing declaration. "I only hope someone was watching to see that performance, because, sweetheart, we deserve an Academy Award for that kiss."

Chapter 4

Suzanne shoveled dirt into a flower bed, displaying the vehemence of a Saturday-night wrestler. Perspiration trailed down her neck onto her back, but she didn't stop to wipe it off. She was working to complete the marine park outside Gruenville Community College, and, more important, she was working at not thinking about Logan.

She stood up and dusted her hands on her jeans. Surveying the area for a minute, she marched over to another planting area and began preparing the surface. This park, which fronted the Travis River, was her biggest project to date. Even though Suzanne's was the smallest nursery that had bid, it had won because of her natural, economical xeric design. The city fathers had wanted to take advantage of the river that flowed through Gruenville. She'd capitalized on that and had planted shrubs, trees and ground cover that were indigenous to the area and so took little care and maintenance.

On a more personal level, Suzanne was glad the council had opted for her design because of its ecological side benefits. She knew they'd voted for it because it had been "politically correct" to do so, but as long as it allowed her to do something for the environment while she beautified it, she didn't care.

She only had three more days until Friday, the official opening of the park. Today she was putting in what she considered the "window dressing," the showy plants. Begonias, salvia, impatiens and shasta daisies created a colorful welcome for visitors.

As she looked at what she'd accomplished this morning, she realized she was one hundred percent of a success at completing the park but one hundred percent of a failure where Logan was concerned. She couldn't erase the Logan of Sunday dinner from her mind. Logan of the passionate kiss and tender caresses. The Logan who had told her she was beautiful and had made her believe it. Almost. His parting comment about the Academy Award had made her realize just how silly she'd been in even thinking about him in any personal context.

She dropped to her knees and began spreading the soil. Working diligently, she forced herself to concentrate on him as the arrogant, know-it-all Logan. She conjured up every cynical, sarcastic thing he had ever said or done. These were the images she needed to keep herself focused on her mission, she reminded herself grimly, so she wouldn't wander into the dangerous territory of "the kiss."

His behavior on the way home had only confused her more. After kidding with her relatives and even given Gram a goodbye hug, he'd been silent and tense during the drive home. He'd kept glancing at Suzanne with a puzzled look on his face. After walking her to her door, he'd said a quiet, restrained good-night and had walked back to his car, looking back only once. Then, shaking his head, he'd gotten into his car and driven away.

What had all that been about? Could he have been thinking about what had happened at the lightning tree?

Suzanne rocked back on her heels and reluctantly admitted that he'd been right all along. She wasn't cut out to be an undercover person. She'd botched their first foray into the world of police work. She couldn't even manage to *pretend* liking him, having practically thrown herself at him and begun to *really* like him, believing in the fantasy.

She shook her head. Really like him? Her thoughts pulled up short. My God, she did! She had liked being around Logan on Sunday. She'd enjoyed watching him play with all her young cousins. Liked being with him out at the lightning tree. Her face heated up as she realized she'd never felt like that before. No one had ever made her feel like a precious jewel, meant for him alone. Until Sunday. Until Logan.

In high school she'd been every guy's best friend. She was just sweet ol' Suzanne. Bubbly and friendly, but no femme fatale. In fact, she'd been the most nonthreatening female in her class. No wonder the guys had always called her with their heartbreak stories.

Her heart still contracted painfully when she thought of her senior prom. For weeks the quarterback of the football team had flirted with her in history class and laughed with her at lunch. Finally, three weeks before the prom, he'd passed her a note saying he wanted to talk after class—about the prom.

She'd been mentally planning what formal gown she wanted when she walked up to his car that afternoon. And somehow she'd managed to keep her true feelings from showing as he'd asked her advice on asking Melody Sanders, the head cheerleader, to the prom. Suzanne had stayed home the night of the dance, watching a movie with her father.

That had been a prelude to her history with men. In college, she'd fallen for a sweet-talker, John Randolph. She'd believed all his vows of undying worship and had trusted him when he'd said he'd always cherish her. She'd found out differently at an after-football game party. He'd lured her into his room and when she'd said no, he'd forced the issue. If his roommate hadn't barged in, Suzanne didn't know how she would've stopped him. She would never trust another man with her emotions and safety again. Christine and Natalie's experiences with men had only confirmed her disasters—men were not to be trusted.

Then why was she beginning to trust Logan? He hadn't asked for her trust; in fact, he went out of his way to make her run from him. Only, instead of running, she felt she was perilously close to falling for this man. And this time she sensed the descent would be steeper and much more dangerous than ever before.

This was *not* how going undercover was supposed to be. She'd thought she would probably just have to keep her eyes and ears open and tell the police what she saw and heard. She really hadn't expected...well...Logan. She almost wished that all she had to do was look at some mug shots and pick out the bad guys. But wishing wasn't going to help catch Natalie's killers. Action was. And, even with the problems of the case, she was still committed to her resolution. She would not let her sister down. She would see justice done.

Having reestablished her goal, she again attacked the dirt, this time with the fervor of a zealot. She'd always used working in Gram's backyard as a way of exorcising her problems. Now she used her job to accomplish the same thing.

She would just pretend that Sunday hadn't happened. That Logan hadn't kissed her and held her and whispered in her ear. Besides, she admitted to herself, she tended to jump to conclusions where men were concerned. She wouldn't do that with Logan. She would be cool and unaffected with him. It was her job. After all, she was sure *he* wasn't consumed with thoughts about Sunday. No, she argued with herself, he was a professional. And, if it killed her, she would be one, too.

"Hey, what are you doing?"

Surprised, Suzanne looked around quickly. "You're burying those poor flowers," Logan announced as he walked toward her. "I was under the impression you were the local expert in horticulture, but even I know that flowers need a little air to survive."

Suzanne looked down and saw a mound of dirt covering her arrangement of petunias. She quickly brushed the loose soil away and straightened the strangled flowers.

"I was thinking," she muttered, her gaze unwillingly moving from the toes of his polished boots up to jean-encased legs and a gray chambray shirt. She wondered why he always managed to look so perfect. Contrasting his clean crispness to herself, she stared at the dirt smudges on her own jeans. Her shirt, stained with grass and flower debris, stuck to her body. "I didn't see you coming."

"I noticed." Logan kneeled down, his knees brushing against her thigh.

Suzanne scooted away from his touch.

She watched as irritation flitted across his face, quickly replaced with a stark stare. She cringed when faced with the amber fire of his eyes. Their intensity made her feel naked, vulnerable. Afraid he would somehow know what she'd been thinking about him, she asked, "What are you doing here?"

"I came out to invite you to lunch. When will you be finished here?"

Suzanne forced herself not to look at him. "In about an hour or two." Then, remembering her resolve not to be overcome by Logan, she said quickly, "but I really need to get back after I finish this planting. We're expecting a big shipment of fruit trees today."

"I'll help with the trees if you'll share a sandwich in my office."

"In your office?" She looked up from tamping down the soil.

"Yeah, it's just about a hundred yards from here, in that building." Logan pointed to the red brick building that would face the marine park once the park was completed. "I'm a professor here—remember? That's my cover. So I actually have an office."

"Oh." Suzanne inwardly rebuked herself at her inane reply. "I don't think I can have lunch."

Logan reached for her hands. When she snatched them away, his irritation was again obvious.

"What's going on? You act as if I'm going to bite you."

"I'm sorry."

"Suzanne—" he lowered his voice "—we're supposed to be a couple. Couples touch. I thought you understood how things worked."

"What do you mean, 'how things worked'?"

"Look, you were great on Sunday. I think the multitudes at your Gram's bought the whole thing. In fact, if I didn't know better, *I* would've believed it."

"That's the point, isn't it?" Suzanne snapped back at Logan. It was obvious he hadn't felt the same as she had about the kiss. For him, it had been part of his duty. She decided to follow his lead. Her determination to make this undercover police investigation turn up Natalie's killers hardened. Now, if only she could keep her heart from exploding every time he touched her or looked at her.

"Yeah. You made a liar out of me. I didn't think you'd be able to pull it off. I thought you'd be spilling the truth before the salad course. In fact, I bet Dan you'd call him on Monday and call the whole thing off."

She ducked her head. "I told you it was hard for me to lie."

"You did. But, believe me, you do it very well. Brandon even had the concerned cousin talk with me."

"He did?"

Logan nodded. "Threatened to kill me if I hurt you."

Suzanne gasped.

Logan continued. "So, for appearance' sake, have lunch with me. We can't talk here." Logan looked around. "I need to fill you in on some things that have happened."

"I'll finish up here and meet you there. What room is it?" She tried to make her tone professional, cool.

"It's on the third floor, 301." Logan stood. "Listen, I can help you here and we'll get there faster."

"No, it'll take me longer to explain what to do than it'll take me to do it myself. But thanks for the offer."

"You're sure?"

"Yes. I'll meet you in about an hour."

As Logan walked away, Suzanne exhaled. She took another deep breath before she mechanically began finishing the section she was working on. She kept telling herself it was a good thing she didn't have to explain herself. Logan's assumption that she'd done such a good job because she was a better actress than he'd given her credit for gave her a little more time. Time to get her "act" more refined. She couldn't allow him to know just how much he affected her.

"Come in," Logan shouted at the closed door when he heard the knock. He knew it was Suzanne. Only she could knock that softly. *Probably hoping I wouldn't hear and then she could sneak off.* But he was ready for her.

"I got cleaned up before I came," Suzanne announced as she entered his office. "I went back home and showered and changed."

Logan looked at her. She was in fashionable blue-and-white-striped short overalls and a white T-shirt. He grinned at her. She looked just right in the updated farmer outfit. "And you clean up very nicely." He motioned to a chair in front of his desk. "Please sit down."

"Thanks."

She smiled at him, but it was without her usual warmth and openness. She was all business. He watched her glance around. Because she surrounded herself with plants, he wondered if the starkness of his office made her uncomfortable.

"I'm going to bring a few personal things in," he explained, "so it'll look like I intend to stay for a while."

"That's good," Suzanne said. "I could lend you some plants to brighten the place."

"Great. But none of those hanging jobs. They make me feel as if I'm in a jungle." Logan settled deeper into his chair on the opposite side of the desk. "Just bring stuff that can sit on this desk or the file cabinet over there."

Suzanne's smile was warmer. "I promise. No jungle stuff." *Even though I see you fitting into a jungle perfectly.*

"I remembered you liked tea." Logan leaned across and handed her a hot cup as he spoke.

Suzanne took the tea and reached for the sandwich he offered.

"I hope you like ham and cheese."

"That's great."

Logan forced himself to eat in silence. He wanted her to relax and had thought that eating companionably together might do the trick. But when she stayed perched on the edge of her chair, he decided to plunge right in.

"We're going to have to go faster than we thought on this deal."

Suzanne stopped in the middle of a bite, and gingerly put her sandwich on its wrapping paper. Swallowing quickly, she asked, "Faster? We haven't even gotten started."

Logan ignored her observation. "We've received information that a group here is trying out a new synthetic drug. We think the main supply line is coming out of Gruenville." He still wasn't sure she would really go through with her plan. Today would tell.

"How do you know?"

"When we met in Dan's office, I told you we've been working on this for a while. We finally got a break. We've got taps on several phones. Someone made a mistake and told the wrong person, and we got the information." He took a long swallow of soft drink, but watched her closely.

"Do you know who's making it?"

"Not exactly. But we do know they don't peddle the stuff directly. It comes through your little town before it hits the streets of Austin, San Antonio or Houston."

"Why would they do that?"

"To convolute the path. To confuse us. Hell, who knows? If we understood why these people did things, we wouldn't need people like you to help us catch them."

"So, how are we going to be involved?"

"You're going to start buying immediately."

"*What?*" Suzanne leapt up, spilling her chair backward.

Logan had known her reaction would be violent. What he hadn't bargained on was his hesitation on telling her. He again felt the overwhelming need to protect this woman, to shield her from the seamy underside of life. And it confused the hell out of him. It was a new feeling for him, and he didn't know how to deal with it. None of his other relationships with women had prepared him for this one. For an instant, he flashed back to Sunday afternoon and the lightning tree.

The feel of her, so small, so fragile in his arms. The way her body had arched into his, so innocently. He was going to send this woman, who nurtured daffodils and roses, out into the streets asking for drugs? There were times, like now, when he wished he'd chosen the crime lab route exclusively, where he could bury himself in its sterile environment. There he could fight the war against drugs with knowledge, test tubes and lab reports, not flesh, blood and raw feelings.

But, instead, he'd listened to Dan, his old mentor and boss, and joined the small-town drug task force. So, here he was telling a wide-eyed innocent to hit the streets. He fought his protective feelings and launched into an explanation. He had a job to do.

"I know it's not what you expected. But Dan and I have talked it over and we feel the folks of Gruenville will sell to you much faster than to me, no matter how close they think we are. And we need to stop this flow of junk."

"In all the conversations I had with Dan, he never, ever mentioned this." Suzanne's accusatory tone made him wince.

"I told you he didn't tell you everything." Logan kept his voice hard. This might be where she decided to exit. "He was so happy to have someone on the inside, he conveniently forgot all the horrors of going undercover with drug cases."

"I want to hear this from Dan." She got up abruptly and moved purposefully to the door. Logan moved swiftly, rounding the desk and grabbing her hand even as she tried to turn the knob.

"No. *I'm* the one you need to talk to. You forget, I'm in charge of this, and if you leave this room, you won't be helping catch your sister's killers, you'll be signing your resignation papers." He glowered at her. "Make up your mind. Deal with me, or you're off the case."

He watched her face. Fear and confusion flashed in her eyes. Several slow seconds dragged by. Finally a look of resolution settled on her brow. She nodded her head.

He led her firmly back to her chair and eased her into it. "Sit down. Let me explain. It sounds a lot worse than it really is."

"It's just that to buy drugs from the same people who murdered my sister seems so... inhuman." Her voice wavered with anguish.

"It's part of what you have to do to get hard evidence," Logan explained. "They'll sell to you much faster than to me. I'll be near you or with you when you make the buys, though."

"Are you sure they'll fall for this? After all, I don't have a wild reputation." She looked earnestly at him as she continued. "I don't want to fail at this and then lose the opportunity to catch Natalie's killers."

Logan shook his head. "You still don't want to admit what we're dealing with here." His eyes held hers. "These people *sell drugs,* Suzanne, not flowers. And they don't care to whom. All they want is the extra cash it will put in their pockets. And they damn sure don't care what happens to the people they sell to."

"I just thought my part was to get you into the social scene and you would do the buying."

"*You* know these people. You'll do the buying." Logan allowed her an extra minute to digest the order, before pressing on. "Do you think Natalie bought her stuff from a stranger? My professional guess is she got it here, at the college, and that same person would have no trouble taking your money. Stop trying to redeem everyone. It's not possible."

Suzanne sat lost in thought for so long, Logan was sure she had changed her mind about the whole thing. Finally she raised her eyes to his. "What do I have to do?"

Logan let out his breath slowly. "We have some ideas on who might be dealing drugs." Moving back to his desk, he settled into his chair once again. "But we need some hits of cocaine and maybe several pounds of marijuana to make any arrests stick."

"And you'll tell me who to target?" Suzanne's quiet voice went straight through him.

"You'll have to buy from several people." Logan bit back a curse when her eyes widened. He felt a renewed pang of guilt at using her for this job, but ignored it. These bastards had to be put out of business and Suzanne had signed on of her own free will. "The word will get out that you're buying. First you'll go for the smaller stuff, marijuana, then the cocaine and, if we get real lucky, you'll score some Cyclone."

"What's that?" Suzanne clutched her hands to her mouth.

"It's the latest in designer drugs. It's worse than angel dust—really goes to your head and makes you feel invisible."

"Oh my God," she whispered. She looked sharply at him. "Do I have to take the stuff in order to make the arrests valid?"

Damn, he hated doing this to her. He cursed again, this time at Dan Rider for putting him in this situation. He wanted nothing more than to erase the image of her sitting here, full of fragile courage. His instincts shouted he should pull her onto his lap and shield her from all of this garbage. Hell, if he were honest, he'd admit protecting her from the muck they were entering wasn't the only reason he wanted her in his lap.

It was all coming down exactly as he'd imagined it would. He was feeling protective toward her, on top of the complication of wanting her. The combination of the two was lethal. When a cop had to keep one eye on his partner, mistakes were made. Deadly mistakes. Worse yet, Suzanne's emotional stake in all this still clawed at his gut. Carla had been just as emotionally involved, had acted foolishly. She'd gone out on her own and gotten herself killed. No way could he let something like that happen again. This time, he would do his damnedest to control the whole operation, including this woman sitting in front of him.

"No, of course not," he answered her coolly. "You just have to buy it. We'll be able to use what you get as hard evidence."

He watched as she reorganized herself. After taking a deep breath, she ran her fingers through her hair, then straightened the straps of her overalls. He waited, knowing what this decision was doing to her. For the first time, she was being forced to admit that the safe, secure world she'd lived in was really loaded with traps, and that she could fall into one of them. With her next words, she would be restructuring her image of reality.

"Okay. I guess I don't have a choice."

"You always have a choice." Logan leaned toward her. "And no one would blame you if you said no. We know you didn't sign on for this."

"No, I didn't," Suzanne admitted. "But I did sign on. And I'm not backing down now."

"Good." And surprisingly, he meant it. He didn't care to analyze why he was glad she had decided to stay in the operation since he didn't want her to, but he knew that she was feeling some guilt over Natalie's death and that staying in the game would ease that. He would just have to see to it that she didn't get in too deeply, he vowed silently. "Now that you've made that decision, I want to show you something. Come with me."

Suzanne followed him down to the ground floor and into a science classroom. "This is my classroom most of the time. But what I really want to show you is back in the lab storage area."

They moved through a connecting door into a smaller area that had shelves stocked with chemistry supplies and a desk area with a computer. Logan sat in front of the computer and motioned for her to take a seat on a stool nearby. He flipped on the computer and as the screen sprang to life, he talked. "I want to show you exactly how important you are to this case."

He jabbed buttons on the computer, creating what looked to Suzanne like spirals, triangles and squares. "Watch."

"What am I looking at?"

"How a drug hits the street and how much damage it can do." He pointed to the spirals on the screen. "These represent thousands of pounds of marijuana, the triangles are cocaine and the squares are Cyclone. Follow the path...."

Suzanne listened as Logan showed her how the schematic took her from labs, to dealers, to street vendors, to customers and how the numbers got bigger as you went down. As he talked, she became conscious of two things. One, she was amazed at how complicated, how sophisticated the network was, and how insignificant she felt next to it.

Her other revelation dealt with Logan. His voice was animated, intense. During the demonstration, he even made the computer, through something called a HyperCard stack, take her through the chemistry of making the new drug, Cyclone. He was at home here in this world of black-and-white images on the screen, of sure results if you followed the correct sequence. It was obvious by the rapt, almost excited expression on his face, that he liked fiddling with computers and test tubes. Things that she found cold and lifeless were intriguing to Logan. She was trying to integrate this Logan into her overall picture of him when she realized he'd quit talking.

She filled in the void. "And I'm supposed to impact that?"

"You're going to help destroy it." He turned and faced her. "And that's why you're so important to this case."

Suzanne nodded. "I don't quite understand all of this. I just want to help put Natalie's killers in jail."

"That's what we both want." Logan waited a beat before he went on. "And, Suzanne..."

"Yes?"

"About Sunday."

He watched her tense.

"What about it?"

"Like I said, you did great. Everyone who saw us together is probably wondering when the wedding will be." Logan stood up and walked over to a counter strewn with test tubes. He turned away from her as he said, "And you're going to have to be that convincing when we go to our first buying party."

There was a long silence. Logan didn't turn around, purposely giving her time to assimilate what he'd said. He knew Sunday hadn't been an act, knew when a woman was responding honestly. What he didn't want her to know was that it hadn't been an act for him, either. God help him, he wanted her like no other woman he'd ever met. But she could never know. For once, her innocence would protect her, because he was sure she'd believe him when he continued to act unaffected. And as long as he kept his professional control over the situation, she would always think he was faking it.

She broke into his thoughts when she said, "Sunday was easy. Don't worry. I can handle it. And everyone is so happy I've finally discovered a man, I shouldn't have any trouble with too much speculation. When do we start?"

He waited a pulse-beat, then turned around. "Tonight. I pick you up at seven. We're going to a faculty party."

"Tonight?"

"Don't worry. Before we leave, we'll spend an hour discussing how you approach someone, what you say. We need you to be as convincing as possible this first time."

"Then you better come earlier. I'm going to need a lot of help."

"Just be ready," Logan demanded. "I'll do the rest."

Chapter 5

He'd gotten there early, at *her* request, and she wasn't even there. Logan mumbled to himself as he pulled on a cowbell with painted bluebonnets all over it. Why couldn't she have a normal doorbell? He probably should be grateful it wasn't a talking flower. When they'd gone to her grandmother's, he'd picked her up at The Good Earth, and it had been too dark to really get a look at her home when he'd dropped her off. Consequently, he was *seeing* it for the first time.

The weird thing was it wasn't a house at all, but an old converted barn. Leave it to Suzanne to take something that was supposed to be filled with smelly animals and turn it into a house. And, if he had to guess, it would be filled to the rafters with greenery.

He was here to take her to the party and to give her some pointers about how to approach people about buying drugs. He flinched even thinking about her doing it. Somehow he just couldn't imagine her pure mouth forming the words needed to buy narcotics.

She was a walking daffodil, a nurturer. And it was his job to turn this sweet thing into something that could attract the sleaze they needed to catch. This was definitely turning out to be his hardest assignment. He hated having to use her.

Shrugging away his doubts, he gave the cowbell one more yank. When no one came to the door, he decided to wander around the barn-house to the back.

He wasn't surprised to see the landscaping miracle all around him. He'd been prepared by the grandmother's house. There were terraces of flowers, a profusion of colors surrounding the barn. When he made it around to the back, he saw a three-tiered wooden deck speckled with hanging plants, flowers and vines. A jungle. Suzanne must have a secret fantasy about Tarzan. Everywhere she'd done her thing, there was enough greenery to furnish the set of any tropical island. Unbidden, the thought of being alone with her on a lush green isle popped into his mind and he fantasized seeing her in a sarong, lounging by a pool, waiting for him.

His thoughts led him to wonder if there was a hot tub tucked away in the decking. He was just getting ready to investigate when he heard a car racing up the road.

He heard her before he saw her. A car door slammed, feet ran through the grass and Suzanne called, "I'm sorry I'm late."

"That's okay. I was just taking a look around." He saw her as she rounded the corner.

"I would've been here sooner except a couple came into the store and wanted a corsage."

Logan noticed the sparkle in her eyes as she continued. "They were eloping. Isn't that wonderful? Naturally, I couldn't *just* do a corsage. So I made this great bouquet for her and a boutonniere for him."

"Of course, what else could you do?" Logan murmured, keeping his eyes from rolling skyward.

"It was so romantic. You should've seen the way they looked at each other."

"Right," Logan said impatiently. "But we need to get to the party. You haven't forgotten about tonight, have you?"

"Oh my gosh!" She hurried toward the back door. "I *had* forgotten for a minute." Her voice lost its lightness, replaced by an underlying tension. "Come on." She opened the door and waited for him to walk in.

"You're going to have to hurry. We're running late."

"I know, I know."

"Tonight is very important. It sets the stage for the rest of the operation. You've got to play your part perfectly." He gave her a level look.

"Logan, I really do understand." Her brow was furrowed in concentration and her mouth was set in a sober line, out of character from its usual sunny smile. He didn't like the change, but steadfastly ignored analyzing why.

"Good." He nodded his head, satisfied that she would try her best tonight at helping to incriminate some of Gruenville's leading citizens in drug trafficking.

"By the way, Logan, make yourself at home."

Logan looked around, and with one glance verified his earlier suspicions. The converted barn was quintessential Suzanne—an indoor flower show. It was one giant room with a loft upstairs. There were flowers hanging and sitting everywhere, and the sofa cushions were made of floral fabric. There was even a sign over the stove that read Annuals, Geraniums, Pansies.

"Are you ever anywhere where there *isn't* wildlife growing inside?"

"I try not to be for long." She pointed toward the tiny kitchen area. "There's cold stuff to drink in the refrigerator. I'll just run upstairs and change. It won't take me long."

He watched her take the steps to the loft two at a time and then turned to wander into the kitchen area. He had to admit he liked the open feel of the entire place. There were no walls, just a giant room with seating areas artfully arranged. Her desk was in a corner and gave her a view of the gardens out back. The couch faced a huge window that also held a view of the countryside. In fact, he doubted that there was anywhere in the place one could sit and not be close to a whole mess of flowers.

She'd created another magical setting for her life. With a dark, impatient sigh, he knew he was back to square one. He was going to teach this person how to buy drugs? Whatever else happened, he knew that this situation would probably destroy the beauty, the magic that followed Suzanne everywhere. And what would he replace it with? A flowery brand of cynicism? Reality, in its starkest form? Was he really prepared to do that?

He answered himself honestly. Yes. He was willing to pull her from her flower cocoon in order to put a dent into the drug business. It was his job, his duty. He'd done worse, to take poison off the streets. Then why the hell didn't it feel right this time?

Unwilling to dwell on his thoughts, he retrieved a beer from the fridge, sighing as he popped the tab. Walking to the couch, he moved a draping plant over and sat down.

When he tipped his head back to take a sip of beer, he froze. There, upstairs, in the reflection of an old-fashioned freestanding beveled mirror, was Suzanne, and she was slipping out of her clothes. The loft was cast in shadow, but the effect was oddly more provocative than any bright light could have created. As though in a delightfully erotic dream, he watched as she skimmed off her shorts, turned and kicked them out of her way. His breathing stopped as he looked at long, slim legs that seemed to gleam with a pale radiance in the dusky light and then it came back in with a whoosh when he saw her curvy derriere covered in a tiny triangle of lavender lace.

He knew that she was completely unaware he could see her; she was being too natural for it to be otherwise. Besides, she was too innocent to stage such a provocative show. And that was precisely what made it so damn seductive. Every decent instinct in him shouted at him to turn away, but his body wasn't answering his mind. He was spellbound. When she lifted the bottom of her T-shirt and began to pull it off, he finally managed to shake himself free. Jumping up, he shakily seated himself opposite the couch in a huge, overstuffed chair, with his back to the loft.

Suzanne called to him. "Did you get something to drink?"

He imagined her without the T-shirt. "Yes," he croaked. After clearing his throat, he tried again. "Yes, I did, thanks."

Forcing himself to dwell on more mundane topics, he asked, "The Good Earth must be a pretty good business for you to be able to decorate this place like this."

"I do pretty well." She peeked her head over the railing of the loft. "But my family helped me with this place. Brandon wired it for electricity, one of the other cousins built this loft, Gram and Christine helped me reupholster the sofa and chairs."

Logan digested the information for a few seconds. Her family was certainly different from his. His family never shared or helped each other like that. They were all separate, unconnected. Whereas this family seemed to be joined and, like the planets revolving around the sun, all revolved around Gram, their own, personal sun.

Suzanne leaned over the railing, belting on a robe, and asked, "What does your family think about your spending months in Gruenville?"

"My dad lives in East Texas. I don't see him much. Mom died years ago. I've got an older sister who I usually spend holidays with. I've also got assorted relatives scattered around the state."

"I bet somewhere in those relatives you've got a lot of little kids who love it when you visit and play with them."

He gave her a puzzled look. "Yeah. How'd you know?"

"You were so good with the little ones at Gram's." She smiled down at him. "Anyone can see you love children. Any child who has you for a father will be fortunate."

He took another swallow of the beer. "I have a son."

"Pardon?"

"A son, Ryan. I have a son. I was married for five years." He stood and paced between the couch and the fireplace.

"Where is he?"

"With his mother."

From her vantage point Suzanne watched Logan stalk the room. She was reminded of her first impression of him, that of a caged mountain lion—all silky muscle, with a wariness toward his surroundings that could easily turn dangerous. In his restless prowling, she could sense he'd been wounded deeply.

He turned his cat's eyes up to her. "Six months after we divorced, Debby, my ex-wife, got a promotion and transferred to Seattle. Ryan went with her. I don't get to see him often now."

"I'm sorry, Logan."

"I am, too." He stopped in front of the fireplace and leaned against the mantel. He shook off his mood by telling her, "Hurry up, we're late."

She hesitated before she complied. "Okay. I'm going to take a quick shower and throw on a dress."

Immediately her words chased away his thoughts about family and he found himself imagining her doing just that— showering. Closing his eyes, he lingered on the fantasy of her in the shower. Only, in his mind, she wasn't alone. He was there with her, and it wasn't a quick shower. He let his mind drift until he could actually feel the water running over them. He would run his hands across those tempting curves he'd seen in the mirror. Her skin would be slick with water, then hot with desire. She'd moan and ask him to... He heard the water shut off upstairs.

Biting back a groan, he forced himself out of his daydream. She was getting to him. Worse than he thought. Even Debby, at the beginning of their marriage hadn't brought on these kinds of fantasies. Yet this small, elfin woman had managed, with her flowers and naïveté, to broach walls he hadn't even known he'd built. Never had the mere sight of a half-clad body glowing in muted light made him this needy, this tight for a woman. And he was disgusted that he couldn't control the instantaneous physical reaction he had to Suzanne.

With an effort, he thought of other things, hoping to tame the bulge in his pants before Suzanne came downstairs. He hadn't been totally honest with her when he'd mentioned Debby. It was true he hadn't given Debby what she needed. He'd given as much of a commitment as he could, and it hadn't been enough. What he'd forgotten to say was that his marriage wasn't the first time he'd left people needing. It had all started with... his father.

His father. He hadn't really thought of him in years. As he sat down again, his father's face materialized in front of him as clearly as if dear old Dad were standing there, frowning.

The same look, the one of disappointment, was there. Logan clenched his teeth at the specter. He'd never been able to be the perfect son his dad had wanted, needed. Logan had always fallen just short. Never the quarterback, just the lineman. Never the straight *A* student, just an average *B* student. Never the millionaire, just a cop.

Letting his head fall back against the chair's headrest, he closed his eyes and remembered one specific incident, a long time ago. He'd been about five or six, running like a hellion with the neighborhood kids, enjoying a rough game of tag. He hadn't seen the vine or felt it wrap around his foot, but before he could catch his balance, he'd tripped.

Sprawling chin first onto the ground, the next thing he'd remembered was his father looking at him with a severe expression and the other kids huddled around him. He could still feel the silence.

"Get up," his father had commanded.

He'd somehow struggled to his feet, and then he'd realized the bottom of his chin felt like it was on fire and was bleeding a glistening, red river down his shirt.

He'd punctured the underside of his chin after falling on a stick. For many days after that he'd been sore and feverish. His mother had tried to fuss over him at first, but his father wouldn't permit it. His father hated messy, emotional scenes.

And his mother's death had been messy. An alcoholic, lost in a world of wine, she had taken too many pills one night and had died before the morning.

The first day after her death, when Logan had been so confused and lost, his father's large frame had filled the doorway of his room as he'd stopped by to set Logan straight.

"Your mother's not worth those tears, boy." His father had walked into the room and stood over him. "I gave her everything. Everything. And what did she do? She left us— on purpose. She didn't give a damn about us."

Logan had been paralyzed by his father's words. *His mother, whom he loved with all his heart, hadn't loved him?*

"Son," his father had continued, "I never want to see you cry. Never."

He remembered immediately swiping away his tears and sniffling.

"Yes, sir," he'd managed to whisper.

"When you feel like crying, whistle instead."

He'd disappeared from the bedroom, leaving Logan with an empty feeling. Betrayed. That's what his mother had done. Betrayed him.

He'd learned several lessons that night. One, you couldn't trust people when they said they loved you. And two, eventually, you were going to be alone, so it was better to hold yourself back from real emotional commitment. Debby, his ex-wife, had tried to build a world with him, but he'd "whistled" her away, too.

He took a long drink of his beer, washing away the bitter memories. He thought he'd dealt with them, finished with them, long ago. But only eight days into this case with "Miss Sweetness and Light" and all his insecurities were there again. Hell, he couldn't even give his own son what he needed—a real father.

He stood in agitation and began pacing the house. He accidentally knocked over a planter. Cursing, he put down his beer, then knelt, to try and repair the damage. Just as he was scooping a handful of dirt back into the planter, Suzanne called to him.

"Logan, I need your help."

"What is it?" He didn't stop his task.

"This zipper's stuck and I can't get it up or down."

The image pierced him. Lord. He gritted his teeth at the current of need and desire that flashed through him at the thought of touching her.

"Logan?"

"Yeah?" He knew his voice was unusually harsh. Slowly he stood up and turned toward the stairs.

"I'll come down there to make it easier for you."

"Stay where you are." He was up into the loft area before she put her foot near the first step.

"Here." She turned around. "Zip me up."

Logan took a step forward and then stopped. Her back was almost bare, with the two sides of the dress hanging open. He swallowed. She wasn't wearing a bra. He clenched his hands to still them before he reached for the wayward zipper. He tried jerking it up.

"Hey, don't yank like that. You'll tear it."

"Sorry." He leaned forward and bent down to see what was caught. Her smell enveloped him. Lilacs—fresh, pure.

A quick glance upward showed him a cluster of them were entwined and pinned to one side of her hair.

Forcing himself to concentrate on the zipper, he located and moved the bit of material that was caught. He had to insert two of his fingers down the dark V below the stuck zipper. Her skin was as warm and soft as a newborn's. Touching her was a mixture of pure heaven and hot hell.

Beads of perspiration dotted his upper lip as the stubborn material refused to budge. After seconds, which seemed more like hours, he succeeded in releasing the zipper. The grating of it moving up sounded like a machine gun to him. He felt her take a breath.

"Thanks." She turned to him with an uncertain smile. "Let me get my purse and I'll be ready."

She started for the stairs, but his husky voice stopped her.

"Not so fast. We have a few more things to go over yet."

She turned to face him, and all thought of his mission evaporated as he took in her appearance. She was wrapped in a white sundress with lavender flowers on it. He hadn't seen her in anything that displayed her form before, but this dress, with its body-hugging bodice and sweetheart neckline, showed him that his fantasies were a pale substitute for the real thing. For all her petite size, her body had been molded by a master craftsman.

"Logan?" she prompted.

He swallowed. "Do you have any idea how you're going to do your job tonight?"

She shook her head. "I assumed you were going to teach me what to do. That is what you said, wasn't it?"

"Yes. I am." He took a deep breath. "Come downstairs and I'll go over the who and what of the party."

Logan waited for her to go down the stairs before he followed. He told himself he was being a gentleman, but he knew it was a cheap bid to give him time to calm down. The sight and smell of her had thrown him. He needed to get his equilibrium back. His professionalism.

"Logan, are you coming?" Suzanne's voice jarred him. He smiled grimly at her choice of words. "Sure."

When they were both standing next to the couch, he took a piece of paper out of his pocket. "Here's a list of the people you should approach."

She took the list, started reading and had to sit down. "All of these people?"

"Yes. We don't expect you to make contact with all of them tonight, but we do expect you to get to the top two. Now this is just a list of suspects—many will probably turn out *not* to have anything to do with the drug problem here in Gruenville. Our job is to find out which ones do."

"How do you know these are the people I should contact? Some of them are pretty important persons in this town." She looked up at him with astonishment and pain in her eyes.

"I told you about having to turn in your neighbors, friends. Who did you expect to see on the list?" He turned away and plowed his fingers through his hair. Damn it. He hated that their case depended on her. He hated that she had to do this.

"I don't know. But most of these people do business with me."

When he turned to face her, he made sure his face was impassive. "Good. Now you can do business with them."

"That's not funny."

"I wasn't making a joke." Logan sat next to her. "Ask me."

"What?"

"If I would sell you drugs." His eyes were hard.

"Just like that? Aren't you going to give me some code or something?"

"Damn, are you really this naive?" Logan's eyes drilled into her. "I want you to be natural. I can't put words into your mouth until I know your approach."

She turned red and twisted her hands together. "Okay." She started to speak, but then stopped. "But I know this isn't for real."

"Suzanne, *do it.*" The hardness in his voice made her jump.

She took a deep breath. Her eyes fastened on Logan's. "I want— No." She started again, her voice firm, resolute. "Logan, I need some stuff. Do you know where I can score?"

Logan's eyebrows went up. He'd expected a more round-about—more wishy-washy—approach. But she'd surprised him again. "Where did you learn that?"

"I watch television." She raised her chin. "Is that good enough?"

He smiled. "It's close enough. Try not to be so direct. Make sure you have your target alone, away from other people. Act casual. You might want to mention that you know Natalie was getting it in town—stuff like that. Take the offensive."

"Logan, I know you think I'm some Pollyanna. And, compared to you, I am." She looked him directly in the eye. "But I really think I can do this. Now let's get going. My career as a drug buster is beginning for real tonight."

"Is the party at the college president's house?"

They were in Logan's Jeep, zipping along the quiet streets of Gruenville.

"Yes. We've discovered that the college is the base of the ring's operations. That's why my cover involves a professorship. We think they're targeting the youth market here." Logan kept his eyes on the road as he looked for the landmarks that would signal his turn. He was looking for a residential street where the houses were large and stately. "This party is in honor of a man who's just given a large sum of money to the college. His name's John Wells, I believe."

"John Wells?"

Logan slanted a quick, curious look at Suzanne. "Yeah. You know him?"

Suzanne shook her head. "I haven't met him, but I've met his wife and daughter. The daughter's getting married in a few weeks, and I'm catering it."

By that time they had arrived at the college president's home. Cars were lined up and down the street, and Logan had to park several houses down from their destination. He hurried around to help Suzanne out of the Jeep and was again struck by how fresh and luscious she looked. He had to consciously force his wayward thoughts away from dwelling on how the bodice of the sundress hugged her curves. This was not a date. Suzanne was his partner in an important and risky undercover operation. They were out together to get evidence against drug dealers and nothing more.

"Come on," he said as he draped an arm across her shoulders and guided her toward a large, redbrick Georgian-style home.

Suzanne gave him a quick look.

"We have to appear to be lovers. Remember that," he said with a frown.

"I'm nervous," she admitted as they moved up the stone walkway.

"Don't be. Just remember, we're the good guys." He gave her shoulders a squeeze just before the door was opened by a uniformed servant who pointed the way to the reception line.

They walked a few steps into the foyer, where a small man with a shock of snow-white hair and a red face pumped Logan's hand. "Logan, glad you could make it."

"President Timsdale, this is Suzanne Stewart."

"Suzanne, how lovely you look tonight."

He proceeded to wrap Suzanne in a bear hug as Logan stood stiffly by her side.

"Edward—" Suzanne smiled beguilingly up at him "—I haven't seen you in the store lately." She felt Logan squeeze her arm and turned to explain, "President Timsdale is a regular customer at The Good Earth. He has a hothouse out back where he raises orchids."

Logan merely raised his eyebrows at her news, but a silent message passed between them. His eyes telegraphed, *Do you know everyone in this town?*

"And let me introduce Gruenville Community College's newest benefactor. Logan Davis, Suzanne Stewart, this is John Wells."

"Nice to meet you, Mr. Wells." Logan shook his hand. "Your gift to the school will reap great benefits for the entire community."

"It's a pleasure to give back to the town," John Wells replied smoothly. He was just as tall as Logan, but a paunch was beginning to spread around his midsection.

"Hello, Mr. Wells." Suzanne shifted the attention to her small frame.

John Wells beamed down at her. "John, please."

Suzanne inclined her head, smiling. "John. Your wife and daughter have been in to see me many times in the last few months—I'm catering the wedding."

"That's fine, fine," he boomed. "Gretchen and Jill couldn't make it tonight. Too busy making plans." His eyes gleamed. "What say I come by your office tomorrow afternoon to discuss costs?"

Suzanne nodded.

More guests were arriving, so Logan and she moved on into an elegant living room off to the left. The room had a high-arched ceiling and tall windows flanking the front wall. A massive fireplace dominated the wall directly opposite them and a glistening chandelier added the final touch of elegance to the room.

"Brandon." Suzanne, spotting her cousin, went to greet him. He stood with a bored expression on his handsome face as he lounged with one booted foot against the stone fireplace.

Logan followed Suzanne a bit more slowly, eyeing Brandon closely. What was he doing here? He watched as the two cousins embraced, before they separated to make introductions.

"Davis." Brandon acknowledged Logan as they shook hands.

"Brandon, darling, don't forget your manners." Long red fingernails appeared on the sleeve of Brandon's shirt as a slim, stunning blonde slithered to his side.

Brandon scowled before he introduced his date. "Sheila, this is my cousin Suzanne Stewart, and this is Logan Davis. Sheila Martin is new this semester at the college, just like you, Logan. She's the new homemaking teacher."

From the calculating look in Sheila's eyes as she limply laid her hand in his, Logan decided she probably made a better home *wrecker* than home*maker*.

"And what do you teach, Logan?" As she spoke, Sheila ran her hand in caressing circles up and down Brandon's arm.

"Chemistry." Logan sensed Brandon's displeasure at the cloying attention of the sexy Miss Martin.

She leaned toward Logan, pressing her generous bosom against his arm. "Oh, I just love chemistry. Especially the kind between people." She looked up into his face, wearing her most meaningful expression.

It was all Logan could do to keep from laughing out loud at her poorly concealed come-on.

After chatting with the couple for several minutes, Suzanne and Logan again moved on. They both knew why they were here. The more people they met and became familiar with, the more information they might be privy to and the easier it might be for Suzanne to make a contact.

Eventually they ambled outside to the back patio. Logan discreetly called Suzanne's attention to a man with thin wheat-colored hair and wire-rimmed glasses who was standing under a huge oak tree by himself. Philip Jones was the professor at the college who had mentioned to Logan that he loved to have frat parties at his house. He was also the second person on the list he'd shown Suzanne.

"This is it. Take it slow, and don't spook him." Logan squeezed her arm. "I'm going to go and mingle. Just casually drift over there and feel your way into the conversation. I'll meet you at the punch bowl later."

Suzanne took a deep breath and smilingly parted from Logan. Seemingly with no real purpose, she approached the man.

"Hi, Philip." Look relaxed, old girl, she told herself.

"Hi, Suzanne. Isn't it?" He smiled at her and Suzanne could detect nothing sinister or menacing in his appearance.

"Yes. I own The Good Earth. You've been in to buy baked goods." So far, so good, she reasoned. Now what?

Seconds ticked by and neither made light conversation.

"Uh, Philip, I was told you might be able to help me...." Her voice trailed off in embarrassed silence.

"With what?" Philip's brows drew together.

"I'm looking for...I mean my boyfriend's looking for...some quality smoke," she said softly. When he didn't say anything, she finally blurted out, "Do you have any reefer to sell?"

His eyes widened and he paled before the chalky color was replaced by a bright scarlet. Veins throbbed in his neck.

For a minute Suzanne thought he was going to have a heart attack, but quickly he spat out, "Are you crazy?" He then turned and disappeared around the corner of the house.

Mortified Suzanne stood quietly under the tree for several minutes, trying to gather her scattered wits and dignity. Fool, she silently chastised herself. Did you really think this was going to be easy?

Squaring her shoulders, she went to join Logan at the punch bowl. At his raised eyebrows she shook her head, but they didn't discuss the incident. Too many ears would make their conversation less than private.

They continued to circulate and mingle, Logan introducing her to the few people she didn't know. Finally she excused herself to freshen up in the ladies' room.

The task complete, she decided that she didn't want to return just yet to the hubbub of the party. Soon enough she'd have to approach someone else about making a buy, but right now she needed more peace and quiet. Entering a room on her left, she found herself in a library that looked like something right out of *Architectural Digest*. Just as she started to browse among the books on the shelves, Margaret Dimpsey and Donna Sue King, whom she knew from her many summers in Gruenville and who now frequented her shop, swept into the room.

Surprised to find the room occupied, the two engaged Suzanne in the usual hellos.

"Suzanne Stewart," Donna Sue, the stocky, athletic-looking one began, "I didn't know you had it in you."

"Pardon?"

"The man, Suzanne, the man," Margaret explained.

"You mean Logan?" Suzanne was uneasy; no telling where this conversation could lead. She had to watch her step. She couldn't say anything to jeopardize their cover.

"Is that his name? Didn't I hear something about him teaching biology or something at the college?"

"Chemistry."

"Chemistry, biology—whatever. I bet the girls in his class outnumber the guys ten to one." Donna Sue winked at Suzanne. "I'd sign up, too, if I had the time."

"How in the world did you two ever get together?" Margaret asked. "You've always been such a shy little thing. I can't imagine such a big, male animal coming on to you."

Margaret Dimpsey had no idea how her words cut Suzanne to the quick. It was just as it had always been. No one believed Suzanne could get—and hold—a man. Of course, she hadn't tried very hard since the incident in college, but then, no one in town knew about that. And Logan *was* just pretending. She felt like a supreme idiot. At that moment she hated her image as the girl-next-door in Gruenville.

"Sweetheart?"

Three pairs of eyes swung to the doorway, where Logan stood like a mountain lion stalking his prey. He advanced toward the three women. Margaret and Donna Sue took a step back. "I was lonely," he murmured huskily. He slid his arm around her waist and pulled her securely to his side. Tawny eyes sparkled with a fire Suzanne didn't understand before he looked over at the two openmouthed women. "Excuse us, ladies. Suzanne and I want to be alone."

Chapter 6

"Dear God, I was terrible." Suzanne leaned back against the headrest in Logan's Jeep and closed her eyes.

"You weren't *that* bad." Logan's voice, rich and deep, reached out to her as he spoke. "At least not for your first time."

Her eyes flew open and green fire spewed from them. "Don't you dare mock me. I know this is crucial to my role and I didn't perform well."

Logan smiled grimly. "I'm not mocking you. And you're right. You do have to do better the next time. For now, let's just say that you were perspiring and looking so nervous, you probably fooled the few people you hit on into believing you're a novice at this."

Suzanne sniffed self-righteously. "It was awful, so nerve-racking. I could barely get out the words." She opened her eyes and stared at Logan. "How do you deal with the pressure day in and day out?" She took in the way he fairly radiated confidence in his casual clothing, while her insides felt as if they were shaking loose.

"I'm not going to lie to you. You never get used to it. You just numb yourself to it, that's all."

"Numb yourself?"

"Yeah. Just control your emotions and do whatever it takes to succeed."

"And that works for you?" Suzanne forced herself to sit up and watch him intently.

Logan turned a corner before he answered. "Most of the time." Yeah, it worked for him. He made it work. His father and mother had taught him well. You couldn't really trust people to be there for you. So you had yourself, and you had your job. And his job was what he saved his real passion for.

"I don't think I could do that, at least not forever. But I'll do it for now because it's the only way I can make those creeps who killed my sister pay." She slouched back down. "I can remember every word, every gesture that happened tonight. I never realized what people were really talking about in those corners before."

Logan frowned, but remained silent, as if giving her time to digest what she'd discovered about her neighbors and friends.

She closed her eyes and thought about the evening. The faculty barbecue would have been fun if their purpose hadn't been so serious. She knew many of the staff and had been greeted warmly. It was just like hundreds of other social functions she'd attended in Gruenville. Only this time, she'd sensed hidden meanings behind every comment and detected secret messages in every glance. And, of course, there was her botched conversation with Philip Jones, which had been dreadfully embarrassing. Logan broke into her thoughts.

"Of course, I'm not in the pressure-cooker position of the street cop anymore now that I work on the drug task force, but it's never easy, especially in drug cases."

She opened her eyes once again and stared at the dark street as familiar landmarks passed by. "All my life I've lived quietly, simply. I've never sought the fast life or danger or whatever it is some people are out there searching for. I thought my life was as close to perfect as it could get. Then Natalie." How could she have been so stupid to give her sister the money? Silently, Suzanne condemned herself for the millionth time.

And how could Natalie have let her boyfriend lure her into doing something so hideous and deadly as taking drugs? Did all men try to control women? She glanced at Logan. Is that what had gone wrong in his marriage? She wanted to believe the answer to that question was no. But he'd just admitted his greatest asset on the job was control.

She sighed, suddenly tired of the game she and Logan were forced to play. "This is foreign to me and I'm afraid I botched it badly tonight. I'm going to need your help to be successful enough to make a difference . . . and I *will* make a difference." She ran her fingers through her curly hair, tucking her legs beneath her.

"We'll practice some more, polish your . . . skills." Had she noticed the hitch in his voice, the pause as his eyes had been drawn to her silken legs in their seductively feline position? *Get a grip on yourself, Logan,* he warned himself. "Uh, by the way, has Brandon been going with the home-economics prof long? I was surprised to see him at the party tonight."

"As far as I know, he's just started seeing her. Why?" She pierced him with a suspicious glance.

"Anyone at these get-togethers is a suspect." He smiled slowly at her. "Even your cousin."

"That is the most ridiculous thing you've said yet, Logan Davis. Brandon would never sell drugs. He was as devastated as we all were with Natalie's death." As she spoke, she uncurled from her comfortable position and planted her feet rigidly on the floor of the vehicle.

"I bet you thought your sister would never take drugs, either."

Suzanne frowned, perversely disgusted with his accurate assumption. Of course, Logan was right. He always seemed to be right. But, in her heart, she hoped he was wrong about this suspicion. Brandon could never be one of them; she didn't think she could stand it if another member of her family was directly involved in this mess.

She stared at Logan again. He was so handsome in a rough, rugged sort of way. His bushy eyebrows lent him a dangerous air while the yellow flecks in his brown eyes added to the effect of a prowling mountain cat, always wary, always alone. His comments tonight about control explained a lot about him, and explained how he was able to play her lover so convincingly.

Knowing that he had a son he didn't get to see very often added to the picture Suzanne mentally drew of him. She envisioned him shrouded in an early-morning fog, lonely but rigid against the elements. He would never admit to feeling alone but would wait until he could claim control and then proceed.

She knew that because he'd been the perfect attentive partner tonight. He'd spent most of the evening with his arm draped casually, possessively, over her shoulders. When he'd saved her from the two busybodies in the library, she'd felt his possessiveness. And she'd wished it was real. She knew that to the people at the party they'd certainly looked like happy lovers. Only she and Logan had known the truth. They'd been doing a job. A little different from the usual nine-to-five job, but a job just the same.

Suzanne envied Logan for the way he handled this assignment. He didn't shiver each time they touched. But she did. It could be a touch as harmless as hands brushing together, and yet she would feel flushed and short of breath. He, conversely, would just turn to her and wink, and then act as if a little explosion hadn't happened.

Once the tips of his fingers had grazed the nipple of her right breast and the sensitive surface had beaded in such quick reaction that she hadn't been able to control the gasp that escaped from her throat. He'd glanced down at her quickly. She only hoped the dim lighting of the hurricane lanterns had shielded her obvious reaction.

At another point in the evening, as they were talking to the dean of women, she'd been acutely aware of Logan's warm fingers gently stroking the top of her shoulder and upper arm. She'd needed a glass of ice tea to cool her down.

She wished she were more sophisticated and schooled in the ways of men. The intimacy of that small gesture had made her stomach do flip-flops, but she was sure Logan hadn't been affected at all as he'd blithely carried on a conversation about minorities and education. However, when he'd arrived to rescue her from the overbearing clutches of Margaret Dimpsey and Donna Sue King, she'd truly felt cherished.

She was having trouble separating the real from the unreal. Her fantasies about Logan were building each time she was with him.

And then it hit her. She lusted after him. There, she'd admitted it. She lusted after Logan Davis, a policeman charged with protecting her, and she couldn't even have a normal conversation with him without thinking about him touching her.

This sensation was so new to her, it jarred her. Lust, in all its connotations, had been ugly to her since the incident with John Randolph. But now it seemed as if she'd broken through an invisible barrier, one she'd created that night long ago.

Earlier this evening was a perfect example. They'd gone over the rudiments of making a drug buy, and Logan had been a friendly yet commanding teacher. On the drive to the party he'd continued his instruction to her in that low, compelling voice of his, and she'd been drawn tighter and tighter into some invisible web that he'd seemed to spin. She ached to run her small hands over his large ones to see if they were as powerful as they looked. She blushed at her unfamiliar thoughts.

"I think your cover as a chemistry instructor is going to work fine." She toyed with the hem of her sundress. "The faculty seems to have already taken you in as one of their own."

"Yeah, things may work out better than I anticipated." He flicked on the turn signal. "By being around the students, I may even be able to find out some interesting facts as to just who's dealing. And I wouldn't rule out the fact that several, not just one or two, of the professors may be in on this thing."

Suzanne inhaled sharply. "I would never have thought that this could be so far-reaching in our little town."

"Greed and money don't acknowledge geographical boundaries." Logan swallowed. He was having a difficult time keeping his eyes on the road and not on the expanse of leg Suzanne had revealed when she'd started playing with the hem of her dress. She often did such things, unconscious of what it did to a man.

All night he'd had a hell of a time with his overheated libido. Seeing her in the mirror, then zipping up her dress, had blasted him into some oversexed zone. At the party he'd been able to separate himself from her, which had helped in controlling his reactions. But now, with her so close, he could feel the warm energy coming from her, and he had no defense against this bombshell.

She flipped the skirt down and leaned toward him. He groaned inwardly as the shadowy cleft between her breasts darkened and deepened. He knew the action, as with all her innately seductive moves, wasn't calculated as Sheila's had been.

"Call me naive," she was saying, "but I will never believe that Brandon has anything to do with this. He's one of the most honest and giving men I know."

Logan shifted uncomfortably and willed himself not to look at what she was so innocently displaying to him. He battled to keep from remembering how instantaneous her reaction had been when he'd brushed his fingers across her breast earlier in the evening. In that second of contact, a bolt of electricity, so strong and powerful they could have lit up the entire city, had passed between them.

He knew she'd felt it when her nipple had tightened and she'd gasped for air. He was astonished by the depth of her reaction, wondered what it would be like to turn all that naive innocence into sensual awareness. How she would feel curled around him.... He took a deep breath, uncomfortably aware of his body's response to her nearness.

When he'd heard those two biddies in the library baiting her, he'd taken a malicious pleasure in intervening. Hell, it had given him even more of an excuse to touch her.

"Why is Brandon such a saint to you?" He hoped that focusing on a potential suspect would divert his attention, because his temperature wasn't showing any signs of abating on its own. "He seems like such an angry, quiet man to me. The rebel-without-a-cause type."

"Well, I guess he is angry and quiet, but that doesn't mean he's a drug trafficker."

Logan frowned. "Just tell me about him. Anyone, no matter what his personality is like, can deal drugs."

Suzanne closed her throat. "He does have a police record." She waved her hands and rushed on to explain. "He was just your typical rebellious teenager. He drank too much and was loud and disorderly, broke some windows in a local store." She looked up at Logan through the thick curtain of her eyelashes. "A liquor store. He stole some liquor."

As Logan started to speak, she stopped him. "Kids do that sort of thing all the time. But what really made him develop his angry-at-the-world attitude was his affair with one of the socialites in Gruenville."

"Ah, a woman enters the picture." Logan's smile was grim.

"He loved her as much as a man can love a woman, I guess, but to make a long story short, she threw him over for a wealthier, more socially prominent man."

"Nothing you've told me so far makes me think he's not dealing drugs." Logan glanced at her upturned face. "In fact, maybe he wants the money from selling dope to buy back his lady love."

"That's absurd! Brandon hocked part of one of his ranches several years ago to use as collateral for a loan to expand my store. Does *that* sound like a ruthless drug lord?"

Privately, Logan admitted to himself that it didn't, but he was still going to keep a close eye on Brandon Stewart. Maybe the payment on one of his ranches was more than he could handle and he'd resorted to dealing.

"What do you think about Philip Jones?" Suzanne asked.

"It's hard to say so far. He's high on our list because he told me he liked having student parties at his house. Said he enjoyed getting to know his students away from the classroom."

"That doesn't sound too good."

"True, but on the other hand, if he's *really* selling to the kids, it doesn't seem likely he would advertise that he liked to have student parties at his house."

Suzanne sighed. "It's all so confusing. Did you find out anything else? I tried to listen in on a few conversations in the ladies' room, but there didn't seem to be much interesting going on. Except, of course, that all of the women think you're a hunk."

Logan gave her a long, bored look and made no comment. Instead he continued his examination of the evening. "I've also got my eye on Sheila Martin."

"I'm sure you do."

Logan sent a swift look in Suzanne's direction and was surprised when a delightful laugh sprang from her throat. He chuckled before he could stop himself. How long had it been since he'd laughed with a woman?

"This is strictly professional, Ms. Stewart." With quick reflexes and barely a pause, he suddenly tugged at the steering wheel to keep from hitting an orange cat that had scampered onto their path. "She seems a bit slick to be a home-economics teacher at a community college. It's just a feeling I have, but she could be one of the peddlers."

"Maybe so, but I still think she's gorgeous and you just want to keep your eye on her."

Logan let the comment pass. They drove in silence for a while before he spoke again. "I was able to take a walk in the parking lot without anyone seeing me and looked around for load cars."

"Load cars?"

Logan shook his head at the pucker of confusion on Suzanne's brow as she asked her question. "Yeah, a load car. It's a vehicle that's been customized to hide packages of drugs in the wheel wells and under the bumpers."

"Well?"

He scowled at the note of childlike eagerness in her voice.

"I could only do a quick check and it was pretty dark so I had to go mainly by my sense of touch. I didn't find anything suspicious."

"Oh." Disappointment was rife in Suzanne's soft voice.

"Suzanne, it's not an easy thing, finding drugs. Scratch that. It is easy to find them. What's hard is building a case against the people who sell them. It'll take time and patience to make all the connections and more to get enough evidence to put these people away."

"Of course. I just wanted this all to be over quickly."

"And there's another thing."

Logan felt Suzanne stiffen in the passenger's seat as she waited for him to impart his news. "A good portion of the people we'll indict won't actually do any time ... and some will only spend a few months in jail." He glanced at her face and saw her lips thin into a tight line. "Hopefully, the big dealers *will* be put away for a long time, but I just wanted to warn you that the system doesn't always work the way we want it to."

Suzanne shook her head. "I'm always so naive about things. I figured I'd go to the police, offer my help and whiz bang, thank you, ma'am, the people responsible for Natalie's death would be put away forever. Now I realize how complicated it all is."

"'Whiz, bang, thank you, ma'am'? Where did you hear that?" Logan smiled. "TV, right?"

"Actually, I heard it from Gram one night when she was fussing about how fast Brandon did his chores when he had a date."

Logan raised his eyebrow. "Really? We'll have to talk about what else you've gleaned from Gram. Right now, I want you to know we'll do the best we can in catching the crooks. Maybe we'll get lucky and the whole crew will go to jail for years."

"Maybe," she agreed.

He turned into her driveway, braked and killed the engine. She made no move to get out but instead sat looking at her hands for several seconds. He followed the direction of her gaze and studied her hands, too.

They were delicate and smooth, although he knew that the palms had a callus here and there from the landscaping work she did. The nails, short, neat and polish-free, reminded him of her and the way she always trimmed things as she went by, without thinking, just following her nurturing instincts.

He lived life on the edge. He was rough and used to fighting crime in any way he could to get a conviction. She was sweet, naive and uncomplicated. Yet this feeling he was developing for her was very complicated, and it definitely wasn't sweet or naive.

He'd closed himself off from emotion and women for a long time. He'd kept them stuffed into a neat corner of his life. Now Suzanne, with her righteous anger laced with purity, was creeping into the corner, invading his peace. She was so different from anyone he'd ever known. And maybe that was it. Maybe the fascination she seemed to hold for him stemmed from the fact that she was so guileless and lived her life in such a simple fashion.

But then what was this other feeling mushrooming inside him? Did he want to explore this emotion? *No.* Should he? *Probably not.* Or would it jeopardize their entire operation? *Absolutely.*

"Logan." Her whisper shook him out of his musings.

"What?" His voice was harsh as he fought the pull of that unknown emotion.

"This...drug thing. I want Natalie's killer or killers to be caught and brought to justice, but I'm having a hard time with actually buying the drugs."

She'd done remarkably well for her first time out, but he knew he wouldn't tell her that. She'd planted some seeds with those people and word would spread that she was looking for a buy. And eventually she'd find it. His eyes narrowed as he studied her, and he refused to give her a kind word. She needed to be toughened up.

Looking away and marshaling his thoughts, Logan leaned his head against the side window, resting the elbow of his left arm against the steering wheel and rubbing his fingers against his eyelids.

He thought about all the many things that could go wrong if she stayed on the job. She could get hurt. He could get hurt. The drug traffickers they were after could conceiv-

ably walk if the department didn't get their evidence right.
He was a professional and he knew she was wrong for the
job. And if he spent his time trying to protect her, they'd
probably both lose.

Instinctively, in the heavy silence that had fallen between
them, he sensed that she was at a crossroads. She wanted
Natalie's killers; he would work that angle. All he had to do
was persuade her she was detrimental to the job. If he
pressed the right buttons, she would give it up.

But he couldn't let her go. He had a feeling that if he let
her quit, she'd never get on with her life. She'd always die a
little more inside when she thought about her sister's death,
and she'd end up wilted and lifeless, like an undernour-
ished plant. Maybe a bit of her had rubbed off on him, but
he couldn't let her quit. And then there was the other side of
the coin. Suzanne might be scared now, but she was nothing if not persistent, and she had a heck of a load of guilt in
her soul—didn't he know all too well what that was like?
Guilt which could lead her to change her mind when he
wasn't around, lead her to try to get close to her sister's
killers...leading her straight into trouble. Now there was no
way out of it. He would have to see to it that she stayed in.

He ignored the inner voice that claimed those weren't the
only reasons to keep her in. He wanted her in his life just a
little while longer. Her incandescence was putting a new
glow in his life and he didn't want to leave her just yet.

He grabbed her shoulders, forcing her undivided attention.

"What?"

He cleared his throat. "You signed on for the duration.
You've had plenty of chances to back out. So get over your
feelings of insecurity. We'll work it out."

"I don't want to quit. But what if I mess up the whole
operation? What if I freeze at a critical moment?" In the
combined moonlight and light from the front porch her eyes
were haunted.

"It's my job to make sure that doesn't happen. Together, we'll make sure it doesn't happen."

"It *was* my only New Year's resolution." Suzanne let her head drop back against the headrest and closed her eyes. When she opened them, Logan saw steely commitment gleaming in the green depths. Her next words confirmed his observation. "I'll learn what I need to, I'll do what I have to, I'll make sure it's not my fault if we fail."

He tightened his grip on her shoulders, grateful she'd made the right decision but cursing the situation that had put them both here.

Suzanne felt the pressure on her arms and before she realized it, she'd whispered his name and moved toward him, knowing only that she needed his reassuring presence. His eyes, narrowed and golden, stared at her. She felt the pull of their promise and knew she was entering into a covenant with this man. When he leaned closer to her, her heart knew they would seal that covenant with a kiss.

Her eyes dropped closed as he lowered his mouth to hers. His lips were soft and warm. She could hear her own blood strumming in her ears as he slanted his mouth and kissed her with subtle pressure.

With gentle urgency, she pulled back from his kiss. She looked at him, waiting for the specter of John Randolph to cloud her mind. It never came. She only felt the pull of Logan's desire reaching for her.

She studied Logan's bottom lip for a moment before running the pad of her index finger across its surface. He hissed through clenched teeth. She marveled at the sound.

Then she pressed nearer to him and laved that same lip with her tongue. Rockets exploded at the touch. He crushed her against him and devoured her mouth for a long moment before sending his tongue piercing into her mouth. She felt herself being pulled into a maelstrom. She gave in to her reactions; she demanded more.

Moaning she let her tongue dance and mate with his. Time and time again he kissed her deeply, his tongue delving and penetrating. Time and time again she met each thrust, each flicker, with a maneuver of her own. Without knowing it, she was answering his call, matching his desire.

As her heated body melted into his, something seemed to snap within him. He pushed her back against the cushions of the seat and somehow his fingers found the top of her zipper. With infinite care he eased it down.

Tearing his mouth from hers, he whispered her name over and over as he peppered searing kisses across her cheek and down her throat. She arched her back and cried out when he reached the pulse point at her neck. She could smell his unique fragrance. Bold, fresh and untamed.

"Let me see you, Suzanne." He kissed her lips again before looking directly in her eyes. "Let me touch you."

"Yes." She whispered the word as a benediction.

He placed fleeting kisses across her collarbone even as he peeled down the top of her dress, pinning her arms at her sides with the straps.

"Suzanne," he breathed.

She felt her breasts swell, as if reaching for his touch. She watched as the pale moonlight bathed his hair when he lowered his head to kiss them.

As soon as his tongue touched the tip of her nipple, she shuddered. He closed his lips around her and suckled ravenously, pulling, teasing. She gasped and writhed at his touch. His hand kneaded and sculpted one breast and then gave the same loving attention to the other.

He started to pull her dress lower, and then his arm hit the gearshift. It stopped his movement and, at the same time, knocked some reason into his brain. Shaking his head as if to clear his heated thoughts, he looked at her. She was primed and waiting for him to finish. My God, he was about to take her right here, in the front seat of a Jeep.

He straightened up abruptly and ran a shaking hand through his dark hair.

"What's wrong?" Suzanne's eyes were huge in her pale face.

"Nothing. Everything's perfect. Too perfect." He was furious at himself for acting like an overheated teenager. "The problem is you don't know what you're asking for and I do. I'm the one who's responsible."

Cursing inwardly, he coldly reminded himself of the facts. He couldn't have a relationship with his partner. It was unprofessional, unorthodox and just plain stupid. He glanced at her and steeled his heart against the wounded look in her eyes. He wanted to explain, but he just couldn't trust himself to speak without hurting her—not just now, anyway.

"Here." He brushed her hands aside as she wriggled, trying to zip her dress. With efficient hands, he got the deed accomplished. "Let me walk you to your door."

"Thank you," she said with great dignity, "but I can make it on my own."

"Fine." He knew that he was acting like a jerk, but that was the way it had to be. "Be ready tomorrow morning at eight. We've got to go over the plans for getting some of the buys on tape."

He was all business again, the professional, but his insides ached. He wanted to curl up around her and tell her everything would be all right, that he'd keep her safe and never hurt her again. But he didn't. Instead he sat stonily as she scrambled out of the car and slammed the door.

He watched until she stood on her front porch; then he backed out of her driveway and screeched away.

Suzanne turned and watched until the taillights of his Jeep were swallowed by the night. Her trembling hands touched her lips, and she knew her world would never be the same.

Chapter 7

By 8:15 a.m. the next morning Suzanne was watching the scenery speed by as she and Logan headed for Austin. An awkward, self-conscious silence filled the Jeep. After last night, she'd expected something different, but one look at Logan's closed face this morning, and she'd known it was going to be a long drive.

She'd never been good at playing games, especially those associated with male/female temperaments. Last night she'd felt something strong and elemental pumping through her, and she'd hoped Logan had felt it, too. But instead of honoring those feelings, he'd treated her like a child, sending her into the house. Why, after all these years, when she'd shied away from men because of what had happened to her, did she have to pick a man like Logan to desire?

But Logan Davis wasn't any man—he was...well, Logan. A paradox of control and concern. He bullied her one minute, then treated her as though she were a fragile gem, precious and rare, the next. In all fairness to him, he'd been clear that they'd have to *play* the part of loving couple, but she thought he'd been as surprised as she had at the way their bodies had responded to each other last night.

For the first time in her life, she'd gone to bed aching for a man, for Logan. Since she'd never known this feeling before, she couldn't help but realize the preciousness of it. This flowering passion had made it impossible for her to sleep last night. The only way she'd finally managed to keep her eyes closed was by hoping that she and Logan could talk about it today. She glanced over at her partner, looked at his set jaw and knew she'd been wrong.

Usually silence soothed Suzanne, but Logan's quietness agitated her. She wanted to know what it was about. Was he angry at her? At himself for responding to her? Did he always just ignore his emotions this way? Was that why he seemed so much more comfortable with computers and drug statistics?

She needed to know, so she decided to force the issue.

"Logan—"

"Suzanne—"

They both spoke at the same time.

"You go ahead," he urged.

"No, you first."

"Okay." He hesitated. "I want to explain about last night—"

"I practically threw myself at you, Logan. It was my fault." She couldn't help interrupting him. Her new feelings were too fragile. She was afraid he would say she'd been foolish.

"No, that's not what happened." His voice was firm. "We both acted like a normal man and woman. It's just that we're in an abnormal situation."

"Yes, but—"

"Hear me out, Suzanne. We're partners in a drug sting operation. Granted, we're physically attracted to each other, but we can't let anything cloud our judgment if we get in a tight situation. I was out of line last night and I took advantage of your innocence.'' He glanced at her and saw her frowning.

"You didn't take advantage of me," Suzanne asserted. "I'm not a child."

He made a scornful sound. "Not in most things. But with sex, you are."

"Logan, I don't want you to feel—"

"What I feel isn't important. Getting the job done is. We need to keep this relationship on a professional level." He waited for her answer. "Suzanne, do you understand?"

He looked at her and she nodded.

"Good. Here's the station house." He concentrated on pulling his Jeep into a parking space.

"Logan, are you sure this is necessary? I don't remember this being part of our agreement," Suzanne muttered minutes later as Logan pushed her through a door marked Shooting Range.

"You agreed to do anything it would take to get Natalie's killers. Remember?" Logan pulled her to one of the cubicles designed for individuals to practice marksmanship and took his own handgun out of its holster, where it had been hidden under his jacket. "I want you to at least be able to hold this thing correctly. Hopefully, you won't ever have to use it, but I want you to be familiar with how it works, just in case."

He knew this wasn't standard procedure, but nothing about this case was standard. Logan didn't know why he wanted her comfortable with a gun, he just did. His instincts told him to do it and he always followed them. Besides, it was his way of giving her some claws.

"I refuse to shoot it." Suzanne looked at the gun Logan was holding in front of her as if it were a snake. She gingerly reached for it. "I'll hold it, but I won't shoot it."

Logan shook his head. "This is ridiculous. Of course you'll do it." His voice was hard, implacable.

Suzanne looked at him closely. She recognized the tone of his voice; Logan, the policeman, was reigning.

"If you won't protect yourself with it, think about me," he said.

"What about you?"

"You might have to save my life with it."

Putting the .22 Magnum into her hands, he curled his fingers around the butt so that she held it firmly in both hands.

She pressed her lips together and gave a quick nod. "You're right. Of course I could use it if I had to save someone I cared about."

They stared into each other's eyes for a moment before Logan swallowed and muttered a curse.

"Here, crouch down a bit, hold the gun level with both hands and line up the sights with the center of the man's silhouette on the target."

He wrapped his body around hers and helped her level the gun. Both stood rigidly. Both tried not to think about being pressed together so intimately. Both worked at being professional in their approach to the day's activities.

Logan sighed. A fine sheen of perspiration moistened his upper lip. It's going to be a helluva day, he thought. Releasing her momentarily, he got them both a pair of ear guards, placed hers gently on her head, then adjusted his own. He placed his finger over her trigger finger and fired. The gun went off and kicked up into the air. She screeched. If Logan hadn't been holding the gun, it would've clattered to the floor.

He took off their ear guards. "Stand with your feet apart more. That gives you a more solid foundation so you'll be steadier holding the gun."

She did as he instructed and brought the .22 Magnum up to point at the paper target. Logan leaned in and placed his right hand over hers again. This time when she fired, she didn't flinch. He nodded to her and stepped back so she could try it on her own.

Logan watched as she closed one eye and fired again. She was nowhere near the target. When she looked back expectantly at him, he nodded, silently telling her to keep firing. She squared her shoulders and did it again, and again and again.

While Suzanne fired, Logan watched intently. He wasn't really paying attention to the target or the gun; he was watching her. This woman who had invaded his safe world. The woman who had breached his defenses. The words *detached* and *Suzanne* didn't go together. No, he was smack-dab in the middle of a mess with this Girl Scout.

His track record with women was bad—in fact, abominable. He never seemed to be on the same wavelength with the women in his life. His mother's alcohol binges had made him permanently wary of females. She had been a bright, charming woman when she was sober, but drunk, weak and cowardly, and had let his father psychologically manipulate her.

When his mother had run away from the family, and then had died, he'd experienced a soul-stinging sense of loss and betrayal. Why hadn't she loved him enough to live? He'd never wanted to feel that deep, bone-scratching hurt again, so he'd never really invested his total heart in a relationship again.

Then he'd met Debby. Soon they were caught up in a torrid affair that had ended in a tepid marriage. She'd also asked what he couldn't give. She'd wanted him to lay all his emotions bare, to commit his soul to the marriage. He couldn't do it. And so he'd failed at marriage.

Since then, he'd stayed away from any serious relationship. It hurt too much to commit his emotions, and then be deserted. Yet slowly, surely, he could feel himself being pulled into uncharted emotional territory. By this wild-shooting woman next to him.

Suzanne was an innocent. Her responsiveness was so natural, so real, but it was still so tentative. Last night they'd crossed a barrier. If they had gone any further, he would have broken every rule in his book. He couldn't let himself do that. But when he thought of another man initiating her to passion, he hardened. Another man—no, he wouldn't think about it. Yes, he was in the middle of a mess with Suzanne.

He felt an elbow in his rib and looked down. She was standing, holding out the gun by the butt. He took it, flipped the magazine release catch, zipped the new cartridges in and gave it back to her. She assumed the stance and began firing.

He did a double take. Her body had gone into a crouch gracefully, and she held the gun with assurance. His eyes followed the path of the next bullet as she squeezed off a round. It hit the shoulder of the target. He watched closely and every one of her rounds hit the target. Watching her be this natural with a gun made him uneasy. He didn't want her becoming so cool and detached as she appeared now, yet he was teaching her a skill that required that to be successful. In the world he was forcing her into, she'd need all the protective skills she could get.

Suzanne smiled as her bullets found their target. It was strange how powerful she felt holding the weapon. Her fingers felt at home on the cold steel as she squeezed the trigger and felt the recoil of the weapon jar her hand. It was exhilarating to realize she was innately good with her aim.

She froze. Was this really her? Suzanne, the earth mother, actually enjoyed shooting this instrument of destruction? How seductive the unknown could be. Was this how Natalie had felt when she'd taken her first drag on a marijuana cigarette? She shuddered and turned to Logan.

"Is that enough?" she asked. "My arms are aching from holding up this gun."

"For today," Logan answered. "I just wanted you to get the feel of it. I don't expect you to really use it. Besides, look at it this way—it'll help build your muscles so you can carry all those plants."

"This really is one of the most difficult things you've asked me to do."

"Not as difficult as what we're going to do next."

Suzanne looked at him, green eyes wide.

"Come on, partner. Don't you trust me?"

She tilted her head, measuring him with a deliberate gaze. "No, I don't."

"Smart girl." Logan took the gun from her and led her out of the shooting range. "We're going to learn a little self-defense."

Suzanne pulled up short. "What?"

"Self-defense," he repeated. "You know, jabbing someone's eyes, kicking someone, rendering a person harmless long enough for you to run away."

"Sounds more like a Three Stooges routine."

"You won't think so when we get finished."

"I repeat, Logan Davis, I don't need this." She had to hurry to keep up with his long stride.

"Let's face it, Suzanne. You're short and light. I want you to learn some of the finer points of how to get away if you're overpowered by an assailant." He noticed her fast pace and slowed his own to accommodate her.

"But, Logan, I know how to escape."

"Really?" His eyebrow arched.

"Yes." She stood her ground. "I'm extremely squirmy."

Logan stopped dead and looked at her as if she'd just turned lime green. "*Squirmy?* Did you say you were squirmy?"

She gritted her teeth and crossed her arms, but she didn't answer him.

"Squirmy," he repeated. Then he tilted his head back and laughed. He kept laughing until he noticed her stony expression. "Forgive me, but I don't want to rely on your...*squirminess* to save you."

Before she could come up with a stinging retort, he grabbed her arm and led her into an exercise room whose walls were lined with mirrors.

He glanced at her in one of the mirrors. She looked gorgeous to him. Of course, she always did. Even today, with no makeup, hair windblown and jeans and T-shirt with bluebonnets painted all over it, she looked beautiful.

He pointed to a door. "Go through there. There're some sweats folded on a shelf. Change into them. I'll go get some on, too."

After Suzanne slipped out of her clothes and dressed in the sweats, she paused for a minute to study her reflection in the mirror over the sink.

Goodness, she thought to herself as she surveyed her tousled hair and squeaky-clean face, I'm so unexciting-looking. How could anyone fall in love with me when there are so many peacocks in the world? She smiled as she remembered something Gram had once told her: a peacock isn't beautiful when it's not displaying its tail feathers, and it takes something exceptional to make that happen. She flashed back to the scene after the party. She'd felt like a peacock then—beautiful, desirable. Her body had exploded with all the sensations Logan had created with his hands and lips. She still felt it when she closed her eyes.

Sighing, thinking herself foolish, she splashed water on her face, toweled it dry and went out to rejoin Logan in the mat-filled exercise room.

"Now what?" Suzanne asked.

"This." He lunged, put his hip next to hers, twisted and before she could blink, had her on her back. He knelt beside her and helped her sit up.

"What a sneaky thing to do! You could've warned me." Suzanne tried to stand up, but he held her down.

"Do you think someone who's going to attack you is going to warn you first? What's the matter? Couldn't you 'squirm' away fast enough?"

"No, damn you. And don't make fun of me." She punched his arm. "Besides, I don't think most attackers know whatever that was you used."

"Never underestimate your enemy." Logan pulled her up. "Now I'm going to warn you. Try to defend yourself."

He lunged again. This time she tried sidestepping, but he just pivoted, and she found herself down on the ground again.

He pulled her up. "Again."

For longer than Suzanne thought her body could take it, Logan attacked and she did her best to feint and maneuver away from him. Each time she was successful, he praised her. But most of the time, he sent her sprawling onto the mats. After a particularly humiliating throw, Suzanne found herself flat on her back—again.

Logan bent down beside her. "Are you getting tired of this position?"

For a minute Suzanne didn't answer, just stared into his eyes. The amber color of his eyes shone like mellow whiskey, and the yellow flecks within them were tiny flames. He watched her with such intensity, Suzanne felt his heat pouring into her. She raised her head to answer him, but he backed away quickly.

"Try it again."

Shaken by his abrupt coldness, Suzanne stood up and faced him in a more aggressive stance. This time when he pounced on her, she managed to deflect him for a moment before he recovered.

"Good," Logan said. "Again."

Finally he began showing her small moves that helped her. He showed her how easily she could twist her hip so the attacker would be behind her and she could run. He drilled her until she knew how to step on an instep, use her fingers to the eyes, jerk her body away and deflect blows with her arms at the same time that she used her knees.

After two grueling hours, he stopped. "That's enough."

Gasping for breath, Suzanne looked up at him from under sweat-drenched brows.

"Are we finished here?"

"Yes. For today." Catching her hand, he said, "Come on. You've earned some lunch."

"Great," Suzanne said. "What's after lunch? Are you going to teach me how to crawl through the jungle, just in case?"

He frowned. "Don't get cute. I might just do that. You might need to 'squirm' through one of your houses on your belly some day."

"Don't even think it." She flashed her eyes at him and pushed the sleeves of her sweatshirt above her elbows.

Logan held up his hands in mock surrender. "Just kidding. After lunch we're going to teach you how to use the wire. Then we'll use your appointment with Mr. Wells today as a practice run with the wire."

Suzanne sobered immediately. "Oh."

"What's the matter?"

"I just realized that revenge is not what I expected it to be. I thought it would heal the sorrow of Natalie's death, but instead I'm disillusioned. I'm going to have to buy drugs from someone I know."

Logan took her hand. "Yes. You are." He looked deeply into her green eyes, catching a wet curl that had fallen across her forehead and smoothing it back. "And I'm going to make sure you won't be hurt doing that."

"I know." Suzanne's low tone told him he should change the subject.

"Go take a shower and put on your street clothes. Then we'll have lunch. I know a place that has the best burgers. And you can get some of that health food stuff there, too, those worm-looking things."

"*Sprouts.* How many times do I have to tell you? They're sprouts."

"Well, they look like worms to me."

Logan surprised himself with how easy it was to talk with Suzanne. Even in the early years of his marriage to Debby, he hadn't tossed jokes about with her. They'd both worked at their jobs during the day, and their evenings had consisted of television and reading. Real communication hadn't been a part of their life. They'd had a good sex life, but it hadn't been enough to save the marriage.

He took a cold shower, needing to cool his body and his mind after a morning with Suzanne. Being with her could become as addictive as the drugs they were trying to stop. He had to make sure he didn't indulge the habit. Laughter came too easy to her, and to him when he was with her. This job didn't require levity; it required serious concentration to a task.

Joining her again, he took her to a nearby restaurant where policemen liked to hang out. After eating they went back to the police station, where Suzanne was ushered into a holding room. Logan went and found Mary, the officer who would put the wire on Suzanne.

"You'll have to take your T-shirt off," said the efficient policewoman with the square body and hair in a bun. "And when you go out tonight, don't wear a T-shirt, wear a blouse. It's easier to hide the wire."

Suzanne knew she was blushing as she stripped off the top. Standing in her bra, she felt more vulnerable than she could ever remember. Just as she was about to crisscross her arms, the door burst open.

Logan stood, openmouthed, at the door. For an instant, he stayed stock-still, freeze-framed in the doorway. Then, with a deep frown, he mumbled, "Sorry," and closed the door.

"I see his manners haven't gotten any better," Mary said as she taped the small mike near Suzanne's right breast.

Suzanne couldn't help her inner tremblings. This was all so foreign to her. As if Mary sensed her trepidation, she tried to lighten the mood. "Don't be modest around me, kid. I've seen it all and probably done it all, so don't think I'm embarrassed about taping this little wire down your front." She began securing the wire as she smoothed it down Suzanne's abdomen and glanced up at Suzanne with a mischievous smile on her lips and a twinkle in her eye. "You've got a nice body, so don't worry about hiding it."

Suzanne could only stare at the top of Mary's head as Mary finished taping the wire and showed her how to hide it under her waistband. Now why on earth had she told her that? Was the sound system on? Could Logan hear them? Her face was on fire with just the thought of it.

"The real trick is to hide the wire," Mary was saying. "That's why loose clothes are the best. You can't see the outline of the wire as easily. Now that we've got you hooked up, we need to do a sound check. Say something."

"Who's going to hear it?"

Mary chuckled. "Some guys in the next room. Are you afraid we'll pipe it through the station?"

"No, this just feels so funny." Suzanne lowered her head and tried to speak into the mike. "One, two, three."

"Don't do it that way. If the only way we can pick it up is for you to talk into your bra, then we're in trouble. Just speak naturally."

Suzanne thought his woman must have a different idea of what natural was. She was standing here in her underwear with a microphone and wire taped to her body and she was supposed to act natural? No way. But aloud she only said, "Okay."

Mary waited and Suzanne said nothing. Mary cocked her head expectantly. Finally she said, "We really need to get on with it. Say something. Give us your bra size or telephone number or something."

Suzanne managed a weak smile at the matter-of-fact policewoman. "I was just trying to think of something. How long have you been a police officer?"

"About ten years."

"Is this what you do now? Put wires on people?"

"Not usually. But Logan asked that I help with this because I'm the best at doing this, wiring people." She spoke with assurance and no false modesty. "I owe Logan, so here I am."

"What did he do for you?" Suzanne asked, for the moment forgetting that she was wearing only a bra, and was speaking into a microphone.

"Logan managed to jump in front of a bullet for me."

Suzanne gasped.

"Yeah, he played the hero." Mary smiled grimly into Suzanne's startled face. "We were investigating a series of robberies and happened to stumble on one in progress. The perps were high on some new synthetic drug and when they saw us, they started shooting. Logan must've spotted the gun before me, because he literally jumped in front of me and got shot."

"What happened then?" Suzanne was listening with wide eyes.

"We managed to bring them down with a few well-placed shots. Didn't even have to shoot them, just over their heads. They dropped their guns and surrendered. Bad guys usually react in just two ways when you chase them. They get real mean and fight dirty, or they go down like whimpering babies. We got lucky that time."

"No wonder you owe Logan."

"Yeah. We were partners. In fact, he was the best partner I've ever had."

"I'm his partner now."

Mary studied Suzanne for a heartbeat. "I know. We were all surprised when he took another civilian on."

"I think Dan Rider convinced him to do it." Suzanne had totally forgotten the wire now.

"Dan can do that. He always knows what button to push to get you to do what he wants."

"What button of Logan's did he push?"

"His protective one. He has a real weakness for playing the knight in shining armor." Mary turned to fiddle with some radio equipment on a table.

Suzanne stood, openmouthed. She couldn't have heard right. Logan, the man who spent more time scowling at her, trying to convince her to give it up and bow out? That was a knight in shining armor? He *had* been fun today, she admitted to herself. Fun? She must be out of her mind. He'd forced her to hold and shoot a heavy gun for hours, had bruised and battered her entire body. *Fun?* Lord, what would a bad time with him be like? She thought for a second and then answered her own question. Being *without* him badgering her would be a bad time.

Mary was speaking again. "I can tell by your expression you're having a hard time with that. But, believe me, Logan will protect you with his life."

Still disbelieving, Suzanne muttered, "I don't think it'll come to that."

"You never know." Mary moved toward the door. "Let me check and see if the sound level is okay." She swung open the door and sauntered out.

Left alone in the room, Suzanne sat down to digest what she'd just heard. Logan, the rescuer. What an odd thought. Be honest, she said to herself. You *have* seen that side of his nature. Remember how he helped Mr. Brown? How wonderful he was around your family? He *was* that knight in shining armor. But instinctively Suzanne knew Logan didn't see himself that way. To him, it was just a job.

And, she forced herself to admit, last night had been a part of his job, too. So, why could she still remember the feel of his hands on her, the way he'd made her move, the ache he'd created in her? She'd never understood what all that tingling stuff the girls in high school talked about was, until Logan had made her tingle from head to toe, completely erasing John Randolph's ugly touch from her mind.

Today, he'd been very careful not to touch her in any romantic way. *He probably knows I have no experience and doesn't want to get involved with an amateur.* But even with no experience, she could tell Logan knew how to make a woman feel special. He did it every time he touched her.

"The sound level's okay." Mary wandered back in, breaking up Suzanne's thoughts. "I'll help you take it off. Then I want you to put it on, so I can see if you can."

Suzanne pulled the tape off and then retaped the wire, all the while concentrating intensely. When she'd done it successfully, Mary declared her ready. Finally Suzanne put on her T-shirt and left the room.

Lounging against the hallway wall was Logan, one leg cocked back. He smiled at her when she walked toward him. "Sorry about barging in there like that."

He didn't look the least bit sorry or embarrassed, she thought. "That's all right." Suzanne had trouble looking at him. "Are we ready to go back to Gruenville now?"

"Yeah, but we're coming back here for a couple of hours every day."

She narrowed her eyes. "I have a business to run, Logan."

"Well you shouldn't have volunteered for this assignment, then. I want you to know a few self-defense moves well enough that they'll come naturally to you in a tight situation." He gave her a smug look with a trace of *I warned you* written in his expression. "Come on. I've got the equipment we need for the wire job in the car. We better get back if you're going to make it to your appointment. I want you wearing the wire during the whole thing."

"You don't suspect John Wells, do you?"

"I suspect everyone, Suzanne. I've told you that a thousand times."

"I know." Suzanne let her gaze drop, unable to meet the amber fire in his. "He just gave money to the university. He's a good community man. It doesn't fit. I think you're imagining things. John Wells isn't going to sell me any drugs. He's just coming to talk about the reception."

Logan took her arm. "So, then we'll at least know the wire works. It'll give you some practice wearing the thing. But remember, this is a big business and money can make people do crazy things. And who knows? We just might get lucky."

Suzanne looked at him doubtfully, but she followed him to the car.

"We're set up," Logan told her as he walked into her office. "You're sure this is where you and Mr. Wells will meet?"

"Yes. But does it matter? I'm wearing this thing." She pointed to her right breast. Logan's eyes followed her motion, darkening. Suzanne noticed his gaze and talked quickly to cover her embarrassment. "And it should work regardless of where we are in the store, right?"

Logan jerked his eyes up to her face. *Get a grip, Logan. This is no time to start fantasizing about the benefits of being that wire, snuggled close to warm, soft—* "Right."

Sara called from the front, announcing Mr. Wells. Logan gave her the thumbs-up sign and slipped out of the office. In just a few moments John Wells's hulking frame was filling the doorway, and he was coming toward her, extending his hand.

"Come on in." She waved him into her office. "I have the file of Gretchen's wedding right on top of my desk."

"Thank you for seeing me on such short notice, but I just wanted to go over the plans and figures with you."

He sat across from her. Suzanne handed him the folder.

"Do you want anything to drink? Tea? Perrier?" Suzanne asked.

Leafing through the folder, Mr. Wells just shook his head and muttered, "No, thank you."

After a short time, he handed the folder back to Suzanne. "Well, I think Gretchen and Jill have thought of everything, and the costs look reasonable." He leaned back as he watched her intently.

"I tried to keep the costs down." Suzanne smiled, but on the inside her smile congealed. *Something about this whole thing is wrong.* He couldn't possibly have looked at everything in that folder. He'd just glanced at it and tossed it aside. He wasn't here to talk about the wedding reception. Logan may have been right; Wells might be here because of drugs. Her heart rate increased suddenly. She nearly jumped when he spoke.

"And you did a great job." Mr. Wells leaned back in his chair. "I think I *will* have that Perrier you offered."

Self-conscious now because of her thoughts, Suzanne nodded. She swiveled in her chair and opened the small refrigerator behind her. "Would you like a glass?"

"No, this'll be fine." He unscrewed the cap on the bottle she'd handed him and took a long drink. "Thanks."

Silence stretched between them as Suzanne wondered inanely if he could see the wire. His voice sounded like a thunderclap, shattering the air.

"Suzanne, how long have you had this business?"

"About five years. Actually, the catering business is the youngest of my ventures. It's only about two years old. But I started five years ago with the nursery." Suzanne knew she was babbling, but she couldn't control herself. What if he offered her drugs? Could she pull off a buy?

"And Logan?" John Wells set the bottle down and looked directly at her.

"What?"

"Logan. You know, the young man you were with the other night." Wells was smiling broadly, but it struck Suzanne as false—too many teeth.

Suzanne started to say something, but nothing came out. Next, she tried clearing her throat. "I met him when I took a class in Austin. He was a professor." Suzanne hoped she was remembering their cover story correctly. This conversation wasn't following any course she could chart. "We've been seeing each other for a few months. Why?"

John leaned back. "Just wondered. Young man like him suddenly appears in a town this size, and I just wanted to know where he came from." His eyes took on the squinty look of a weasel and there was a glitter in them that didn't match the bland smile on his lips. "He seems like a nice enough fellow. I'd sure like to get to know him better so I can include him on some of the city boards, committees—that sort of thing. Is he planning to stay in town?"

"He's teaching at the community college, as you know. I'm not sure how long he plans to stay after the present semester is over."

"Hmm . . . interesting."

Wells sat quietly for so long after that that Suzanne felt compelled to get the conversation back to a topic she could handle. "Did you want to see some of the samples of the flowers your daughter picked out for her bouquet?"

"Flowers . . . ? What? Oh, no. I'm sure Gretchen made a beautiful choice." He frowned at her suddenly. "Are you and this Davis serious about each other? Is your gram going to be planning *your* wedding soon?"

It was an innocuous question, but Suzanne felt an underlying edge to it. Besides, John Wells didn't play the part of the teasing uncle with any conviction. Still, he was a customer and she couldn't be rude. "Not anytime soon, Mr. Wells. Logan and I aren't that serious yet. We're still in the having-fun stage."

He stared into space for several minutes. Suzanne wished she could transmit the look in his eyes through the wire for Logan to see. His face appeared friendly enough with that toothy smile glued on. But his eyes. There was a look in them that she'd never noticed before today. They were as cold as bullets. He looked . . . threatening. Involuntarily her hand raised in a defensive gesture to her throat. Without warning, he stood up.

"I've got to get back. Thanks for everything."

Suzanne walked around the desk and opened the door for him. "I'll see you at the reception."

"Sure will."

Suzanne watched him leave, puzzled by his odd behavior. Shrugging, she admitted she was probably just disappointed he hadn't offered her drugs, and his behavior wasn' that bizarre after all. She turned back into the office, took the file off her desk and put it into the cabinet. Just as she was shutting the file drawer, Logan came in.

"You can take off the wire now."

"Oh." Suzanne looked down, then reached inside her blouse and slipped it off. "Did you hear everything?"

"Yes, dammit."

"What's the matter with you?" Suzanne questioned "Are you angry because he didn't offer me any drugs or even mention them?"

Logan glared at her. "No. But I *do* wonder why he was asking all those questions about me."

"I don't know, just being small-town nosy." Suzanne shook her head. "For a minute, there, I was definitely nervous. You must be rubbing off on me."

"I hope you're right." He took her arm. "Let's get the wire back to the people in the truck."

"I've got to talk to Sara first. Wait here for me. I'll be right back."

Logan watched her walk away, his mind on what he'd heard. It was too pat, he told himself. Small-town nosi ness? No. John Wells was after something else. It had sounded like a fishing expedition to Logan. His instincts told him he was right.

His thoughts switched to Suzanne and he smiled grimly. She'd dodged Wells's questions like a veteran. He was probably the only one who could detect the slight catch in her voice that signaled her nervousness.

With a cop's unfailing radar, Logan knew this encounter wasn't what it seemed. At best, the dealers were looking for a connection to him; at worst, they'd made it and were trying to determine if Suzanne knew anything. They were getting too close to finding out the truth about her involvement. Damn, but small-town gossip traveled fast. He uttered a dark, low curse. The seamy world was closing in on his innocent, unsuspecting partner.

Whatever it took, he wouldn't let Suzanne get hurt—even if he had to protect her with his life.

Chapter 8

The sun was a dazzling white-hot ball in the blue April sky. The day promised to be unseasonably warm in an area of the country where heat and humidity were a way of life. The Good Earth van gobbled up the ribbon of asphalt with steady precision.

She and Logan were headed to Mr. Brown's to return the plant he'd left in her store the day of his attack. It was a way for her to make sure he was all right.

Suzanne stared at the highway, allowing the blurring motion of the scenery to keep her mind focused on her driving, while Logan—the man sitting so nonchalantly beside her—steadily caused a racing inside her. Could it be that he felt a little something for her? Was that why he'd come charging back into her office the way he had after her meeting with Wells? He'd had such a predatory look on his face when he'd found her. On the other hand, did she want all that intensity searing her? It was all so confusing. One minute she thought she might be falling in love with the man, and the next she wanted to chuck the whole situation.

One thing was for sure: they *were* like two explosive devices when they touched each other. Even yesterday, when everything was supposed to be just business, she'd felt it every time he'd moved her one way or the other during the karate lesson he'd given her. And there were times when he'd had her on her back, that she'd wanted to arch into him just to feel his strength. She hadn't, of course. But the temptation had been nearly impossible to resist....

"Now tell me again why we're going out to visit this old guy." Logan's rich drawl rose above the wind streaming in the open windows, forcing her back to the reality of the moment.

"The *we* you refer to could have been just *me*. I didn't hold a gun to your head and insist you come with me." Suzanne flexed her fingers around the steering wheel.

"That's true, but it's all part of the act. We're supposed to be inseparable, which means as much time together as possible. I don't have classes today, so here I am." He rested his arm on the window casement. What he didn't tell her was that he would've found a way to come along, regardless. He was going to stick to her like the proverbial glue from now on. After that visit from Wells yesterday, he wasn't leaving anything to chance.

As if reading his mind, she interrupted him with, "Are you still worried about Wells?"

He glanced at her and frowned. She must have picked up on his agitation yesterday. She was getting good at reading him and he wasn't sure he liked that. His feelings about her were too raw, and he definitely didn't want her messing around in them, although this protective streak in him was natural, given their circumstances.

Unbidden, a brutal vision of Carla's lifeless body drove a spur in his side. It was quickly replaced by a picture of Suzanne, helpless, at the mercy of a killer. No, he was right to be this protective. He'd sworn nothing would happen to her, and by damn it wouldn't. He scowled deeper, concentrating on answering her question.

"I'm not sure about Wells. We're checking into his background a bit more, but until we know anything, I don't want to take unnecessary chances."

"You still didn't need to come with me today."

"Let's just say I didn't want you lifting that heavy plant."

Suzanne rolled her eyes. "Mr. Davis, I've been lifting plants, heavy wedding cakes and all kinds of stuff for years before you came along."

"Yes, but I'm along now, so humor me. When I'm around, I want to lift the heavy things." Logan raised his eyebrows in a parody of male arrogance. "So let me. Will you, sweetheart?"

Suzanne just shrugged, but said nothing, secretly pleased that he should want to help her. When he lapsed into his "knight in shining armor" routine, she found it endearing. But she couldn't let his lovable charm seduce her, so she headed for neutral territory.

"You're lucky the college is letting you help students who are doing independent research and giving you such a light class load. That gives you a great deal of time off to help me lift heavy plants."

"The entire operation's proceeding smoothly. We just need to start making some buys soon so we can get some evidence that will stand up in court." He shifted his long legs. She watched as his jeans stretched tight across the hard muscled planes of his thighs and again had to try and calm her racing heart.

"You said Mr. Brown was out of the hospital and doing okay, right?" Logan's abrupt change of conversation didn't throw her nearly as much as the hand he rested on the back of her seat. She squirmed uncomfortably.

"Yes." The word came out as a reedy whisper. She cleared her throat and said more distinctly, "Yes." She smiled as she thought of the kind old gentleman. She'd missed his regular trips to the store and had visited him in the hospital. "The doctors say he only had a scare. He didn't have a stroke or heart attack. He seems to be under a lot of stress and needs to rest more."

Logan shook his head. "I still can't believe you're delivering his plant to him. That seems above and beyond the call of a good retailer."

Suzanne shot him a piercing look. "I'm also his friend, and besides, that's the way neighbors do things in Gruenville."

A dark scowl marred Logan's features. "I'm more interested in how Gruenville runs its drug operation. But if you think this house call is necessary, I'll go along with your judgment."

"I do," Suzanne told him. "Besides, Mr. Brown is thinking of starting an herb garden, and I want to help him with his plants."

"An herb garden?"

"Surely you've heard of herbs?"

"It's the stuff that goes into those teas you drink, right?"

Suzanne laughed and nodded her head. "That's close enough."

"You're a strange woman, Suzanne Stewart. How many women do you know who give a damn about herbs, or plants or old, sick men for that matter?" He shook his head again.

"When Mr. Brown comes in for one of his visits, we talk about lots of things. I mentioned to him one day that I'd bought a book on herbs and was experimenting with herbal teas and vinegars." She hazarded a peek at Logan and immediately looked back at the highway. Logan was staring a hole through her.

"And Mr. Brown probably wrote the book you bought, right?"

"Wrong." Suzanne turned off the main highway onto a gravel county road. "He just seemed to be fascinated by the whole conversation and said he'd like to try his hand at it. I've been thinking about expanding my store to include specialty items like the herbal products, and Mr. Brown could become a supplier." Her voice dropped in volume. "Anyway, it will give him something to live for."

She met Logan's eyes briefly. He was still looking at her keenly. "Always the nurturer, huh?"

"Pardon me?"

"Never mind."

"By the way, Gram called me last night."

Logan's head swiveled quickly in her direction, and she sensed a heightened awareness from him. "Did she question you about us?"

"Yes. How did you know?"

"I told her to. She gave me a little talk at her place. I suggested she call you. Remember, I talked to you about it at the dinner on Sunday? What did you tell her?"

She could tell from his tense body language that how successfully she'd lied to her grandmother was vitally important. A test of some sort. "I said we'd just had a couple of friendly dates when I was in your class in Austin. I didn't tell her because I was embarrassed to be dating a professor." She glanced at the rigid set of his jaw and saw it relax.

"That was inspired. Anyone who knows you as well as she does would believe you wouldn't want it spread you were dating a professor. They might think you were pandering for a good grade. Good job."

Suzanne smiled at his unexpected compliment.

"Do you think she believed you?"

"Yes, I think so." She nodded. "I told her that you got in touch with me when you moved here, and we'd just started dating again."

He looked at her briefly. "I need to know you can think on your feet—everything can't be scripted. Some things have to be spontaneous. You did great, so don't worry about it."

Suzanne was quiet for a minute before she pointed to something in front of them. "There it is."

A rambling old house set among a grove of oak trees came into view. With paint peeling and screen door slightly askew, it looked like something out of a John Steinbeck novel. There were a few straggling flowers beside the front steps, but for the most part, the house and grounds looked sad and lonesome. Like a racehorse suddenly turned out to pasture with no one to groom it.

Suzanne tried not to notice and parked the van by the front gate. She jumped down out of the vehicle and found Logan had already gotten to the gate and opened it for her. Mr. Brown was shuffling slowly out the door.

"Suzanne, how nice to see you." With his eyes glowing with warmth at the sight of his friend, he turned to Logan. "And who is this? Have you been keeping your love life secret from me?"

Suzanne couldn't stop the blush she knew was spreading across her cheeks. "This is Logan Davis, Mr. Brown. He's teaching chemistry at the college. He and I are seeing one another."

Mr. Brown clasped Logan's hand. "Suzanne here is a fine catch." He wagged his finger in Logan's face. "Consider yourself lucky and take good care of her."

Logan's eyes smoldered with a fierce fire as he gazed into Suzanne's eyes. "Yes, I'm well aware how special she is."

Shocked and thoroughly confused by his heated look and romantic words, Suzanne almost stepped away from Logan. Forcibly, she reminded herself that this was a job to him, an acting job, and that he was shooting for an Oscar.

Her blush deepened, but she was saved from having to make some inane reply when a snazzy red sports car zipped up beside her van and braked a mere hairbreadth from the fence. Out of the sleek automobile that looked totally out of sync with the dilapidated farmhouse, jumped a young man, who vaulted over the fence.

"David." Mr. Brown's pleasure was obvious by the rush of emotion in his voice and the broad smile on his mouth.

"Hi ya, Pop." The young man loosely embraced his father.

Suzanne stared at David. He was short and lean, with a lanky build that most girls would find extremely attractive. He had long sideburns and his hair combed in a perfect pompadour, emulating the newest male sex symbol on TV. His shirt and slacks were both obviously designer, and the boots on his feet looked like they were made of expensive alligator. He exuded money and . . . sullenness.

"David, I want you to meet my friend Suzanne Stewart and her beau, Logan Davis." Mr. Brown had unclasped his son but still had his arm draped around the younger man's shoulders.

"Dave, Pop. You know how I hate that David crap." David shrugged his father's arm away and shook Logan's hand with a bored nonchalance before turning his full attention and what he thought was high-voltage charm on Suzanne.

"Suzanne Stewart... Oh, yes...you're the chick Pop goes to see in Gruenville all the time. Don't you own a feed store or something?" He had captured her hand between both of his and was giving her suggestive looks.

Logan moved to her side and slipped her hand out of David's.

Now why had he done that? Suzanne smiled at the younger man, trying to telegraph a casual friendliness to him. "I own The Good Earth. There are three parts to the store, but I don't sell feed in any of them." She looked at Logan for an instant. "But that's a great idea. Maybe that'll be my next addition."

"Yeah, well I knew it was something like that." He seemed to instantly forget his flirting and turned back to his father. "Jeez, it's hot out here in this godforsaken country. Let's go into the dump."

Mortified by his hurtful words, Suzanne tried to soothe things. "Let me help you, Mr. Brown."

She placed an arm protectively around the old man while Logan held the door open. David rushed through before his father. Suzanne felt Logan's body tense beside her and she glanced quickly into his face. His gold eyes popped with fire and were directed at the back of the rude boy, and his lips had thinned to a tight slash across his face. The set of his granite jaw made Suzanne afraid Logan was going to grab the younger man and cause a scene. Instead, Logan merely looked over at Mr. Brown and shook his head.

As they entered the cool interior of the house, David was heading down a hall that probably led to the kitchen and calling over his shoulder, "Pop, do you have any beer in the fridge?"

Mr. Brown looked pained, but he smiled at Suzanne before raising his voice to call out to his son. "No, son, but there're some sodas. Why don't you bring everyone one?"

"Oh, no, thanks, Mr. Brown." Suzanne managed a weak laugh. "Logan and I just came out to deliver that plant you called me about. I've taken good care of it."

"I'm sure you have, dear."

The three settled in the living room, where the furniture was as old and sagging as the rest of the house.

"I also brought you some herbs to get you started on your garden. I spoke with one of your doctors and he said that herb gardening was the perfect activity for you because it doesn't require much chopping and lifting and things like that."

"You are such a dear, Suzanne. How can I repay you?"

Before Suzanne could answer, David burst into the room with a cola in one hand. "Pop. Can I have a few minutes? I need to talk to you privately. *Now.*"

Mr. Brown glanced at Logan and Suzanne. "David, please . . ."

"Look, Pop, it's urgent."

"David, not now."

Logan broke in. "What did you say you did, David?"

David lowered his eyelids and looked at Logan speculatively. "I didn't say, but I'm a student in Austin."

"At the University of Texas?"

"Ah, no." David glanced quickly at his father and for the first time, he shifted in his sleek boots and looked uncomfortable. "I'm going to business school."

Logan didn't seem to want to let the matter rest. "There are some fine business colleges in Austin. Which one do you attend?"

A black scowl colored David's face. "Hey, what is this? A police interrogation?"

Suzanne coughed into her hand. How close the fool had come to the truth!

Logan was as cool and confident as always. He actually smiled an icy smile. "Sounded like it, didn't it? Naw, I just went to school at the university and thought we might be fraternity brothers or something."

That seemed to pacify David because the thundercloud that had been building on his forehead dissipated and he relaxed his rigid posture. He grinned and looked straight at his dad. "The truth is, I just hang out on different campuses looking for the coolest chick to pick up." He winked at Logan. "The action's happening in the big city. These country chicks don't know how to please a man."

"David." Mr. Brown looked like he was truly going to have a stroke. His face was red and his eyes shone with an unnatural glow.

Suzanne jumped up from the faded chair where she'd been sitting. "If you don't mind, Mr. Brown, Logan and I will check out your backyard and see where the best place to start your herb garden is."

"That would be very nice." Mr. Brown looked as if he'd aged thirty years in the last five minutes.

"We'll just get your plant and the herbs I brought out of the van and set them on the front porch." Suzanne knew she was talking too loud and too fast, but David Brown made her skin crawl. She felt guilty that her feelings about kindly Mr. Brown's son were so negative.

"Thank you, dear."

Logan got up and followed her out the front door. Neither spoke as he hefted the large plant up to the front porch and she carried a tray of herbs. They circled the house until they got to the backyard. It was a pretty area, where, no doubt, Mr. Brown must spend most of his time. There were two well-tended flower beds and several fruit trees dotting the landscape.

"There's plenty of space here to build some raised herb gardens." Suzanne glanced at Logan but knew by the frown knotting his forehead that he wasn't listening to her. "You and I might spend a morning out here getting things set up for him, and then he could take over the actual care of the garden."

"Hmm? Oh, sure that sounds great."

"Let's walk back this way." Suzanne pointed in an easterly direction. "Mr. Brown mentioned a creek that runs through his pasture. I bet it's this way." She lowered her voice. "That'll give David time to talk in private with his father."

"I have a feeling whatever David wants, he'll get."

"Shh!" Suzanne glanced up at the house, but she doubted any of their conversation carried to its occupants. Grabbing Logan's hand, she pulled him toward a line of trees she was sure signified a creek.

Logan didn't put up any resistance and allowed Suzanne to guide him to the edge of a small creek that only had a trickle of water running through it. The bank was covered with a mossy grass and shaded by large oaks and sycamore trees.

Suzanne sat down and hugged her knees up against her chest. Logan walked a few feet away and stretched out an arm, resting his hand on the trunk of a tree. He stared into the bark as if he could read the secrets of the universe there.

"I feel so sorry for Mr. Brown." Suzanne broke the silence.

"Yeah, that's a tough situation, I guess, to have a bratty kid." He didn't turn to face her and his stance seemed tense.

She stared at the corded muscles in his arms and suddenly it dawned on her that his body had been like a coiled spring since they'd left the Brown house.

"What is it, Logan? What happened back there to upset you this much? It's more than David, isn't it? He's a jerk and a creep, but there's something stronger than that bothering you?"

Then he did turn around and look at her. "You're very perceptive."

She just stared at him with wide, green eyes.

"I got a letter yesterday. Actually, I got two letters. One was from my ex-wife and the other was from my son."

His mountain lion eyes hazed over. Suzanne knew he must be thinking about Ryan. By the look on his face, something was terribly wrong.

"What is it, Logan?" she asked gently. "Is Ryan sick?"

"No."

He stopped and stared into the tiny creek for so long, Suzanne didn't think he was going to explain anything more to her, but finally he continued.

"Debby's getting married again."

"Oh."

"Yeah—" he glanced at Suzanne and she could read guilt and hurt in his eyes "—but everything is okay with Ryan. He said that he loves this new man and wants his mother to marry him."

The haunted expression in Logan's eyes was almost more than she could stand. "He won't take your place in Ryan's life, Logan. You'll always be his father."

"I've tried to tell myself that, but the truth is that this guy needs to take my place. He needs to be a father to Ryan because I'm not there with him." He reached down and pulled a chunk of grass out of the soil and twisted it through his hands.

"Don't punish yourself because your ex-wife moved away and you can't be with your son for long periods of time. That's not your fault."

"Intellectually, I know that my home has always been Texas—that's where my job is, and all of the trappings that come from living in the same area all of your life. But I can't help thinking, I should've followed him to Seattle." His voice carried on the gentle breeze with heartrending clarity.

"No one blames you for not pulling up your whole life and moving to a place far from everything you know. I bet Debby would have fought you if you'd tried to follow her."

Logan's amber eyes roved over her face. "That's true. She warned me to leave her alone and let her make a new start. She assured me I could see Ryan whenever I wanted to drive or fly up there. And she stood by her word. I've always gotten to see him when I could get away for a few days." He threw the tuft of grass he'd been squeezing into the creek bed.

"Life doesn't always turn out the way we assume it will as children. Does Ryan seem well adjusted?"

"Yeah, he seems to do all right. He's done a thing or two that I chalked up to normal kid stuff. He threw a rock through a neighbor's window one time. Another time, Deb found him sneaking in a snake because he wanted it for a pet."

"That sounds normal to me, too. I guess every kid has to test his wings a bit."

Logan walked over and sat down next to her, stretching his long legs out in front of him and lying back on one elbow. "I feel like a failure as a father. Old man Brown and I have more in common than he could ever realize."

"Logan—"

Logan held up his hand, effectively silencing her. "This man Debby's going to marry has gotten Ryan involved in soccer and T-ball. I'm really happy for him, but God help me, I wish it were me who was there to take him to practice and games." He tunneled his fingers through the grass again.

Suzanne leaned toward him and covered his hands with hers. "It takes too much energy to worry about what you can't fix. He sounds happy, so leave it at that. You're doing the best you can as a long-distance father and you have to learn to live with that."

He looked up at her and the bleakness in his eyes softened. "You don't have to nurture me, too, Suzanne. I can handle this on my own." He could hear his father telling him to whistle. He'd already opened up too much to her.

"I know." She ran her hand lightly up and down his forearm. "But it's easier if two carry the load instead of one."

"Your shoulders aren't wide enough to help me," he said. "You can barely handle your own problems right now."

She traced his jawline with her fingers. "Try me."

He groaned and pulled her to him, kissing her. The kiss was so poignantly sweet that Suzanne thought she would faint from the exquisite simplicity of it. He was wounded and she wanted to heal him. He was suffering and she wanted to make everything all right.

With aching urgency she returned his kiss.

This kiss was different from the ones they'd shared that night in the Jeep. Those had been full of lusty passion. This one contained passion certainly, but there was something richer and deeper about this kiss. Suzanne recognized it even though she wasn't sure that Logan even felt it.

Love. She was falling in love with Logan and this kiss was her giving that love to him.

She drew back and stared at him in wonder while he watched her under hooded eyes. Then she stretched out beside him and crooked a hand around his neck, silently guiding his mouth to hers again. This time she opened her mouth and sent her tongue questing. He groaned from deep in his chest and slanted his mouth across hers.

He drew back his head after a long, wet kiss and shook his head as if trying to clear it of cobwebs. "Sweetheart, you don't know what you're doing. You're making it tough for me to control myself. You don't have to offer yourself to me like this."

"Logan, I...I..." She couldn't say the words. She couldn't tell him she loved him. He would probably think it was a girlish fancy, anyway.

"Just let me hold you a moment longer." He kissed her nose, eyelids and forehead as he looped his arms around her so they lay entwined in each other's arms.

The breeze in the trees created a natural symphony for them and the wildflowers perfumed the air. They lay in peaceful silence as Suzanne listened to the beat of Logan's heart under her ear.

After a few minutes, she said in a quiet voice, "Maybe it's time for you to fly up for a visit with Ryan. Nothing can beat a face-to-face, man-to-man talk." She shifted slowly against Logan's side and heard him groan again. Unsure of his reaction, she rushed on with her idea. "After he's reassured you that you'll always be his father, you'll feel better."

Suzanne sat up halfway and leaned across Logan's chest, staring down at him with green eyes shining. She waited for his answer.

Then she shifted slightly and, feeling her warmth pressing into him, Logan had to bite back a moan. Didn't she know what she was doing to him?

Trying to concentrate on their conversation, Logan couldn't help but notice his voice was abnormally husky. "I can't leave in the middle of our sting operation. And afterward—I don't know—I don't want to mess things up between Debby and Ryan and this new guy. But I'll give it some deep thought."

Hoping to lighten his mood, Suzanne smiled and rearranged herself on top of him.

"Damn, is this some special torture of yours?" he whispered.

"Torture? What on earth—?"

Her words were swallowed up when Logan framed her face with his hands and claimed her lips with his. She sighed and complied fully with the demands his mouth and tongue made on hers. Then he swept his hands down her back and on to the naked flesh of her thighs. Wanting to get closer, she pressed herself into him, settling her body more fully on his, and she thought his breath rasped in the back of his throat.

When his warm hands moved up under the hem of her short overalls and under the lacy wisp of silk that passed for underwear to cup her buttocks, she was the one who couldn't stifle a whimper. As he kneaded the soft flesh, her body grew taut and a sweet feeling akin to pain but promising pleasure spread from the bud between her thighs and blossomed throughout her body. No man had ever touched her this way nor made her feel this wonderful, this heady.

"Logan, Logan." She chanted his name between kisses.

"Do you feel what you do to me, Suzanne? Do you feel it?"

Through the confines of their clothing she did feel the hard ridge that pressed with life and heat against her softness. The knowledge that she had brought him to that state made her quiver and fall over the edge just a little more. She planted her palms against his shoulders and rose up, arching her spine, eyes closed, russet curls thrown back. His fingers worked a magical massage on her buttocks as he bucked slowly, erotically, beneath her. She was breathless and totally caught up in the delicate sensations that sparked from his fingers and his sinuous movements. She couldn't hold back the cry that escaped as she felt a small explosion between her thighs overwhelm her.

When she looked down at Logan, he was watching her with wonderment lighting his eyes. "You're beautiful."

Suzanne stared dreamily into his eyes and shook her head. "No, *you're* beautiful. Especially when you let your guard down like this. You should do it more often." She reached up and cupped his jaw.

Logan's eyes clouded suddenly and he broke away from her touch. "That's not part of my job, Suzanne. I'm paid to be wary, alert—not to be relaxed. If I get any looser with you, I'll hurt you, and I don't want to do that." Facing what was happening between them, he knew he had to be utterly truthful with her. "If we make love, you've got to understand that it's not a fairy tale. I'm not the beast that's going to turn into the handsome prince."

"I don't want a handsome prince, Logan. I want a man—you." Even as she spoke, she was unhooking the fasteners on her overalls and lowering the bib.

"Suzanne, I'm not a shallow kid. You can't tease me." He grabbed her hands as she began unbuttoning her blouse.

She looked him straight in the eyes. "I'm not teasing you."

He let her hands slip out of his grasp then and watched as she finished unbuttoning the blouse. She started to pull it off, but stopped and looked at him. "Don't you want to do this?"

He swallowed and closed his eyes for a minute and she knew he was warring with himself. The breeze sighed through the trees and her shallow breaths mingled with it.

"Hell, yes, I want to do this. Just a taste... Even if the sweetness torments me every night when I remember it," he said as he opened his eyes.

Then he reached out and gently brushed the blouse from her shoulders. Her bra was pale blue and barely covered the peaks of her breasts. Logan unsnapped the fastener in the front and watched as her bounty spilled into his hands. In the dappled light filtering through the trees, he thought her breasts were the most beautiful things he'd ever seen. He thought of smooth white marble, polished and perfect. Tiny blue veins radiated from the apricot crests. When he ran the pads of his thumbs over the tips, they became pearls to his touch.

He drew her up to her knees and eagerly nuzzled first one tip, then the other. They immediately stiffened and Suzanne clutched his head and cradled him closer to her. He pulled back and chuckled when the breeze hardened the wet crests even more.

"Umm, unbelievable," he said as he watched his hands mold and reshape her breasts.

She moaned softly and let her head drop back. Her reaction let him know how incredibly sensitive her sense of touch was. Leaning close again, he nibbled along the silken skin of her throat, not stopping until his lips reached the delicate lobe of her ear. There he took the skin between his teeth and tugged gently before plunging his tongue into the cavern above. Suzanne shuddered in his arms and rubbed her naked breasts against his chest.

"Yes," Suzanne urged him on.

Unable to stop himself, Logan trailed hot kisses down the valley the hills of her breasts made. He felt her trembling hands fumbling with the buttons on his shirt and his manhood straining against the confines of his jeans. Her inex perienced movements and the sweet ache of his loins assaulted his senses as nothing else ever had. But then, at the edge of sanity, a vision of where they were, vulnerable to the prying eyes of the Brown men, made Logan lean back and take several deep breaths to clear the sensuous haze from his brain.

He looked into her eyes and smiled ruefully. Kissing her once more, he said, "As much as I'd like to open you to passion right here, I'm worried that Mr. Brown or his charming son will come looking for us at any moment."

Suzanne glanced through the trees and realized the wisdom of Logan's words. "This would be a beautiful place to have this happen—among the trees and grass and flowers, and the wide-open sky."

His smile deepened. "Yes, another of your perfect settings." They stared deeply at each other for a few minutes before he spoke again. "Come on, sweetheart, let's repair these clothes."

"Logan, I..."

He put a hand over her lips. "Suzanne, please don't say anything. We've already said and done more than we should." He waited until she nodded; then he pulled her up and helped her straighten out her clothing. He let the questions spilling from her eyes go unanswered.

He knew he was the one who had to stop this... this attraction they had between them. He was older, wiser and more experienced than her. She was new to these feelings, but he knew where they could lead and where they *shouldn't* lead. It was his job to be the one to stop this physical thing because she didn't know that he could never stay for the long haul, and that's what she would want.

He didn't need her thinking that what they'd just experienced—open communication—was a normal habit of his, either. This rare moment had surprised even him. He knew his inability to communicate had killed his marriage and he also knew it would doom a deep relationship with Suzanne.

"Suzanne, I can't let this happen—not between partners," Logan said tersely. Without looking at her, he turned and began walking back toward the van.

"But it already has," she said softly to his retreating back.

Chapter 9

Later that afternoon Suzanne was startled from her dinner of fresh fruit salad by an insistent pounding on her front door. It couldn't be Logan. He was teaching an evening class at the college. Whoever it was, was not being polite about wanting her attention. Jumping up from the table, she scurried to the door and flung it open.

"Christine." Suzanne was shocked by the haunted look in her cousin's gray eyes. She had seemed to be rejoining the world lately. But today her face was a stricken mask.

"What on earth, Christine—?"

Christine rushed inside. "Don't you 'what on earth' me, Suzanne Stewart." She pushed a dark strand of hair behind an ear. "What are you doing buying drugs?"

Startled, Suzanne turned her back to Christine, not wanting her to read the secrets she knew she had to keep hidden. Her thoughts were a topsy-turvy tornado for a minute. Somehow or other, Christine had heard something. Oh, Lord. How could she get herself out of this and at the same time calm Christine's fears? She took a breath and tried to think clearly. Finally, over her shoulder, she asked Christine, "How did you find out?"

"Then it's true." Christine flopped down in the nearest chair like a puppet whose strings had been cut.

"What did you hear about me, Christine?" Suzanne knew she'd have to tread lightly, not give anything away.

"Philip Jones from the college pulled me aside at the public library board meeting today." Christine searched Suzanne's face. "He said you'd tried buying drugs from him at the faculty party."

Suzanne stared unblinkingly at Christine.

"It's true, isn't it?" Christine shook her head. She stood up and began pacing in front of Suzanne. "I didn't believe it until right this minute."

Suzanne knew that her next words would be among the most important she'd ever speak. She had to protect the operation and keep Christine's trust. But if one had to be sacrificed, the latter would have to go.

"Philip told you the truth as he knows it."

"What the hell does that mean?" Christine bristled, coming to a stop in front of her. "You either asked him to buy drugs or you didn't."

Suzanne shut her eyes momentarily. There was no way out of this. "I did."

Christine sank back into a chair. She put her head in her hands and just sighed. "How could you?"

Trying to give herself more time to think, Suzanne turned and headed for the kitchen. "Let me get you some herbal tea. Then we'll talk about this." She had only taken three steps when Christine stopped her with words deadlier and more painful than any knife could cut.

"It's Logan."

Again Suzanne whirled around. "What?"

"*Logan Davis*. He's poisoning your mind and spirit just like Curtis did me. That's it. I just knew it." Christine got up and wandered listlessly around the room before she turned to Suzanne again. "We Stewart women don't seem to be very lucky in love, do we?"

"Now just a minute, Christine. Logan has nothing to do with this." Suzanne couldn't keep the sharp edge out of her voice.

"Don't try to fool me. You'd never buy drugs on your own. And for goodness' sake, don't protect him—he doesn't deserve it."

"Listen to me, Christine. The world is not all black and white. There's a lot of gray and every other color of the spectrum. What Philip Jones saw on the surface is much different than what really was. Logan Davis hasn't influenced me to do anything I haven't wanted to do. You've got to believe that." Suzanne's voice was calm, but underneath her heart was in turmoil. She hoped fervently her cousin would believe her.

"Natalie's boyfriend led her down the wrong path and now you. I just wish when the Stewart women fell in love, they wouldn't—"

"Who said I was in love with Logan?"

Christine smiled sadly. "You did. From the moment I saw you together in The Good Earth, I knew it. You're verifying it with the way you're rushing to defend him. At Gram's you gave yourself away every time you looked at him and with the way you melted every time the man touched you."

The room was so quiet that Suzanne could hear the wind rustling the trees outside. Suzanne's mind and entire body froze. She was in love with Logan! Everyone knew. Did he?

Christine touched her arm gently. "Suzanne, I don't believe *you're* taking the drugs. I know Logan is pushing this issue with you."

Suzanne backed away from Christine, forcing herself to say calmly, "I'll tell you again. Logan doesn't—"

"Don't." Christine cut her off. "Please don't tell me how wonderful he is or how misunderstood." She began pacing again. "Suzanne, I understand. I did things for Curtis I still haven't told anyone about. But in the end it didn't help.'' She looked pleadingly at Suzanne. ''You can't save him, you know.''

Suzanne closed her eyes for an instant. How could she let Christine continue to think this way about Logan? Technically, what Christine was saying was true. Logan *was* the one pushing this. But not in the way she thought.

Surely if she told her the truth, Christine could keep it a secret. She was about to open her mouth when she remembered Logan's warning: Don't trust anyone. Their success depended on it. She couldn't let her partner down.

Suzanne smiled reassuringly. ''For the moment, Christine, you'll just have to trust me. As soon as I can, I'll explain everything to you.''

''I trust you,'' Christine told her. ''It's Logan I don't. I once loved a man with the same fervor and fever you have now. I don't want you to make the same mistake I did.''

''I won't, I promise.''

''Then get away from him. Please, before it's too late.''

Suzanne tried one more time to ease Christine's fears. ''I know you don't understand, but I've got to stay with Logan. Trust me.''

Christine's gray eyes probed Suzanne for several seconds and then she said, frustration coloring her tone, ''Okay, for now. But remember, be careful and don't get into anything that will get you hurt.''

''Don't be so dramatic.''

Christine shook her head. ''I hope you're right. It's taken me a long time to begin getting my life back together. I don't want that for you.''

Suzanne nodded. ''Gram told me about the school you want to open.''

Christine smiled for the first time. ''Yes, I think I've found a site. Now I just have to work with the state. There are so many forms because it's going to be for special children.''

"You'll be great at it," Suzanne assured her.

Christine walked toward the door. "I know, but thanks anyway. And remember, I'm here if you need me," Christine called over her shoulder as she walked to her car.

"I know that," Suzanne said. After she shut the door, she leaned against it and gave her heart a chance to get back to its normal rhythm. Lying to her cousin had been hard. But hearing her talk about how obvious her feelings for Logan were had been even more difficult. She wanted to shelter her feelings about Logan; they were still too fragile. She had hoped to keep them secret, away from public scrutiny. Apparently that wasn't going to be allowed.

Suzanne rushed past the small hand-painted Parsons table by her front door, intent on going to the kitchen for that cup of tea she'd offered Christine. She was also trying to keep busy so she wouldn't have to think about her drug-buying actions and what they would mean in the town that she called home. Having her reputation ruined had always been a risk, but now that it was becoming a reality, she was beginning to feel real loss.

She brushed against the piece of furniture and sent her purse clattering to the floor. When the bag hit the tile, its contents spilled out. Immediately Suzanne's attention zeroed in on a plastic Ziploc bag.

"What in the world?" she whispered out loud.

Scooping the pouch up, she opened it. Her hands were shaking, and her mind flew into overdrive. Inside the plastic was a white powdery substance with small crystals interspersed throughout it. She knew it hadn't been in her purse before. When had it been put there—and by whom?

She tried to reconstruct her day. It was impossible. Her purse had never been out of her sight. She couldn't pin any one name down as to who might have been around her purse.

What was this stuff, really? In the movies the police always tasted a fingertip of powder to see if it was the right thing. Suzanne giggled rather hysterically. She wouldn't know the taste of cocaine from powdered sugar.

She held the bag away from herself, almost as if it would bite. Even her limited experience told her this was some sort of breakthrough. She didn't know what sort, but she knew who would know. Logan.

Glancing at her wristwatch, she saw that he had another hour in his class before she could talk to him.

She clutched the cache to her chest and closed her eyes. *Someone was taking her drug buying seriously.* Maybe now she and Logan could begin to piece together some real evidence that would put the sellers behind bars.

As she held the sack close, she felt a lump and quickly fished around in the white powder until she found a carefully folded one-dollar bill. Easing it out, Suzanne gingerly unfolded it and stared dumbstruck at more white powder. What in the world is all this? she asked herself.

Logan would know.

Gently refolding the bill and putting it back into the plastic bag, Suzanne scooped up the contents of her purse and hurried out the door to see her partner.

On the drive to the college, she focused all of her energy on the bag in her purse, as if it could tell her answers. Instead, all she came up with were questions. What did it all mean? Did the drug dealers trust her now? What would Logan's reaction be to her apparent success? What if this had happened when Christine had been there?

Suddenly Suzanne felt chilled and shivered while the hairs at the nape of her neck stood up. Involuntarily she glanced in her rearview mirror and saw a tan sedan following about fifty yards behind her. Not understanding what motivated her, she turned right at the next corner instead of going her usual route to the community college. She breathed a sigh of relief when the car went straight.

"Goodness, Suzanne," she admonished herself out loud, "you're starting to act as silly as a heroine in a B movie."

Nevertheless, she couldn't shake the chill that had enveloped her. Finally she turned her thoughts to Logan, hoping they would calm her quivering nerves.

When Christine had attacked Logan, Suzanne had jumped to his defense. And during her speech, it had become clear to her. She'd meant it. Logan, for all his rough, bullying behavior, was a kind man. Suzanne knew that events in his past had led him to shut people out. But there had been moments when she caught the twinkle in his eye, or the slow smile that harbored no bitterness, but just as quickly, they had been gone. Something always seemed to trigger the return of his stoicism. Whatever forced his control to surface, it didn't hide one thing. He loved his son.

One day soon this case would be over and Logan would go back to his lab in Austin, and she would go back to The Good Earth. A deep ache in the region of her heart throbbed at the thought of ending their tenuous relationship. She thought of the way he insisted she learn the rudiments of self-defense, the way the webbing of lines around his eyes deepened when he smiled at some mistake she made in the course of her training. How would she face day after day in her sunny shop without ever seeing Logan again?

Once more an eerie feeling shimmied up her back and she scanned the streets for any sign of danger. She didn't relax until she got to the college. As she ran up the steps to the science building, she glanced over her shoulder in time to see the tan sedan that had been cruising behind her pull into a student parking space. She laughed at her fears.

Hurrying down the quiet hall that led to room 104, Suzanne forgot everything in her excitement to show Logan what was in her purse. Her footsteps clicked on the hard floor in the tomblike building. When she finally arrived at the classroom, she halted and bent down, peeking in through the narrow rectangle of glass that rose above the doorknob.

Logan was standing beside a computer with some device attached to the top of it that allowed the images he was drawing to be reproduced on an overhead screen. Her eyes swept the students and everyone seemed to be busily writing in notebooks except for two young women who sat right in front of Logan. Their attention was centered on the man himself and not on what words of wisdom he appeared to be imparting.

Suzanne could see only profiles, but both looked to have smiles—glowingly outlined in red and hot pink—trained on Logan. He smiled back at one of them, and the lucky recipient turned to wink at her girlfriend, who, in turn, stretched out long, tanned legs that seemed to go on for miles from under her short shorts.

Why were coeds allowed to wear shorts these days, anyway? Suzanne fumed. And, since it was obvious they were more interested in the professor than in chemistry, why were they even allowed to take the course? *I need to screen the applicants for Logan's course,* she thought irrationally. *And I'd only let in men and very old, overweight women,* she added crossly. Smushing her nose against the pane of glass, she stared at the creamy skin on the thighs of one of the women.

Suddenly it dawned on her that Logan had quit lecturing. Her eyes lifted to his face, and she found he was staring at her in disbelief. Glancing around, she realized everyone in the room had turned to see what his or her professor was looking at. Ruby Lips and Fuchsia Lips were giggling and pointing at her.

Suzanne straightened abruptly and pivoted from the window, flattening herself against the wooden part of the door. She was such an idiot. Why couldn't she act like a normal, mature adult and wait patiently for Logan in his office?

She knew the answer to that one. She wanted to be with Logan all the time now. She wanted to share her news with him. She wanted to share...everything with him. That thought brought Suzanne away from the door, terrified. Christine had been right. She couldn't hide her feelings—even from herself. Feverishly she prayed: Please, *please* don't let him come out right now. With his keen perception he'd see exactly what she was thinking. And what she was thinking made those two coeds down front look tame....

What in the name of hell does Suzanne want that can't wait until later? Logan asked himself as he tried to get the class back to their discussion of the latest advances in DNA testing. Did she have any idea how charming and silly she looked with her nose pressed against the glass like a child looking in Neiman Marcus's window at Christmas?

Her kind of sweetness was unaffected and he knew she hadn't planned her actions to distract him, but, Lordy, how they had. He wanted to tell the two simpering women in front of him to get a life and not waste their time fawning over him. He'd take a woman who owned her own business and put her life on the line for her family—and really, the entire town of Gruenville—any old day over these two. They seemed to think their worth was in what they could offer with their bodies.

Not that he wouldn't love to be able to crush Suzanne's lush body to him and take what she kept offering, but he couldn't. She needed a man who could offer her soft words and security and emotional ties. He could offer none of those, but that knowledge didn't keep him from aching for her. If he didn't watch his thoughts, he'd embarrass himself in front of this class.

"Okay, that's it for tonight, class." He shut down the computer. "Get yourselves some coffee at the student union building and read the next three chapters before next week."

Books slammed, pencils scattered and chairs scraped. Logan gathered his book and papers off the desk and looked up to find the twosome from the front row standing in front of his desk.

"We're buying the coffee tonight, Professor Davis." The one with the red lipstick smiled to show a true orthodontia masterpiece. "Want to join us? I didn't understand the part of your lecture about DNA and proving paternity and stuff. You could explain that more fully."

He glanced at each and then at Suzanne, who stood in the hallway peering at him through the small window in the door. He scowled at her, shaking his head discreetly. Turning back to the artificial-looking pair, he said simply, "Thanks, ladies, but I have other plans for this evening." He nodded toward Suzanne. "See ya." He didn't give them another thought as he went to join his partner.

In the hall, Suzanne noted wryly, "Getting numbers for your little black book?"

Logan gathered her against him and marveled at how she fit so perfectly against his side next to his heartbeat. "Never. You're the only woman for me and you know it."

Suzanne smiled up at him and wished it were true. It felt wonderful to be held close to him where she could feel the beat of his heart. Even though she knew it was all a charade, a part of her pretended it was for real.

When they were behind closed doors on the third floor in Logan's office, Suzanne said, "Sit down, Logan. You're not going to believe this."

He sat down at his desk, all sign of the lover-boy facade erased from his face. "Okay. What's all the suspense about?"

"This afternoon Christine came to see me." Suzanne leaned across his desk in her excitement.

"She and I talked for a while and then, after she left, I was busy getting some tea."

"Suzanne, what does all this—"

"Hear me out, Logan. I was hurrying around and I knocked my purse to the floor. This purse." She held it up triumphantly. "Everything spilled out."

She set the purse down on his desk and opened it, fishing around for the plastic bag. "This fell out. I think I've finally scored."

Logan snatched the pouch from her hands, opened it and tasted a bit of the powder. He looked up at her grimly. "It's cocaine. Not a very high grade, but I don't suppose the folks in Gruenville care."

She sank down farther in her chair. Somehow his confirmation had pierced a hole in her enthusiasm. Things were getting very real now, maybe too real. "How did that get in my purse?"

"You'll need to make a list of everywhere you were today and yesterday and where you set your purse down." He ran a hand through his hair. "We'll probably never know where or who put this in your purse, but it's a start."

"Logan, there's more."

"More?" His eyes narrowed.

"Yes, in the bag." She pointed to it.

"Dear God," he breathed when he pulled the dollar bill from the powder. He barely looked at her. "Let's go into the lab."

She followed him closely as they went into the room where, only a few weeks ago, he had explained the booming world of illicit narcotics. Sitting down on a stool near him, she watched as he booted up computers and lit lights on machines she couldn't identify. He worked quietly, absorbed in the identification of the powder that had been stashed in the money.

She watched him as he fiddled with the computer, then put the powder into some liquid. He recorded what was happening to the substance. She recorded in her mind what was happening to him. The muscles in his back bunched, then relaxed as he worked. His intensity as he mixed ingre-

dients was fierce, and for a moment she remembered th
heat he'd generated when last that laserlike focus had bee
directed at her. She shivered.

His eyebrows furrowed as he studied the data he fed int
the machines, and she wanted to smooth away the wrinkle
with the tips of her fingers. Then she wanted to trace th
planes and contours of his face, pausing to feather his thic
eyelashes and then to map the outlines of his lips. And whe
her fingers had had their fill of charting the intricacies of h
handsome face, she wanted to record it all with her lips. Sh
wanted to know him as well as he would know the whi
powder he was now exploring....

"See here, Suzanne." His voice brought her out of he
sensuous musings. "These machines aren't exactly like th
ones I have in my lab in Austin, but I'm reasonably certai
that this drug isn't Cyclone but Super K."

"Super K?" Suzanne squinted at the computer scree
where Logan was pointing, but none of the formula co
figurations or words on it made much sense to her.

"The official name's ketamine, but on the street it
known as Super K." He continued to punch data into th
computer.

"I've never read anything about that or heard it used (
the TV news."

"It's not nearly as potent or deadly as...say, PCP
Ecstasy, but it seems to be the drug of the moment in big ci
clubs. I've been receiving a lot of information about it ba
at my office." He glanced up at her, his eyes dark, broo
ing. "I guess it's finding its way to small towns, too."

"You said it wasn't as deadly as PCP. Does that mean i
not as dangerous?"

He frowned ominously at her. "That's probably what
lot of sellers are telling their customers, but it's lethal in
own way. A person can overdose on it just like any oth
narcotic, and people with depression or other emotion

problems can totally trip out on this stuff and turn violent or commit suicide.''

"Oh, Logan.'' Suzanne couldn't help that her eyes filled with tears. ''What's happening to Gruenville?''

Logan covered her hands with his and squeezed. ''That's where you come in. You're working to rid your town of this filth.'' God help him, but he had to keep using her so they could clean out this viper's nest. It shouldn't bother him as much as it did.

Suzanne liked the feel of Logan's warm hands caressing hers and was mildly disappointed when he removed them and turned back to the computer. Her thoughts strayed to her sister's sweet face on the day she died. At first Suzanne had said ''no'' when Natalie asked for money to go out with her friends. But her sister had looked so forlorn, Suzanne had reached into her purse and pulled out a twenty-dollar bill. Natalie had hugged her and then Suzanne had given her another twenty, telling her sister she'd worked hard around The Good Earth and that she deserved a reward. *Why, oh why, had she been such a fool?*

Hesitantly, she asked Logan, ''Do you think this could have been something Natalie dabbled in?''

Logan looked up from the computer screen, alerted by some nuance in Suzanne's voice to the inner struggle she was waging. He was sure it had something to do with Natalie's death. What else was locked inside her? He'd wondered the same thing when he'd first met Suzanne in Dan's office and now he questioned again—what details hadn't she told him about her sister's death? There had to be some element in the scenario that wouldn't allow Suzanne to lay her sister to rest and get on with her life. Maybe one day soon she would trust him enough to confide in him and he could help her work out her problem. Maybe...

''What does this stuff do for a person?'' Suzanne asked, bringing him back to the problem at hand.

"It's a mild hallucinogenic. It gives you an energy burst that only lasts for a few hours. You could take a hit at a party, have a tripping good time, come down from the high and go home with no one at home being the wiser." He stood up and began shutting down the equipment.

But Suzanne had more questions she wanted answered. "Does it come from South America?"

"No." He looked at her for several minutes before he continued. "It's used as an anesthetic by many veterinarians."

"Veterinarians?" Suzanne echoed in a thin voice. "Then it might be Dr. Adams?"

"Probably not," Logan replied. "That's too simple a solution and too easy to trace. The source isn't usually that stupid. But the department will run a check on the doc anyway."

"Maybe it's someone who works for him." Suzanne tried to visualize the various people who worked for the local vet.

"Maybe, but it's probably coming from a larger source. Hospitals have it, too. Someone steals it from a supply room where it's in liquid form and then boils it down to powder."

"Why do you think it was put in my purse?" This was all too confusing and upsetting for Suzanne right now. Her enthusiasm over the find had disappeared. She wanted the perpetrators caught red-handed and put in jail. This game they were playing was fraying her nerves.

"It's likely some sort of test, to see how you respond, if you keep trying to buy, et cetera." He faced her and drank in the green of her eyes. "This is a social drug, meaning it's accepted at many upper-class parties, like LSD was in the sixties. Maybe you're going to start getting invitations to all kinds of parties."

"It's unreal that some narcotics are acceptable to the rich and some aren't." Suzanne shook her head. "But this is what we want, right?"

Logan nodded.

"I'm barely reliving my high school days, where beer was the big taboo and kids had to try it." She crinkled her nose. "I never could stand the taste of the stuff and, come to think of it, I never went to that many parties."

"Whoever is behind this probably figures this is a good drug to bring into a small town. Besides the fact that it's not as dangerous as some, it's also not very expensive, so lots of kids can buy it."

"Dear God," Suzanne whispered and covered her mouth with a trembling hand.

"One bump like this—" he motioned to the white powder on the lab table "—will only cost about twenty dollars. Then you're robbed of your sense of time and space and you float for a couple of hours. Pretty great stuff, huh?" The expression on his face told Suzanne he thought it was anything but great.

"On the one hand I'm excited that I've finally gotten the police some hard evidence, but on the other, I'm terrified of this whole thing." Her eyes were large and frightened.

"You should be." Logan walked over to a briefcase and opened it. Inside was a phone system. Automatically, he punched in some numbers, keeping an eye on Suzanne the whole time. Then he turned his back and talked quietly, calmly explaining to someone on the other end what had happened.

It took all of three minutes. Suzanne stared at his rigid, warriorlike stance. Suddenly she realized the truth. To him, this *was* a war. Logan's weapons weren't guns or knives, but they were just as effective—a high-tech laboratory with computers and test tubes. He trapped his enemy with intelligence and cunning. This Logan scared her a little. Her face must have registered her fear, because when he turned around and saw her face, he smiled slowly.

"Suzanne. You did it." Logan crushed her against him, trying, through the sheer strength of his body, to give her courage. He ran his hands lightly across her back and she snuggled closer.

"Your heart's racing," Suzanne informed him. "I can feel it beating against my cheek."

"You're right." He picked her up and swung her around, smiling into her eyes.

"Logan, what are you doing?" she squealed as she clutched her arms around his neck, holding on for dear life.

"I'm excited, too. This is a real breakthrough." But he didn't tell her the whole truth. He didn't tell her that his heart was about to beat right out of his chest because she felt good and right fitted against him. He couldn't tell her that he wanted to do more than swing her around. He wanted to lay her across the hard lab table behind them and then bury himself in her. No, he definitely couldn't tell her that.

Her small hand moved along his side and he groaned out loud.

"Suzanne, you make me crazy," was all he could say before he locked his mouth over hers.

She responded immediately by clasping her arms around his neck tighter and pulling him even closer, escalating the excitement of the kiss. He met her challenge with one of his own. Sliding his hands down to cup her derriere, he lifted her and cushioned her soft V against the steely length of him. She moaned, but didn't pull away. Instead she rubbed herself intimately against him, while running her tongue along his bottom lip.

Logan responded by deepening the kiss, seeking the honey of her mouth. He stroked her back with feathery caresses, slowly making his strokes harder, more intense. As she leaned into him, he brought his hands forward to cup her breasts, teasing her nipples with his thumb. When they beaded in response, he pressed his palm against them.

Suzanne arched against his hand, asking for more. With his need at a firestorm level, Logan began unbuttoning her blouse, searching for her warm, lush flesh.

The clackety-clack of the printer serving up information brought him to his senses. Setting her gently on the floor, he backed up. He searched his brain for a clever remark to neutralize what had just happened between them. But the cool chemist, comfortable with computers and petri dishes came up empty. So he relied on the cop in him to get the job done.

"We'll celebrate when we put some of these people in jail," he said neutrally as he turned off the printer. "But, right now, you better get on home. Tomorrow we're going to the mayor's dinner and you might score big there. That will be the first real test."

Suzanne, still caught in the foggy haze of desire Logan had wrapped her in, blinked and then backed away slowly. "I'll be ready," she whispered, and, picking up her purse, she walked out of the room.

Logan watched her leave and felt a raw ache spread somewhere in his chest. Someday she would exit from his life, just like that.

Chapter 10

"Let me help you with that." Logan took the tilting boxes from Suzanne as she walked carefully down the porch stairs and headed for Wells's huge backyard. "Where are the bartenders who are supposed to be setting this up?"

"They're right behind me with their arms full, too."

Two college students bounded down the stairs, arms loaded, and came over to where Suzanne and Logan were standing. "Over by the champagne fountain. Right?" one asked.

"Yes. And please stack the glasses carefully. It's supposed to look like a pyramid." Suzanne steered Logan, with his cargo of crystal flutes, to the designated spot. The champagne fountain stood under a stand of giant crepe myrtle. Next to it, on a table draped with white linens, sat a four-tiered wedding cake.

"This is where they'll cut the cake. The background of flowers will make a great picture," Suzanne explained to Logan. She surveyed the rest of the setting with a critical eye, making sure everything was ready for the bride and groom. In the middle of the yard stood the huge tent complete with dance floor, seating for several hundred and the stage for the ensemble imported from Austin for the occasion. Along with the champagne fountain, three bars were set up so the guests wouldn't have to wait in line for drinks. The food would be served from a makeshift kitchen located in the garage. Flowers, dark pink and baby blue, were everywhere. The only thing missing from the picture were the guests and the bride and groom, who would be there in about four hours. Suzanne was satisfied with the job. But she wasn't happy about having to wear a wire during the reception and knowing she would be searching for people willing to sell her drugs.

In the past two weeks their sting operation had shifted into high gear. Ever since the discovery of cocaine in her purse, she'd been scoring. She was working her way down Logan's list. With every buy she made, Logan was able to piece together the pattern of distribution. They were close to identifying the two top suppliers, but, with every victory she had, a sadness grew within her. Her world, so protected and safe, was slowly slipping away. And she wasn't sure she liked what was in its place. But today was not the day to dwell on dreary thoughts. After all, the bride and groom deserved a perfect setting for their love.

Suzanne walked over and rearranged the bouquet at the head table and then turned to Logan to let him know she was ready to go home. She smiled when she saw him sitting behind the drum set the band had put out, tapping quietly on the cymbals. His head was bowed and his eyes were half-closed; he was in his own world. How relaxed he looked. This was not the same man who had methodically worked in his lab to identify the drug found in her purse and then had reported his findings in a cold voice to the other operatives on the case. No, this was the man who, only seconds after the phone call, had kissed her with such wild abandon. She could still feel his arms around her as he'd swung her around. She moved closer to the dais and saw him smile a slow, seductive smile.

"A secret fantasy?" Suzanne teased.

Logan's head jerked up and his grin widened. "You caught me. I've always wanted to be a drummer. One of those guys who just bangs away, hair thrown back, earring dangling, tattoos visible under a black muscle T-shirt."

Suzanne laughed. "Well, I can picture you in the shirt, but the earring and the hair are a little harder to imagine." What she didn't say was she'd love to see him in a black muscle T-shirt, sweating from the exertion of pounding on the drums.

"Yeah." Logan put the drumsticks down, stood and jumped off the stage. "My son loves the drums. I like to think he inherited it from me."

"Maybe he'll live out your fantasy."

Logan stopped to think for a second, and his eyes narrowed. "I don't know if I want him hanging around with the kind of guys I just described."

Suzanne sighed, sorry to see the man from the lab return. "Logan, you can't control everything." She gave him a small smile. "Some things you just have to trust will be all right."

Logan was about to answer when a man came around the corner of the house and headed straight for them.

Something about the man's forbidding demeanor caused Suzanne to stiffen.

Logan turned to her. "It's all right." He shook hands with the guy. "Suzanne, this is Steve. He'll be in the truck during the reception, listening to what's going down."

Steve nodded in Suzanne's direction. "We're set up. It's the catering truck right across the street." As he pointed to the truck, he seemed to notice the yard for the first time. "Hey, this is really something. It doesn't look this big from the front." He looked at Suzanne and motioned for her to follow him. "We need to run a test. Can you come with me"

We'll show you the equipment, the setup and run a sound-level check."

Logan took her arm. "I'll bring her over in a minute." He watched as Steve headed back to the truck. Then he faced Suzanne. "I know you don't think this is necessary, but it's a perfect opportunity for us."

Suzanne nodded. "In my head, I know you're right. But my heart wishes I could just enjoy the reception."

"I agree. But the whole town will be here. You've been successful breaking into the buying ring—you need to keep doing it. Remember, we're still trying to trap the main suppliers. Plus, this gives us more 'time on stage' for the community. It will help verify all those things you told John Wells. We *need* to use this time."

Suzanne nodded again and they began walking in the direction Steve had taken. Before they made it to the end of the yard, Logan stopped her with a hand on her arm and looked soberly into her eyes. "Suzanne, it's almost over and your world *will* go back to normal."

She smiled sadly as she whispered, "It'll never be normal again, and you know it."

Logan watched Suzanne as she mingled with the crowd. She looked beautiful in another one of those filmy dresses that floated around her when she walked. The fabric looked like a Monet watercolor, mixing blues, greens and pinks. Her wide-brimmed hat was decorated with the same flowers scattered on the tables. She fit perfect into the scene.

He straightened away from the pillar he'd casually leaned against the moment he'd seen her follow Fred Johnson, one of his college colleagues, to the side of the house. They reappeared quickly, and he knew she'd managed to score something from him. No one else would be able to tell, but Logan did because he'd made watching her every mannerism a career. He noticed her shoulders weren't as straight as they usually were and the easy flow to her walk was gone.

Only he knew what caused the slight frown on her forehead. When he'd picked her up, she'd dismissed his com-
pliments with a shrug. On the drive to the church she'd been
quiet, and during the wedding ceremony she'd never smiled.
Damn. He hated what this was doing to her. He was watching her metamorphose right before his eyes—from a sweet,
naive girl, to the pensive, quiet woman gliding among the
guests—and he'd been the cause of it all.

She was changing in other ways, too. He remembered the
sweet, tender kiss they'd shared at the lightning tree. Every
kiss since had been harder, filled with a yearning desire he
wasn't going to be able to resist much longer. Logan hoped
he was right and that it would only be a few more weeks.
They'd coordinated all their efforts with the federal Drug
Enforcement Agency, through the Austin Police Department, and now had a command post set up in Logan's house
with communications equipment linking Gruenville to the
South American country of Colombia. If the infrastruc-
ture held in Colombia, they would have the connections in
both the U.S. and Colombia nailed down. And if it happened fast enough, Suzanne might hold on to some of that
warm, innocence that had scared him so in the beginning.
Funny, now what scared him was how cool she had become. Cursing inwardly, he started over to where she was
standing, chatting with some friends.

"Suzanne, do you want some champagne?" he asked
when he reached her side.

She looked up at him and smiled. "I'll come with you."
She turned to her friends. "Excuse me." She followed Logan toward the champagne, her gossamer skirt swirling
around both their legs as they walked.

When they were safely away from the crowd, he leaned
down and whispered to her. "What was it?"

"Cocaine, I think." She looked up at him and he flinched
from the pain shadowed in her eyes. "The word must really
be out. We did it without ten words being exchanged. I just

gave him money and he gave me what I asked for. I'm amazed who's involved in this." She looked up at Logan, subconsciously imploringly. "Can't I trust anyone?"

"Suzanne—"

"It's okay. I'm a success. Can you believe after all these years of living in this town and being known as the town saint, it's only taken about four weeks for them to believe I could be using this stuff?" She tried to smile but it looked more like a grimace.

Logan wanted to reassure her that the town didn't believe it, but he remained quiet. She was right. With his help, she'd been able to sacrifice her reputation to retaliate for Natalie's death. He only hoped when this was all over, she would still think it was worth it.

He almost wanted to remind her of their first conversation when he'd tried warning her away from all this. But he couldn't. He was stopped by the look in her eyes and the fact they needed her to continue what she was doing. It would get worse, and he would push her the whole way, because that was what he was being paid to do.

"Where is it?" Logan asked, getting down to business.

"In my purse." Suzanne put her hand to the clasp and was nearly done opening it when Logan's hand closed over hers.

"Not here." He pointed toward the house. "Let's go in there. You can pretend you're checking on something. After all, you're helping to cater this thing." He put his arm around her and maneuvered her through the crowd toward the back door, refusing to delve too deeply into why he was doing it. But being noticed could only add credibility to their cover.

They slipped inside the house and then wandered into one of the back bedrooms. Suzanne reached into her bag and gave him the packet. Logan frowned.

"What is it? Is it fake?"

Logan opened the plastic bag and put some of the sub
stance on his little finger. He licked it off. "No, it's real."

"Then why did you frown?" Suzanne stepped away from
him to better gauge his reaction.

Logan felt the weight of the pouch. "It's just more than
we usually get. How much money did you give him?"

"The usual. Why?"

"This is more than you should've gotten." Logan
wrapped it up and stuffed it into his suit pocket. "I'm going to take a little walk and get this to the boys in the truck.
I'll be back."

"Logan, what is it?" Suzanne asked tensely.

"Nothing." He lowered his eyes, shielding them from her
and walked toward the door. "I'll meet you out back in fifteen minutes." He left, five seconds later he stuck his head
in the door. "Don't worry. I always get overcautious when
we're this close to the end of a case."

"You're sure?"

"Absolutely," he assured her grimly. "Now please try to
enjoy yourself. You've put on one helluva party." He waited
for her to smile at him before he turned and went outside.

Logan was on his way back from the truck after having
passed on the cocaine when Brandon stepped in front of
him. He stood like a rock, blocking Logan's path. "I've
been looking for you."

Logan noticed Brandon wasn't smiling, but then, he'd
never really seen him smile unless he was talking to Suzanne, Christine or Gram. He was either brooding or
scowling the other times. He was scowling now.

"You've found me." Logan stood his ground. This wasn't
what he needed right now. Even though he knew Brandon
had been watching him and Suzanne during the entire reception and had even been expecting this confrontation, he
still wasn't ready for Brandon's first comment.

"I should kill you for what you've done to her." Brandon swayed on the balls of his feet, ostensibly just taking a deep breath. Logan wasn't fooled; he recognized the movement. Brandon was balancing himself, readying for a fight.

Logan squared his own stance before he asked sarcastically, "What *exactly* have I done?"

Brandon raised an eyebrow. "I don't know *exactly*, but I will as soon as some friends of mine verify what I suspect. But I do know one thing. You're using her. And she doesn't deserve that kind of treatment."

You're right, Logan thought to himself, she doesn't deserve it. I've told her that myself. However, he kept his expression bland, carefully camouflaging his reactions. He didn't need Brandon poking around and finding out the truth. With Brandon's protective instincts, he'd probably blow the operation to rescue Suzanne. Logan had to prevent that.

"I really don't know what you're talking about, but I can tell you that whatever's going on between Suzanne and myself is going on because she asked for it."

Brandon took a step forward. "You son-of-a-bitch. Suzanne was an innocent until you appeared on the scene, and now—"

Logan rushed in before Brandon could voice his suspicions out loud. "Maybe Suzanne isn't as innocent as you believe."

"I should break your nose for that remark," Brandon said through gritted teeth, his hands clenching and unclenching at his sides. "And I would if we were somewhere else besides this damned wedding reception."

Logan shrugged. "You're right. This isn't the time or the place for this. And I'm not the one you should be talking to. Talk to Suzanne. She'll tell you I haven't forced her to do anything."

Logan watched as Brandon relaxed. He admired the man's control. "Don't worry, I'll talk to Suzanne. But not until I have all the facts." He turned and stalked away.

Logan wished he could call him back and explain everything to him, but it was too dangerous. He already suspected that his cover with Suzanne was tenuous enough in the community. Besides, it actually helped that he and Brandon were at odds; it added credibility to their story. Sighing inwardly, he watched as Brandon went up to Sheila Martin, took her by the elbow and propelled her onto the dance floor.

He didn't blame Brandon one bit. He'd have done the same thing if Suzanne were his cousin. She'd been a sweet innocent until he'd soiled her by agreeing to let her see the seamy side of life. He hated it that, once this was over, she would never again look on life in the same unspoiled way she had when he'd first met her.

He was disgusted with himself. Why should he care what he was exposing her to as long as they were going to catch the bad guys? This was business, pure and simple. Or was it? The feelings about Suzanne that kept sneaking up to zap him whenever he least expected them were far from business.

The trauma of his mother's betrayal had kept him insulated from real commitment for so long that the soft feelings he was experiencing for Suzanne terrified him. Could he risk himself for her? His protective instincts plus a deeper feeling—what was it?—were blazing where she was concerned. He needed to see her, drink in her subtle scent, hear her voice, touch her. He went in search of Suzanne.

He found her standing by the cake table, arranging some of the flowers along the border. Reaching around her, he stilled her hands and whispered into her ear. "Come dance with me." He fitted his body against her back and said, "People will think you don't like me, if you don't spend more time with me."

He felt her lean back into him for a minute, before she righted herself and turned around, still within the circle of his arms.

"You're the one that's been dashing off every time we're together," she said.

"Let me make up for it." He pulled her gently toward the tent, removed her hat, laid it on a table and then took her into his embrace. "Come on. It's a slow song."

Suzanne went into his arms as easily as spring flowers gave themselves to the morning sun.

Logan held her, breathing in the freshness that was Suzanne. He closed his eyes and let the music wrap itself around them, and for a minute he allowed himself to believe that they were just two people enjoying a wedding reception. He felt her hips sway with his and felt her fingertips curl into the hair at the nape of his neck. Her breath warmed his throat and he let the sensations of the moment engulf him as he fantasized... letting the dream that deliciously haunted him take shape.

He saw her standing in front of her mirror, shadowed, naked. He saw himself standing behind her, encircling her with his arms. He watched in the mirror as her eyes darkened and her lips parted when his hands weighed and massaged her breasts. He held her tighter. He was brought back to reality with Suzanne's soft sigh, and when he opened his eyes, he saw Brandon across the dance floor, glaring at him over the head of his partner. He loosened his hold on her.

Suzanne looked up at him, searching for an answer to his odd behavior. For a minute she'd felt his heat, had felt the way they melted into each other. But in the next instant, he'd backed away and was now looking over her head at nothing in particular. She wasn't so innocent she didn't recognize that he felt something for her. His touch was like fire, and his eyes had a hunger in them when he looked at her that she knew meant he desired her. What was wrong, then?

She knew what was wrong with her. She was confused. Every day that she spent with Logan only confirmed what her heart had been telling her—he was going to be hard to forget. But she had to. This was all a game to him and he would leave as soon as the case was over. She would go back to...what? To her life? She didn't even know what that meant anymore.

She noticed they'd stopped swaying and looked up at Logan. He smiled down at her. "The quartet's on a break." Taking her elbow, he shepherded her off the dance floor. He led her to the table with her hat on it, and sat down, pulling her onto his lap.

"Logan, have you lost your mind?" Suzanne pushed against him, trying to break away.

He held her firmly. "No. I'm just trying to give the gossips something to talk about."

A little voice in his brain whispered that he should stop this silliness, this delicious torment he was putting himself through by insisting on holding her so close. But a stronger voice, its source near the region of his heart, overruled the other. He was powerless around her. He wanted to run his fingers over the smoothness of her cheeks, drink in the shining glory of her copper-tipped hair, taste the wine of her lips.

She finally broke free. "We do that without little displays like this." Picking up her hat, she walked briskly away from him, finding herself in the middle of the crowd watching the bride and groom cut the cake. Suzanne stopped and watched as the bride put a piece of cake dripping with icing into her new husband's mouth. She smiled when the young missus rose on her tiptoe to lick the icing off the corner of the groom's mouth. The crowd broke into spontaneous applause, with a few hoots and hollers thrown in.

Just as Suzanne was about to inch closer to see the rest of the ceremony, she felt someone tugging on her skirt.

Thinking it was a small child, she glanced down, ready to pick the youngster up. Instead she looked straight into the eyes of old Mr. Brown's obnoxious, spoiled son, David. He sat, guarding a glass of bubbly liquid.

"David, what do you want?"

He leered at her. "I want you to come with me for a minute." He was still tugging on her skirt. His slurred voice told Suzanne he'd had way too much to drink. She gently disengaged his hand and backed away from him. He lurched after her and took her arm. He leaned closer to her and she could smell the alcohol on his breath.

"Don't think you're too good for me. I know about you and what you're into."

Suzanne glanced around to see if they were attracting a crowd. No one was paying any attention to them—yet.

She pulled him away from the crowd. "David, I think you'd better sit down."

He looked puzzled at her suggestion but followed her docilely. When they got to a table, he yanked her backward toward him.

She looked into his flushed face and a chill ran over her.

"No, I don't want to sit down. I want to show you something, and I can't do it here." David glanced around the yard. "You're going to love it. It's better than the stuff you've been getting from everyone else. I get the best stuff. This is hot."

Suzanne felt her heart accelerate. He wanted to show her dope. David. She looked quickly and found his father, in the crowd. She couldn't believe he would do this with Mr. Brown so close. Then she stopped and thought about her own relatives, who were also close by. What made her any different?

She was doing it for the right reasons, that was what. But David didn't know that. He thought she was just like him. She shuddered.

When he listed toward her and had to balance himself on her arm, she made a decision. She had to get away from everyone. They couldn't see what was happening here, and David was too drunk to realize that. She pulled him to the side of the house. Luckily the guests were all enjoying the dancing and the food. No one was nearby.

"Okay, David. What have you got?" She purposely made her voice sound bored.

"Before I show you, I want a kiss."

This guy was unbelievable, she thought, mentally shaking her head, just like a kid in his approach to women. She backed away, unwilling to play his game even to make a buy. "Forget it." She spun around to leave, but he grabbed her with amazing speed for one so inebriated.

"What's the matter? Think you're too good for me." He pushed his face within an inch of hers. She leaned back, sickened by his crude behavior. "I'm better than that college professor you're sleeping with."

It flickered across her mind that Logan's cover was working, but the pressure David was exerting on her arm brought her soberly back to her present predicament. She tried reasoning with him. "Let me go, David. You're drunk and out of control."

"Not that drunk." He moved to kiss her. She pushed against his chest.

"Stop it!" Suzanne bit out through clenched teeth. "If you don't let me go, I'm going to scream, and then everyone will know what you're doing."

David paused for a minute, but then he shoved her against the wall and sneered. "Go ahead, scream. Then they'll all know what you've been doing, too. I'll show them this." He backed away slightly to show her what he had in his inside pocket. Suzanne didn't take the time to look but tried to wrench away from him. He slammed her back against the wall. "Not yet. I want to see what that guy is all hot about over you. You must really be something in the sack. I'm not finished with you yet."

He mashed his body against hers, grinding his pelvis and closing in for a kiss. Suzanne strained away from him and was just getting ready to slam her foot down on his instep when he was yanked away and thrown into the fence. She looked up into Logan's furious face.

Before she could stop him, Logan had grabbed David by his shirtfront, pulling him to within one inch of his face. In a deadly calm tone, he said, "If I ever see you touch her again, for any reason, I'll—kill—you."

He then proceeded to hold David in this precarious position, giving him time to digest the message. Then, he gave him a little shake. "Understand?"

When he got no answer, he slammed him into the fence again. Frightened by the dark intensity radiating from Logan, Suzanne tried to intervene.

"Logan, he was just..."

He cut her a brief glance, then said, "Suzanne stay out of this, it's between him and me."

He refocused on David, pressing his knee into his unprotected groin. "I'll ask you one more time, do you understand?"

"God, yes," David squeaked. "Let me go, please."

Logan let him drop to the ground. David scrambled up and ran away, never looking back.

Logan turned to Suzanne, his usually impassive face alive with a maelstrom of conflicting emotions. Suzanne read fear, anger and... a softer feeling?

"Did he hurt you?"

"No." She took a deep breath. "How did you know where we were? Did anyone else see us?"

"I always know where you are. Besides, the guy in the truck alerted me that something wasn't right. And no, I don't think anyone else saw."

"He was trying to..."

"I saw what he was trying to do." A muscle ticked furiously in Logan's jaw.

"He wanted to sell me something. He told me it was better than what I'd been getting."

Logan frowned. "Did he?"

"No. You interrupted him." Suzanne, still somewhat shocked by the whole incident, frowned back at Logan. "I was about to kick him and get away when you interfered."

Logan gave her a hard look. "I can't believe it. I rescue you and you blame me."

"It's just so typical of you. You mistake a rescue for always trying to be in control." She warmed to her subject. "Logan, trust your training. If I can't get away from a joke like David, then you did a really poor job preparing me." By this time, Suzanne had worked herself into a snit. She put her hands on her hips. "Next time, let me handle it myself."

The rational part of Logan's brain warned him to back off, but the right side of his brain kept replaying what he'd seen. He hadn't been able to stand seeing David touch her. Logan was quiet for a moment, but then he leaned in, backing Suzanne against the wall much as David had earlier. His voice was slow, dangerous. "You're upset about what happened. I understand that, but don't take it out on me. I remember just how 'squirmy' you are and how you can handle everything."

"Don't patronize me," Suzanne snapped.

Logan gritted his teeth. "We're going to be noticed by our absence. Come on. It's almost time for the bride and groom to leave." He urged her forward, but Suzanne wouldn't be mollified. She jerked her arm out of his grasp.

"If you're so *smart*, then you should know that this will be good for our cover, Mr. Know-It-All-Policeman. People will just think we're back here kissing. We're lovers, remember?"

"If you don't come with me, it'll be more like me putting you over my knee." His voice was hard, filled with frustration.

"You wouldn't dare."

"Just stand there and see."

When Suzanne didn't budge, Logan took a step toward her. She shrieked and ran from him. Cursing, he watched her fly through the crowd, her dress a multicolored cloud. He started to follow her, but then stopped. He needed control before he got anywhere near her again. Suddenly, he laughed mirthlessly. Control. Yeah, right. His famed control was at a breaking point, and he wasn't sure he could rely on it much longer. But he had to.

He couldn't guarantee her safety if he didn't.

Chapter 11

Stony silence reigned as they drove back to Suzanne's cozy barn-house. The tension between the two was a palpable thing. It ate ravenously at Suzanne's already flagging spirit and brought a growl from Logan every time they brushed each other as he shifted gears.

At first Suzanne hadn't been able to stop from remembering Logan's behavior with David, fuming that he'd acted like a barbarian and a bully. She *could* handle herself without Logan's interference. Why, he'd shown himself to be exactly the kind of man she had always avoided.

But sometime during the short drive to the house the air in the Good Earth van began to change from that of angry silence to that of charged awareness. The metamorphosis came slowly but steadily. Suzanne felt the atmosphere crackling with a current as strong as the lightning bolt that had hit the tree in Gram's backyard. The emotions engulfing them were slowly transforming into a yearning, a desire, a need.

Logan turned into her driveway and stopped the van. Suzanne didn't wait for his help but scrambled out and practically ran to her front door. Logan was right behind her and followed her inside when she opened the door.

He slammed the door shut with his foot, causing Suzanne to jump. She turned to face him. "Logan, I don't think..."

He grabbed her and held her at arm's length, his sinewy forearms taut with his restraint. "Thinking has nothing to do with what's going on here." With that one movement, he again reminded her of a mountain lion—primal, electrifying, stalking its prey.

"I shouldn't be here," Logan said, his voice low. "Lord help me, but I wanted to explain what happened today. When I saw that bastard—that creep—David, touch you, something inside me snapped. I don't ever want to see another man touch you." He paused for what seemed endless seconds. "And I know I shouldn't be feeling that way, but I can't seem to stop myself."

Suzanne swayed toward him. Logan kept her away from him but moved his fingers up to her shoulders and then cupped her face in his hands. He smoothed his thumbs over her parted lips.

"Suzanne, honey, please listen to me." His golden eyes begged for her attention. "I'm very different from you. You believe there's good in everyone."

She sighed, and opened her mouth to speak. He stopped her with a finger to her lips. "I've learned not to believe in anyone. My life is sharp and hard and controlled. Yours is round and soft—God, you're so soft." He stroked her throat with the tips of his fingers.

Suzanne reached up and tenderly touched Logan's face. She leaned forward and kissed his eyes, his chin, his mouth. Logan stiffened under her gentle assault. Then he broke away.

"Stop," he said, his voice unrelenting. "God help me, I want you touching me," his eyes, dark with need, held her hypnotized, "everywhere—anywhere. But you need to understand that I've never been good at keeping a relationship going, so this isn't hearts, flowers and forever I'm offering. I know I should be out the door, but where you're concerned, I can't seem to control myself." Then he added huskily, "And that's a new emotion for me." He took her hand and brought it to his lips and kissed her palm, gently biting the pulse point at her wrist.

"If you touch me again, I won't be able to leave after a few kisses. If you touch me again, you're giving me this night to make you mine." He dropped his hands and backed away from her. He waited.

Oddly reassured by his whispered words, Suzanne didn't have to think. It took only one heartbeat for her to know what her decision would be. She had nothing to fear from Logan. He wasn't John Randolph, or Natalie's boyfriend. No, this was Logan and she'd been waiting a long time for this moment, hadn't she? Yes, she knew to the depth of her soul what her answer was, and had known since Logan had kissed her at the lightning tree. She drew a deep breath and moved into his arms.

She threaded her arms around his neck as he lifted her off the floor, bringing his searching, starving mouth on line with hers. As his lips crushed hers, she lost the capacity to breathe, to think, to do anything but revel in the hunger of his kiss.

She clung to him, wanting to feel his hardness, his warmth, along every inch of her body. Her fingertips kneaded the tops of his shoulders and a slight trembling in the muscles there told her he was holding himself in tight restraint. She moaned softly and he gathered her even closer to him.

Logan drew such a sweet, generous response from Suzanne's lips, he was overwhelmed. Along with the sweetness was a passion that threatened to rob him of rational thought. He focused on giving her pleasure, but found that the honeyed reply of her lips sent him ballooning into a sky filled with puffy clouds, blue skies and sunshine. He relished her gift, sending his tongue to linger and draw from Suzanne a passion so astounding he'd never forget this time, this place and her. He wanted to hold her forever, to shelter her from the rest of the world, to protect her . . . from him.

Finally, he drew back and she slipped down his torso. He groaned and closed his eyes as she slid down the length of his arousal. Unable to control himself, he gripped her hips and ground softness against hardness for a second before gently settling her on the floor. Placing his forehead against hers, he drew deep cleansing breaths of air as he tried to steady his careening world.

"Thank you," he breathed.

Suzanne leaned back to stare at him. She smiled shyly. "For what?"

"For that incredible, mind-blowing, hold-nothing-back kiss." He kissed her on the tip of her nose. "With that kiss, you showed me you really want me." He looked deeply into her eyes. "The way you're looking at me right now tells me you want me."

Suzanne eagerly studied his face. "If you liked it that much, let's do it again."

Logan chuckled. "In a minute. I need to get a little better control. You hold nothing back, and it makes me want to bury myself in you right here." He ran a hand through his hair.

Suzanne watched Logan with a mixture of puzzlement and concern in her eyes. "And that would be bad?"

"No, sweetheart, it wouldn't be bad, except I have no way to protect you. I didn't expect to be making love tonight, so . . ."

Suzanne interrupted him. "I don't understand."

Logan hesitated a moment, then, watching her face carefully, he asked, "You're a virgin, aren't you?"

Now she blushed a deep crimson, but held his gaze. "Yes, but I don't think it's a disease or a reason to shun me."

"You're right," Logan agreed. "It's quite an accomplishment in this crazy world we live in. To be honest, I expected it of you. It fits you perfectly."

"I'm not ashamed that I've waited this long. It's just that, before now, I've been . . ." She couldn't seem to finish her sentence under his steady, heated gaze. She hadn't told anyone about the incident with John Randolph, she'd been too ashamed.

Logan coaxed her on. "Suzanne?"

"Afraid," she blurted out.

Logan stilled. "Afraid? Of what?"

Suzanne closed her eyes briefly before beginning her story. "I almost became a statistic in college. I was probably thirty seconds from being raped . . . by a boy I was dating."

White-hot anger flamed through Logan, but he forced himself to appear calm, knowing that what Suzanne needed now was tenderness. He gently touched her cheek. "Sweetheart. I'm sorry."

Golden eyes, warm and sympathetic, bathed her with an unspoken assurance that whatever happened, Logan wouldn't hurt her. She wanted to thank him for his understanding. She also wanted a verbal assurance that her confession wouldn't matter.

Suzanne lowered her lashes. "Does what I've told you change tonight?"

Logan wished he could tell her yes, that he was going out the door, leaving her as innocent as when he walked in. It would be the right thing to do. But he'd known when he came inside tonight that they would become lovers. And nothing short of a bullet could stop him now. He pulled her into his arms and said, "No, it doesn't. If I was a decent person, I'd let you go safely to bed—without me." He pushed her hair away from her ear and told her softly, "But I can't."

Suzanne breathed a sigh of relief. "I'm glad."

"I'm just afraid of bumbling this and hurting you."

Now it was Suzanne's turn to search the depths of his eyes. "The only bumbling that will be going on tonight will be that of any bee in the area."

Logan smiled, but then sobered abruptly. "I want you to tell me if I do anything that scares you or reminds you of..."

Suzanne rushed to reassure him. "You could never do anything to—"

"Promise me," Logan demanded.

"I promise."

He leaned down until his lips were a mere fraction away from hers. The warmth of his breath misted her lips. Suzanne waited in anticipation. His earlier kiss had sent her world spinning crazily on its axis. What would this one be like? Would he teach her new and erotic secrets?

"Logan, kiss me. Please."

Logan groaned as his mouth came down to claim hers. He didn't know who was the expert and who the novice as each had their lessons to impart. He plunged his tongue into her velvet mouth and Suzanne responded with a naive passion that made his own flame burn higher, brighter.

He knew he should withdraw from her and go slower; he was rushing it already. But even as he tried to draw back, she melted into him. Rockets exploded in his groin. If this was insanity, lock him up.

He slid his hands down her back to cup her buttocks, half-lifting her and molding her to him, unconsciously beginning a rocking motion that threatened his control even as their mouths continued to mate, dance and play. Her responses, at once innocent and openly sensual, were more inflaming than the most skilled courtesan's.

Breathing heavily, he tore his mouth from hers and looked at her through half-closed eyes. "Feel me, Suzanne." He pressed into her so she could feel his arousal. "This is what you do to me with just a look, a kiss."

He kissed her again, slowly, languorously. The flame rose ever higher, its searing temperature threatening to shoot right out of them. Strong and sure, Logan's tongue pillaged her sweetness. And all the while he moved his hips against hers, making slow circles with his pelvis, letting her know just how much he desired her.

A tiny sound gurgled deep in Suzanne's throat, and she clung to him. When he finally lifted his head, a sound close to a sob escaped her red, thoroughly kissed lips. A trembling spasm shook her body, and Logan smiled at her heated, unguarded response.

With great care he set her feet on the floor and let one hand glide up to caress one of her breasts through the material of her dress. Fascinated, he watched as his fingers lifted and cradled the hot fullness. Through the fabric the tip knotted into silken hardness. Again, ripples of sensations swept through Suzanne's body.

"Suzanne," was all Logan could choke out before he took possession of her mouth again. His tongue stroked hers in an intoxicating rhythm of penetration and withdrawal. Against his chest, he could feel the lushness of her breasts, the rigidity of her nipples. Shifting slightly, he tortured them both by slowly rubbing his chest against the tips several times.

"Logan—" her voice was a fevered whisper "—what's happening to me, to us?"

He grinned down into her clear, green eyes. "We're teaching each other about loving and pleasuring. Do you like it?"

"Oh, yes, yes." She pulled his head down to join their lips once more and snuggled tightly against him. She felt the heat and strength of his manhood and was awed by the power of his desire.

"Ah, Suzanne, I need to be inside you. But, tonight, kissing is the only way I can do that."

He held her at arm's length, looking at all of her, from her breasts straining against her thin bodice, to the fluid lines of her hips and thighs accentuated by her flowing skirt. Something hot and animal-like burst free within him and he couldn't help it—he pulled her close again and proceeded to thoroughly ravage her mouth.

Suzanne could barely breathe, her world suddenly narrowed to this man, this place, this time. Her body strummed with sensations, making her feel as if she were spinning out of control. Her breasts, swollen and aching, felt as if they were on fire. Unconsciously, needing more, she moved her legs, expanding the juncture between them. His hot kisses continued to nourish the need within her, his gentle strokings inciting a riot of emotion that made her tremble with yearning. She was ready for the next step.

Clinging to him, she kneaded the corded muscles in his shoulder and ran her hand experimentally down the rough hairiness of his arms. He murmured dark erotic words as he rained kisses along her jawline.

A tiny voice whispered in Logan's ear that Suzanne was inexperienced and didn't know that he was teetering on the edge of control.

The same voice told him to stop before they were both sorry.

He chose to ignore the voice.

Suzanne had gone from sweet innocent to raging siren and was luring him into her. He wanted her with a frenzy that left him shaking.

He zeroed in on the pulse point at the base of her throat. Nibbling on her silken flesh, he shuddered. "I feel like a drowning man, Suzanne. You're pulling me deeper and deeper into a whirlpool."

"No, Logan. I'm throwing you a lifeline." She smiled dreamily. "Take it, Logan...please."

He smiled and bent to nuzzle her breasts through her clothing. When his mouth encircled one tight tip and pulled on it, Suzanne gasped and dug her fingers in his hair to draw him closer to the throbbing flesh. Even hindered by the fabric and bra, she felt the flick of his tongue, the pressure of his lips, the heat of his mouth. And she wanted more.

He looked at the wetness of the cotton fabric and chuckled.

"What's so funny?"

Logan caught the shyness, the hesitancy, to Suzanne's voice. "Nothing, sweetheart."

Reassured, Suzanne smiled at the old-fashioned endearment that she loved to hear him use.

"It's just that now that spot is wet on your dress, it's also transparent."

Suzanne glanced downward. He was right. The dusky center of her breast made a pebbly peak on the left side of her chest. Instead of blushing like Logan expected, she looked up at him through the veil of her lashes and said, "Well, I guess you'll just have to blow it dry."

Logan's brow quirked. "I'm supposed to be the teacher here, remember?" Gently he blew on the nipple, causing it to contract even more. Logan and Suzanne's eyes locked.

"Take me to bed, Logan. Now."

Wordlessly, he picked her up and carried her up the stairs to the loft, laying her tenderly on the great bed that dominated the room. Straightening, he studied her. She looked like something out of a painting, her natural beauty sprawled against the backdrop of the flower-bedecked comforter, rusty curls falling across her forehead, lips swollen from being thoroughly kissed.

"Logan."

His eyes slowly traveled back to her beautiful face. How could she not know how gorgeous she was? How could anyone not know?

"Undress me."

"Suzanne—" He cleared his throat. "I can't promise I'll stop if you're undressed. It might be too much." *I know it'll be too much. I'm already on the brink.*

"I trust you. You would never hurt me."

I wish that were true, Logan thought. But could he keep from taking all that she was so sweetly offering? He lowered his lashes. He didn't want to frighten her with the force of his desire.

He sat on the side of the bed and placed his hands along her throat. Gently he bent his head to hers and nibbled her lips as his fingers worked to unfasten her buttons. Finally he straightened and brushed the dress back, and she shifted to let the garment slip from her shoulders. Her lacy bra came next and then she was revealed to his appreciative gaze.

"Oh, but you're more beautiful than I remember, all cream and satin."

"Do you *really* think so?" she asked anxiously.

"Yes. I *really* know so."

Her smile was radiant and she lay back against the pillows, relaxed and sensual. Logan knew he should stop now, but he remained at her side, kept there by her trust and his need.

His hands, powerful and gentle, skimmed across the smoothness of her curves. She shuddered and arched, restless for more. Smiling inwardly, he slowly traced his way back to her breasts and kissed each peak. Then he skillfully squeezed the silken mounds together and ran his tongue back and forth, back and forth across them. Suzanne whimpered with pleasure and writhed against the plush coverlet.

"Do you like that?" He looked up at her. "I don't want to do anything that hurts you."

For an answer, she caught his hands and spread his fin gers, whisking the rough-textured surface against her nip ples. They stiffened.

"I want to teach you the ultimate pleasure," Logan whispered into her ear. "If you want me to stop, this may b your last chance." He nipped her earlobe.

Suzanne felt her world spin out of control. She anchore herself by reaching up to touch Logan. "I don't want yo to stop." She traced elaborate circles on his shirt. "Tell m how to help you."

Logan smiled wickedly. "This is one time you don't hav to do any nurturing. It's my turn to nurture you."

"Mmm, that sounds wonderful."

Buoyed even more by her faith in him, he twisted an quickly flung off her shoes. Bending, he licked a trail of fir up each instep. Then his hands glided up the silkiness of he legs.

"It's time I saw all of you."

"Yes, Logan, yes." Her voice was husky.

He kissed her lingeringly and only when he stopped di Suzanne realize he had skimmed her dress off and one of hi strong hands was lying possessively on her stomach. H leaned down and sipped from her navel, then nibbled dow to the tops of her panties.

Returning to her lips, he kissed her again as he slowly re moved the last barrier between them. Finally she was com pletely naked...and suddenly felt very vulnerable under hi heated stare. She shifted to cover herself but was stopped b his hands.

"Trust me, sweetheart. I won't do anything you don want me to. I just want to touch you. To taste you."

One of his hands nestled in the russet curls between he legs even as he spoke, and Suzanne was lost in a cloud o sensations.

He palmed her mound gently. She was already slick an humid and he increased the pressure of his hand as h rocked against her. She cried out, once, twice, three times and ground herself against his hand. He felt the tension break inside her, and he heard himself groan at her uninhibited response to his questing fingers.

When he sensed the wave of her passion had subsided, he whispered in her ear, "Open up for me, Suzanne. I want you to feel me inside you."

He dipped his tongue in her mouth and between her legs Suzanne felt the stroke of his finger. She gasped at the intrusion into virgin flesh, but the breath became a sigh as passion took over. Continuing his slow, erotic invasion of her mouth, he deliberately paced his caresses in an equally slow cadence timed to give her the utmost pleasure. He'd reverted to the primitive male. He wanted her to always remember he'd been the first man to please her.

As he increased his rhythm, he felt the magical waves shimmer through her. Releasing her lips, he took love bites out of her exposed throat and then suckled hungrily at a pouty breast. No longer shy, Suzanne arched her neck and called his name over and over. Delicately he raked his thumb across the heart of her passion, hidden amid the slick curls.

Quicker and quicker he moved, and the sweet tension ballooned within her. Sensing she was near the edge, he gently nipped her hardened nipple...and felt her come apart in his arms. Again and again, he felt the waves ripple through her body. She was like a fire out of control.

Carefully he drew her into his embrace. His own need made him shake as he held her and he cursed himself for getting carried away. Even now he breathed in her scent, he felt her warmth, and it was driving him crazy.

"I feel as though I've been struck by lightning, Suzanne." He closed his eyes and held her tighter. "I should never have joined you in that tree. It's done weird things to me. I feel as torn in two as that damn tree. I must be insane."

Suzanne looked up from where her head rested on his chest. "I was just thinking the same thing. A moment ago I did things I never realized I wanted to do with a man. But it wasn't crazy—it was wonderful."

"Don't ever believe you're not beautiful." He looked her deeply in the eyes. "You're beautiful in every way possible—body, mind and soul."

Suzanne smiled the dreamy smile of a satisfied woman. She looked down the length of Logan's body. The bulge behind the fly of his jeans was unmistakable. She glanced back at his face and noticed the tense lines around his mouth. She kissed him lightly on the lips.

"I may be beautiful, but I'm also selfish."

"Selfish?" Logan's brows drew together.

"Mmm..." Suzanne was busily sending her tongue skimming over Logan's bottom lip and then she shifted slightly to let it forage in his left ear.

"Uh...sweetheart." His voice was a harsh whisper. "Be careful what you're doing.... My control will only go so far."

She peeked at him from beneath her lashes. "And how far is that? This far?" She unfastened his top button and placed a kiss where his chest was exposed.

"Or this far?" The next button was dislodged and she repeated the process.

"No? Then, maybe this far?" she whispered and moved to open the next section of shirt.

"Suzanne, I'm warning you." But his threat was far from frightening, and the look in his eyes made heated promises.

She studied the way his belt and the waistband of his pants stopped further disrobing. "It looks as though we have a lot farther to go."

She scrambled up and quickly unlaced his shoes, sending them crashing to the floor. Then she swung back around and started unbuckling his belt. Logan's hands shot out and stilled her fingers.

"Be very sure of this, Suzanne. Very sure." His eyes were molten gold and his breathing was shallow.

"I've never been more sure of anything, Logan. I want to see you naked." She met his eyes squarely. "Does that shock you?"

He waited a minute before he answered. "I guess not, and it sure makes me happy."

In the end, he unfastened and unzipped and slid his trousers off, but left his briefs in place. Suzanne seemed happy with that situation for the moment.

"Does a man like to be touched in the same ways as a woman?" she asked.

He gritted his teeth. "Definitely."

She smoothed back the crisp hair around one of his nipples and gave it a tentative swipe with her tongue. Logan hissed his pleasure and so she applied more pressure. He couldn't control his groan of pure need.

"That's it, Suzanne. You have to stop." His voice was tinged with a desperate harshness.

She moved up his body and slowly ground her breasts against his. She felt her nipples harden again as they were abraded by his crisp chest hair, and she laughed. "I'm learning new things every minute."

Whispering into his mouth, "Logan, I want it all," she kissed him, losing herself in the heat of his immediate response.

His lips were hungry in their exploration as his hands glided over the silk of her back. Suzanne met each thrust of his tongue with an improvised movement of her own. She let her hands drift down the sides of his body and secretly gloried in the tremor that shook him.

"Come here and ride me for a while." Logan placed his hands around her waist and helped her straddle his body.

Unashamed, magnificent, Suzanne was overwhelmed by the fiery approval and wanton desire she read in Logan's eyes as they memorized the taut fullness of her breasts, slight rounding of her abdomen and lush richness of her rust-colored curls.

Logan rose, propping himself on his elbows and suckling her breasts. "Sweet Sue..." he murmured.

As he continued to manipulate one apricot crest, he felt her thighs tighten around him. Happy at her quick response to his touch, he mentally smiled and pulled her breast even farther into his mouth. Suzanne moaned.

Framing his face with her hands, she stilled his movements. "I want to give you pleasure."

"You already have."

Shaking her head, she scooted down to remove his briefs. Gently she reached out and touched him. Immediately he groaned.

She sat up straight, alarm written in her expression. "What is it? Did that hurt?"

He chuckled grimly. "No. It felt great."

"Oh." She smiled. "Then it's okay if I do it again?"

He just gave her a smoky look and she quickly decided that was a yes.

Delicately she traced the contour of his manliness. It seemed to her to represent life itself as it surged with power under her touch. Awesome, that overused adjective, seemed the best way she could describe it. Very awesome.

Fascinated, she bent down, kissing her way to the heat of him. Worshiping him, she reveled in the way Logan's body tensed and quivered. Looking up, she said huskily, "The male body is beautiful. I just never knew how much until right now."

"Suzanne, this is pure torture for me." He nodded toward his middle. "Right now I'm as dangerous as a .357 Magnum in a child's hands. And, sweetheart, the safety catch is off."

She lay atop him again, looking seriously into his golden gaze. "I said I wanted it all and I meant it."

The dam broke for him. He was going to regret this; it went beyond the bounds of being stupid. But he was consumed by the feel of Suzanne's lush breasts pressed against his chest and the way her sultry delta crushed against his straining arousal. Rational thinking was impossible.

In a heartbeat, Logan had reversed their positions. Now she reclined against the pillows and his hot nakedness was wedged between her thighs.

"Yes, this feels right," she whispered as, moving purely on instinct, she opened her thighs farther to feel more of Logan's length pressed against her.

"I can't hold back." Logan positioned himself and pressed gently into Suzanne's waiting body. Beads of perspiration dotted his forehead and upper lip as he tried to enter slowly, taking it inch by excruciating inch. *He mustn't hurt her.*

"More, Logan," she demanded. "I want more."

Her words and enthusiasm shredded what little remained of his control. Quickly, with a fluid lunge, he pierced the barrier of her innocence.

At the moment he stroked away her girlhood and swept her into womanhood, she called out his name. He stilled and lay breathing harshly against her ear.

"Logan?"

"Don't move."

She felt so good around him. No one else had ever fitted him so perfectly. As dangerous as his thoughts were, her slick, hot body incited him to finish what he'd begun.

Easily he withdrew. Frantically, Suzanne clutched his buttocks, urging him to continue. Mindlessly now, she uttered passionate phrases, fragmented sounds, all begging him, entreating him, not to stop.

He pressed into her again, withdrew, penetrated again, drew back. The walls of her body were quivering and clinging to his body, sending delicious sparks skittering like fireflies across his body.

Again and again he entered her and withdrew, each time thinking it would be his last. He had to stop before it was too late. But each time, his traitorous body plunged back to delight in the closeness, the heat, the softness that was Suzanne.

Suddenly she cried out his name again and pitched wildly beneath him at the same time he felt the wetness of her release. There were no reserves of control for Logan to find. He gave an agonized groan and thrust once, twice, then surged to fill her with his seed.

Afterward, they lay replete and sated in each other's arms. Suzanne's coppery head was curled on Logan's chest, her breath warm on him as she drifted into sleep.

Cooled down from his earlier passion, Logan cursed himself. Why had he let it get this far? He'd broken every rule he'd ever had. Now he'd taken *all* of her innocence. My God, what had he done?

The man in Logan wanted to stay, gather her to his heart and hold her until she awakened, then start loving her all over again. But even though he wished one night in Suzanne's arm could erase a lifetime of guarding his emotions, it couldn't. And the policeman in Logan knew he needed to get the hell out of there or risk blowing the entire case.

Quietly he eased Suzanne off him, dressed and left.

A persistent ringing brought Suzanne out of a deep, sensuous haze. She reached for the phone, at the same time realizing Logan wasn't in the bed.

Dragging the receiver to her ear, she murmured a distracted "Hello?"

"If you want that boyfriend of yours to stay in one piece, stop doing his dirty work—stay out of our business."

Click. Dial tone. It was a threat against Logan. Where was he?

"Logan?" Suzanne called as she eased the phone back into the cradle and sat up. When there was no answer, she knew he had left her without saying goodbye. The soreness in her body reminded her of the evening's events. She'd shared passion with him, her soul with him, and he...might have made her pregnant. She stopped breathing. His child, their child. Surely not on the first time. She exhaled and forced herself not to think about it right now. Her mind had to be clear about the immediate situation.

Logan had left her. She should have expected it. After all, he'd warned her that he couldn't give a promise of forever. But just one night wasn't too much to ask, was it?

Suzanne shuddered and faced harsh reality. She had to do something about the phone call. But she also had to do something about Logan. She could think of only one solution for both problems. It was time to get off the case. Not because she couldn't do it, but because staying meant endangering Logan. And that was something she would not do.

Chapter 12

Logan paced in front of Dan Rider's office. The early-morning call from Dan meant something had broken with the case. He guessed it was from their operatives in Colombia. When he'd poked his head in to say hello, Dan had told him to wait until Suzanne came and then they would talk.

Suzanne. Damn, he wasn't ready to see her again after last night. He didn't know if he could sit in a confined space with her near and not burst, literally and figuratively. He couldn't face her and see the hurt in her eyes—pain he had put there with his cowardice. He had hardly been able to face himself this morning, but he still knew there was no way he could have been there when she opened her eyes.

He would have been back inside her in an instant.

Even now he craved the sweetness, the softness of how she made him feel. He imagined her awakening, russet curls tousled, with a half smile on her face, reaching for him. He had to stop walking and wait for the bulge in his jeans to lessen. When he heard the click of a woman's heels, he turned around and watched as Suzanne walked toward him.

She was dressed much like she had been on their first meeting, in one of those outfits that made her look cool, like sweet ice cream on a hot summer day. She avoided looking at him and went straight to Dan's door and knocked. She opened it after he called out for her to come in. Logan followed, trying to decide if it was better this way. Her ignoring him. Hell, no, it wasn't better. It was hell on earth.

He sat down and waited for Dan to talk. He almost jumped out of his chair when Suzanne spoke.

"I want to officially resign from this case."

"What?" Logan said sharply.

She refused to answer him, but spoke directly to Dan. "I don't think I'm going to be able to help. In fact, I think I'm a hindrance. So, in the interest of the case, I'm withdrawing my voluntary services."

"Are you crazy? We're just about to make a deal." Logan looked over at Dan. "Talk to her. Tell her she can't withdraw."

"I've already talked to her. Early this morning when she called to tell me her decision."

Logan stopped and stared at Dan, and then he turned to look at Suzanne. She had called early this morning... when she'd awakened and he wasn't there. She was taking herself away from the case because of him and the fact they'd made love. Damn, he couldn't have screwed it up more if he'd had a script.

He swiveled in his chair until he faced Dan. "Look, Dan, let me talk to Suzanne in private. I think I might be able to straighten this out."

Dan looked at both of them, shook his head and directed his question to Suzanne. "Will you talk to him?"

"I don't have anything to say to him."

Dan sighed. "I want you to." He levered himself out of the chair and came out from behind his desk. "I'm going to catch up on some news down the hall. Come get me when you're finished." He looked pointedly at Logan. "And don't leave until I've talked to you."

After Dan had closed the door, Logan turned to Suzanne. "I'm sorry I wasn't there this morning."

Suzanne stared straight ahead. "That's okay."

"No, it's not." Logan clenched his teeth, frustrated by the profile of her face. "Could you please look at me?"

"No."

Logan stood up and walked in front of her and hunkered down. "Dammit, Suzanne, I need to see your eyes."

She averted her face. "Why?"

"Because all you're feeling is reflected in them, and I need to see them this morning." He cupped her chin gently in his hands. "Don't hide from me."

She lowered her lashes, but not before he saw the hurt, confused look and the wetness that spoke of tears. "Oh, sweetheart." He took her in his arms, but she stiffened and backed away.

"Don't touch me," Suzanne said, her voice quavering. "If this is what you wanted to talk about, we're finished." She tried to stand, but he wouldn't let her.

"This *is* what we have to talk about and I'm not going to let you leave until we do."

"You'd use force against me?"

Logan didn't move. "What do you think?"

Suzanne looked him fully in the face this time, her eyes brimming with unshed tears. "I don't know what to think."

"I know." Standing up, Logan pulled his chair over closer to hers. Once he sat down, they were knee to knee. "I don't know what to think, either."

"Why? Was it so bad that you couldn't stand to be around me? Was I so clumsy?"

Logan cursed under his breath. "Oh, baby, just the opposite. You were so good, I would've had you underneath me again in seconds. We would've exploded from the first kiss."

Suzanne looked at him innocently. "And you didn't want that?"

He shifted in his chair. "Hell, yes, I wanted that." Logan took a deep breath before he continued. "But . . . I was terrified."

"Of what?"

Of loving you totally—body and spirit—and then having you walk out when you've lost interest or I can't be what you want. Logan's thoughts settled like a rock in his heart, but he didn't voice them. Instead, he said, "Of you. Of me. Of how you made me feel. Suzanne, what happened last night was special . . . it was wonderful, but it should never have occurred, and it can't occur again."

He pushed his chair back and walked over to the window. Being this close to her was killing him. He wanted to take her into his arms and comfort her. But that would only make a complicated situation more complex.

"Look, I told you before we got started, that it wouldn't be flowers and rings and forever. Lord, I should've known you'd never be able to handle it." Even to himself that excuse sounded lame. And from all appearances, she was handling it fine. He was the one who was losing it.

"I understand."

He flinched at her hurt tone, knowing she really didn't have the faintest idea what was going on with him. Hell, *he* didn't know what was going on with him.

"Good. Then you can tell Dan we'll be back on the case again."

"No."

Logan turned to stare at her. "Suzanne, don't get stubborn about this."

"I'm not. I didn't quit the case because of last night. Well, I did. But it's not what you think."

Logan said stiffly, "I'm having a little trouble following you. Exactly why did you call Dan this morning and quit?

And, by the way, I'm the one who hired you. I'll be the one who fires you.''

"I got a call late last night."

"So?"

"The caller told me to stop doing your dirty work. That I could get you hurt if I didn't."

"Damn." The drug traffickers must not believe his story that he was a visiting professor and that he and Suzanne were having a relationship. Suddenly he remembered John Wells asking all those questions. Dammit, Suzanne's answers must not have convinced him.

On the other hand, this was a good sign. When threats like this started coming, a case was usually breaking. It meant they were getting too close. He felt his adrenaline start to flow. The negative part was that if they thought he was a phony, they would assume—hence their threat—that Suzanne was tied up with him. It wouldn't be long before they would add two and two and come up with a Magnum .44.

Which meant that if he and Suzanne were going to convince the traffickers that they were wrong, they would have to turn up the heat of their "public" romance and shore up their cover story. He cursed everyone and everything that had to do with this case. He was doing exactly what he'd predicted—hurting her in every way possible. He'd seduced her, and now he was going to continue to use her to close the net. He hated himself, but knew he really had no choice. More rode on this than his personal feelings for Suzanne. He would do everything possible to protect her from the danger, but he wouldn't take her away from it now. They needed her now more than ever before. Her next comment broke into his thoughts.

"So, you see, you were right all along. I was wrong for the job. How did you put it? Too sweet. Too pure." She dropped her gaze from his.

Logan paced the small confines of the office. "Oh, you were the right pick all right." He chewed the inside of his cheek. "And don't think I don't hate admitting it. What exactly did your caller say?"

"I just told you." She cocked her head to the side as if trying to remember something else. "The only thing that seemed strange to me was he was whispering."

"Whispering? Like he had a cold or something?"

"No. Like he didn't want anyone to hear him."

"When did he call?" Logan was focused on her face, piercing her with those predatory gold eyes.

"I don't know. He woke me from a deep sleep." She blushed. "I guess it was about midnight."

Logan noticed the blush and knew she'd been thinking about why she'd been in such a deep sleep. Determinedly ignoring her reaction, he continued with his speculations. "I'd only been gone for about fifteen minutes then."

"I don't know. I mean, I don't know when you left." She looked down at her hands. This time, Logan couldn't stop the wince at her embarrassment. Even after last night, she was still very much the innocent.

"It's almost as if someone was watching your place and they knew when I left."

"Logan, you're imagining things. Why would someone be watching my house?"

"To see who goes in and out." He turned to the door. "I'm going to get Dan. Don't leave."

"I'm not going to change my mind."

Logan stopped and said over his shoulder, "Just don't leave."

Suzanne got up after Logan left and expelled a great breath of air. It had been harder than she thought, seeing him again. When she'd been jarred awake by the telephone it had taken her a while to realize he wasn't there. Then, when she had, the ache she'd felt had almost killed her. She had felt so full, so cherished when he'd made love to her, but to wake to an empty bed . . . It was like jumping into a rapidly freezing lake and not being able to find a chink in the ice through which to escape.

This morning she had been a little surprised to see him here. Even though she'd tried not to, her blood had started running faster and her heart had beat louder the second her eyes had landed on his back. And when he'd spoken to her, she'd almost run for cover.

She twisted her hands together. She knew this emptiness would go away. In a million years if she was lucky. And until then, she had to keep focused, keep working, keep breathing.

She wanted to get Natalie's killers, but not if her being on the case would hurt Logan. She couldn't live with that. Her guilt over Natalie's death swamped her again. If only she hadn't given her sister the money. But she wouldn't take chances with Logan's life. She wouldn't do something stupid and endanger another person. Especially not Logan.

She turned when the door opened and saw the very serious face of Dan Rider before Logan followed him in.

"Logan tells me he's having trouble talking you into staying." Dan sat down behind his desk. He steepled his hands together and looked over the top at her.

"I told him I wouldn't reconsider."

"You may not have a choice."

"Why?"

"I have to ask you a few questions before I answer that one." He leaned forward. "Why didn't you tell me about the call you got last night?"

"Didn't I?"

Dan sighed. "No, you didn't mention he told you to stay away from Logan."

"Oh, well, I guess it didn't seem important." She glanced quickly at Logan. "Maybe I was a little embarrassed."

"About what?" Logan interceded.

"That you had been right all along." She turned to him. "It was in this very office where you enumerated all the reasons I shouldn't be on this case, and, unfortunately, you were right."

Dan looked at them both and shook his head. "I don't care who's right or wrong. What I *do* care about is this case. We are this close—" he held up two fingers about an inch apart "—to breaking this one."

"How can you be? I haven't bought that much yet. How could you have all the evidence you need? We don't even know who the main supplier is."

Dan glanced at Logan and shrugged his shoulders. "You've done fine and our other operatives have scored big since you've entered the picture."

"Other operatives?"

"We've got two other people hidden in Gruenville and they've been having a heyday."

She stared at first one man and then the other in disbelief. "But if you could do this without me, why did you let me get involved?"

"We couldn't do it without you." Dan sat back and smiled, looking like the cat who'd found a bowlful of cream. "As soon as you got started, our other operatives were able to break through another layer of couriers."

"What?"

"We think you broke the trust barrier for us. Everyone was focused on you, so our undercover people were able to gather a lot of dope, both literally and figuratively." Dan leaned forward, as if letting her in on a secret. "At bars and pool halls in Gruenville, pushers are telling your story. You're such an upstanding member of the community, everyone's been speculating why you'd do such a thing. Fortunately for us, their wild guesses also included the dropping of several names of other upright citizens who are dabbling in the stuff. Yes, our men in the field have been privy to some pretty juicy stuff as they told your story."

Suzanne whirled on Logan. "Why didn't you tell me this was going on?"

"Because it wasn't necessary. You were doing your job, and they were doing theirs. Besides, it's better you don't know the whole setup."

Suzanne closed her eyes against the pain. All of it—every last conversation, every touch—everything had been a lie. For the first time in her life she understood why people constructed shells around themselves and hid in them. She wished she had one now.

"You didn't trust me?"

"Good Lord, no," Logan exclaimed. "Suzanne, you're making this out to be something it's not. This is usual procedure in a case like this. Everyone except the people calling the shots are on a 'need to know' status."

Suzanne was not placated. "Then why didn't you explain that to me?"

"Because you didn't need to know." Logan threw up his hands in exasperation.

Dan Rider broke into the conversation. "Look, Suzanne, we were handling this with correct police procedure. Remember, you came to us asking to help. And you really helped. Leave it at that."

"You're right. I just wish I'd known."

Dan nodded his understanding. "But even that's not important anymore."

"Then what is important?"

"You staying on the job until we're finished," Dan said forcefully.

"Why? Simply find another sucker to pull in and finish the case off."

Dan glared at her. "We don't have time to find another 'sucker.' And besides, something is funny about that call. We think one of the kingpins may have figured out what was going on, and that was why they were watching your house."

"So?"

"That means you may be in some danger."

"Oh, come on. It's me. Sweet old Sue, the girl next door. No one would hurt me." She gave Logan a pointed look.

"That's what we thought. But we need to be careful about this. So I've made a decision." Logan, who'd been pacing throughout the entire conversation, now stopped directly in front of her.

Suzanne waited.

"I'm moving in with you. Today." His voice was hard.

Suzanne's eyes snapped with green flames. "You are flat out of your mind. You will *not* move into my house. I forbid it."

"You either do it or we take you into protective custody until we figure it out. And if we do that, we blow the whole case." Logan folded his arms across his chest and narrowed his eyes in a silent challenge.

Suzanne looked from Dan to Logan, trying to figure out if they would really jeopardize the entire case over her.

Logan knew it was time to really push. "I thought you wanted to help get Natalie's killers."

"I do." She remained quiet for several heartbeats. "And you would really jeopardize the whole thing for me?"

Logan looked at her and for a minute she saw the man of the night before. His eyes darkened and he stepped toward her. He checked himself and cleared his throat. "Yes, we would. You're more important. We could always rebuild the case. These creeps always come back."

Suzanne wanted to believe him. She needed to believe him. And she wanted to follow through with her New Year's resolution. "If you can't think of any other way, I guess it would be all right."

Logan breathed a sigh of relief. "Great. We'll pick up my things this afternoon."

Dan came from behind the desk and shook her hand. "Thanks, Suzanne. I know this isn't what you bargained for, but you'll be glad you did it when we round up those lowlifes."

"I hope so." She took one last look at Logan and left the office.

The first thing Logan asked when he dumped his duffel bag and computer by the front door was, "Are you okay?"

"I'm fine," Suzanne said, her voice flat, lifeless.

Logan surveyed the straight line of Suzanne's back. It was as if she'd changed from the girl in Dan's office to this apparition standing in front of him.

"You don't sound fine," he said.

She looked at him passively.

Logan swore. "Okay, I'll back off." He headed for the back door. "I've got to go to my office at the college to pick up some files. You can reach me there. I'll be back in an hour."

Suzanne watched him leave, then looked at his bag resting on her floor. He was actually here, in her house. It had only been about three hours since the decision had been made in Dan's office. And in that short span of time, her life had changed. She wished . . . she wished he were living here under different circumstances. And in her secret heart, she hoped that last night would happen again, no matter what Logan thought.

She'd gone into the kitchen to see if she had anything for dinner when she heard a car drive up. Thinking it was Logan back again, she looked out the window, but instead she saw Gram marching up her driveway. Suzanne met her just as the older woman walked in the door.

"I guess you didn't learn anything from Christine," Gram stated without preamble as she went straight into the kitchen and sat at the table. Before Suzanne could collect her thoughts, Gram continued. "You're letting him live here aren't you?"

"Gram, I . . ."

"Don't try lying to me."

Suzanne turned away so Gram couldn't see the blush she could feel spreading across her face.

Gram shook her head knowingly. "Make me some ice tea, and come outside with me. You always think better outside."

Suzanne did what Gram asked and found herself sitting on a bench by a stand of crepe myrtle.

"Now tell me why my most levelheaded grandchild is running around town asking for drugs."

Suzanne gasped. "Did Christine tell you that?"

"No. The man in the supermarket did, and the woman at the movie house and the paperboy. It's all over town."

"Oh my God."

"That's what I said the first time. The second time I just shrugged, and with the paperboy, I just told him to mind his own business."

Suzanne smiled as she imagined that scene. "Gram, I know I owe you an explanation—"

"Yes, and everyone else in this family." Gram took a sip of her tea and then folded her hands in her lap. "And I'm going to wait until I get one."

Suzanne looked into Gram's weathered face with its shrewd eyes and hoped that her story would hold. Not for an instant did she consider coming clean. And that scared her a little. Lying to her family had become easier. Or her need to protect Logan had become greater. Whichever, she took a deep breath and started.

"I know what I did looks bad."

"Listen young lady, I don't think *you* look bad, I think Logan is the one." She leaned toward Suzanne. "Don't get me wrong. When I first met him I really liked him. He's got a strength about him I appreciate. But this business with the drugs and now moving in here, that's too much. If he cared about you, he wouldn't jeopardize your reputation like this."

"Gram, Logan isn't forcing me to do anything."

"Then explain why this is going on."

"I love him, Gram." Suzanne nearly drew back in surprise at her own words. But now that they were out in the open, she went on. "Is that so hard to understand? I've fallen in love, and I want him here with me."

There was a silence after that, broken only by the sound of the evening song of a few birds. Suzanne felt lighter, more centered than she had during the past few weeks. The truth was out in the open. She loved Logan and she was glad he was here. At that moment, she vowed to enjoy the days they would have together. It was all she would have. And she'd be damned if she'd give it up.

Gram finally broke into her thoughts. "Suzanne, you've never been with a man before."

"No, I haven't. Does that make a difference? Is it all right for Christine to fall in love, for Natalie, for everyone except me?"

"Now, you know I didn't mean that."

Suzanne softened her tone. "I know. But I want you to trust me. I love Logan and I know everything will work out."

Suzanne watched Gram close her eyes, then, when she opened them, glance behind her. "What do you have to say about that?"

Suzanne whirled around and saw Logan there, one foot on the step, frozen in midmotion. He looked at Suzanne before he answered. "I think you should trust your grand-daughter." He came the rest of the way onto the deck and sat next to Suzanne.

"It's not Suzanne I don't trust, it's *you.*"

"Gram, don't."

Logan stopped her with a hand on her leg. "No, it's okay." He spoke to the older woman. "You heard Suzanne. We fell in love and decided to move in together. We want to test our relationship."

Gram stood. "I know I'm old, but I remember what being in love was like. But I can tell you one thing. This business doesn't sound, look *or* feel right to me." She walked down the steps. Logan and Suzanne followed. "I'm not satisfied—not one bit. But I do owe Suzanne my trust, so she's got it." She turned and pointed at Logan. "But let me tell you one thing. If you hurt her, you'll have to deal with me."

Logan looked her squarely in the eye. "Yes, ma'am, I understand."

Suzanne and Logan watched her drive off, then walked silently into the house. Their words hung between them like a string of firecrackers, just waiting to be set off.

Logan spoke first. "I know that was hard for you. Thank you for sticking to our story."

Suzanne smiled sadly. "It's my job, remember?"

"Suzanne, it's almost over."

She looked at Logan. "What if I don't want this part of it to be over?"

"It has to be over. My God, I just promised I wouldn't hurt you." He turned away. "And believe me, it would only hurt you."

Abruptly Logan stopped speaking. Memories of Suzanne's natural sensuality played through his body. She'd given herself to him, freely, with no constraints. He'd felt her pureness reach into his past, threatening to destroy all the barriers he'd erected to protect himself.

He wanted to run from what she offered but instead found himself rooted next to her, pleading with her not to coax him back into her arms. He had no defenses against her vulnerability.

"You don't understand," Logan continued, facing her once again. "I can't give you what you want, what you deserve."

Suzanne looked at him through a glimmer of tears. "Let me decide what I want, what I deserve." She reached for his

hands and then held them up to her face. "Let me decide t
love you while I can."

"No." Logan spoke harshly. "Don't give yourself to m
for a few days or weeks. Because that's all it would be. I'
accept responsibility for last night. Hell, I'll pay for it in m
dreams, in my nightmares, for the rest of my life. But I'll b
damned if I'll compound it by making love to you again."

"You're already damned," Suzanne whispered. "You'v
damned yourself to a life without real love, without laugh
ter, without sunshine. Don't do the same to me."

"Suzanne . . ." Logan was lured by the yearning in he
voice. Losing control, he pulled her into his arms and al
lowed her warmth to flow into him, around him.

Suzanne waited for his touch to go from comforting t
caressing. When it didn't, she sighed and stepped out of hi
embrace. "It's all right, Logan."

"No, it's not." His eyes radiated need. "This whole setu
isn't right, but it's what we've got. And we've got to try an
make it work. Please."

Suzanne's smile was bittersweet. "I'll do my best. But
want you to know I'm here if you want me. I'm willing t
take whatever you can give."

"Hell, Suzanne, how can you?" Logan's voice betraye
his anguish. "I've tried to be honest with you."

"Because I was telling Gram the truth when I told her
loved you." Suzanne had to turn away from the look of pai
that flashed through his eyes. "And since I've never been i
love before, this is the only way I know to handle it. Wit
honesty." Suzanne looked at him with her clear green eye
and something in him snapped.

"Honesty. *Honesty.* You want honesty?" Logan spok
through clenched teeth. "I'll *give* you some honesty."

He yanked her to him and kissed her with a ferocity tha
shattered her world. He devoured her mouth, feeding on he
warmth, her sweetness. After he felt her melt into his arms

he aligned her with his body so she could feel his arousal. He rocked against her.

"Feel that?" he whispered into her ear. "*That's* honesty. I want you like I've never wanted another woman in my life."

Silently she prayed that her love could turn his wanting into something more. But regardless, she needed him. "I'm yours."

Her words sent his professionalism flying out the window. All he could do now was try and gentle his actions so he wouldn't hurt her, because restraint and common sense and promises of denial were forgotten in the glow of her green eyes.

He lifted her as though she were a doll and carried her up to the loft, laying her on the coverlet. Quickly divesting himself of his clothes, he saw that she was doing the same thing.

"Suzanne, this is crazy," he whispered as he joined her on the bed.

"No, Logan, it's honest. It's what we both want."

His hands swirled across her satiny skin, titillating. His fingers were followed by hot, openmouthed kisses. Her fingers clenched in his hair as he dipped his head down to her breasts to make them achingly full of sweet sensations. He could hear her whimpering his name between breathless sighs as he kissed every inch of her skin. When he nipped love bites down her hip, she shuddered and cried out.

She was the sweetest wine he had ever drunk. Her reactions intoxicated him with their potency, and he dipped his tongue into the secret place between her thighs and sent her careening over the edge into sweet nothingness.

When she lay panting and spent, he slanted his mouth across hers again, sinking into her honeyed sweetness. Their bodies were sheened and slick with sweat. She closed her eyes and flowered under him, opening herself, inviting his maleness.

"No," he gasped. "Open your eyes, Suzanne. Look at me."

She focused on him.

"This is honest."

Hot and full, he glided into her. They kept their eyes locked even as the rhythm increased tempo. In the split second when they climaxed, she knew without a doubt that this man was her dream come true.

He knew without a doubt that he'd bought a ticket to a heavenly hell.

Chapter 13

"Miss Stewart? Miss Suzanne Stewart?"

The disembodied voice at the other end of the telephone line had a slight lisp on the sibilant sounds of her name. Suzanne smiled to herself as she thought of grammar school and the fun she and her friends had had thinking up tongue twisters with her name. "Yes, this is Suzanne."

"I've just bought the old Perkins place out on Freeman Road. I wondered if you could come by sometime this afternoon and look over the yard and make an estimate on completely overhauling the landscape?"

Suzanne glanced at her watch. Her stomach had been growling for thirty minutes, signaling it was past lunchtime. She usually let Sara take her lunch hour first, and the girl wasn't back yet.

"I'm afraid not. I'm really busy this afternoon." A great rumble from her abdomen punctuated her sentence. Logan had given her strict instructions not to go to any job site alone, but he was teaching a class this afternoon. "After lunch I'll be busy overseeing the unloading of a shipment of summer perennials we're expecting today. Could we set it up for sometime later in the week?''

"Today's it. My wife is moving down in a few weeks, and I want to surprise her. I'm off work today to see you."

The story of the gift to his wife worked on Suzanne's romantic nature, and she found herself leaning toward meeting with him. Logan would never know she'd gone since they'd hardly spoken to each other since he had moved in with her. After that one afternoon of lovemaking, Logan had become a monosyllabic roommate who went to great lengths not to touch her or in any other way show he cared about her.

Realizing she had left the man on the other end of the telephone line waiting for an answer, she gave him her decision. "Okay, I'll zip over during my lunch break. See you in a few minutes."

It was only after she hung up that she realized she hadn't gotten the man's name. "I will soon enough," she told herself out loud. Moving to the front of the store, she gave instructions to the returning Sara and asked for directions to the old Perkins place.

"If I'm not back by two this afternoon and the shipment of flowers gets in, tell them to start unloading in the spot at the back where we cleared out the spring annuals." She turned toward the door but halted abruptly and swung around. "Find Sweet Thing and make sure that skunk stays out of the way." She smiled, waved and was off.

After making a quick stop at a fast-food drive-through, Suzanne munched on the unhealthy but oh-so-tasty fare as she drove the van through the small town and out onto Freeman Road. The wind was blowing strongly and the sky was overcast and gloomy, so different from the usual bright, sunny days they had been having. A late spring storm was probably approaching, Suzanne surmised as she sought to keep the van headed squarely down the country road.

The forbidding skies reminded her of Logan's disposition. His temper was hair-trigger, and he spent as much time as possible outside in her yard working in the flower beds. He would usually come in late, take a shower and then collapse on her couch. He refused to even consider any other option. Dark circles were showing under his eyes, testifying to what she already knew—he wasn't sleeping well and neither was she.

Their public intimacy made their private time hell. He would kiss her and stroke her in front of people, but behind closed doors, he kept a tight rein on his emotions. She tried to tell herself she would eventually break through, that her love would reach him and he would come to her. But, so far, he had resisted every overture, adamant about her not becoming a living sacrifice for him. She told herself she could wait.

It was a lie.

He wasn't changing; in fact, she could feel him pulling away farther and farther every day.

Where was the Perkins place? Sara had said to follow the road about two miles and then turn left onto a gravel thoroughfare marked Perkins. Had she gone two miles? Just when she thought she'd missed the turn-off, the sign and road loomed in front of her.

The gravel lane was deeply rutted and weeds grew in its center. Suzanne slowed down and concentrated on keeping the van in the deep grooves. The trees that shrouded the road were whipping in the wind and scratching the top of her vehicle. Maybe the man she had spoken to would agree to let her send out some of the high school boys she employed for special projects, to let them trim the trees.

The road wound back farther and farther away from the main highway until she rounded a curve and had to pull up quickly. In front of her was a dilapidated fence and a house that was so in need of repairs that it listed to one side. A rusted screen door attached to the house by only its top hinge waved in the wind and banged against the house.

Something prickled along the fine hairs at the nape of Suzanne's neck. This house wasn't livable. Why would anyone be putting in landscaping?

Suddenly a man appeared at the door and motioned for her to come in. She got out of the van, pushed through the wind and found herself standing in a ramshackle living room. There was no furniture in the room except for a dusty potbellied stove in the center.

Suzanne swung around to stare questioningly at the man and had to clamp down on her bottom lip to stifle a gasp. He was short and wiry, but what made her want to cry out was the wild, crazy look in his blue eyes. In spite of herself she backed away from him. He smiled at that, showing to-bacco-stained teeth.

He stuck out his hand for her to shake and even though she had a courteous and friendly nature, Suzanne had to tell herself that he was a human being and nothing to be afraid of. She held out her hand. Just as he grabbed it, she smelled a combination of axle grease and gasoline on him. Fighting the urge to gag, she held her ground.

"Miss Stewart, thanks for coming out today. I was afraid this weather would keep you away."

He turned to look out the door at the bent trees and Suzanne sighed. He really wasn't so bad. He just didn't make a good first impression.

"Mr. . . ." She looked at him expectantly until he turned back to her.

"Jim. Just call me Jim."

She took a deep breath. He still had that wild-eyed look, but she'd plunge right on, she decided.

"Okay, Jim, this place needs a lot of work. I'm sur-prised you want to start with landscaping."

He moved toward her and she couldn't help it, she backed away from him. "Jim?"

He didn't stop but stalked her until she felt the rough boards of the wall at her back. He paused right in front of her, and she fought the urge to bolt out the door. His fetid smell permeated the room. When his hand touched her cheek, she jumped. Knocking his hand away, she started around him, headed for the door, but he quickly posted his arms on each side of her, blocking her path. She froze.

"Jim, this is silly. You're scaring me. I want to leave now, so put your arms down and let me pass." She tried to keep her voice calm and authoritative.

It didn't work.

He smiled and his eyes lit up with some inner glow that mocked her with its evilness. "Scaring you? That's good. I like to scare little girls."

"I'm not a little girl. Now let me pass." Her voice rose, filled with anger now.

"No, you're not a little girl." His eyes swept down the front of her body, and Suzanne grew sickened as his gaze settled on the curves of her breasts. She couldn't control her labored breathing, and he seemed fascinated by the heaving of her chest.

Suddenly she knew. She had to get away from him or die. With barely a conscious thought, she pushed hard against his torso and tried to rush past him. He had quick reflexes and was able to catch one of her arms and throw her back against the wall with amazing force. The back of Suzanne's head hit the old boards and she was stunned for a second. It was just long enough for him to cover her body with his, pinning her against the wall.

One of his legs insinuated itself between hers, and Suzanne felt him rub his thigh against the cleft between her legs.

Bile rose in her throat.

"You like that honey?"

"Look—" she began.

"No, *you* look." He interrupted her and his voice was razor sharp. "I've got a message to give you, but before I do, I mean to have me a little fun."

His hand came up and groped her breast, squeezing painfully.

Suzanne tried to think about her quick lessons in self-defense. Her brain was still fogged from the hit on her head, but she had to do something. Without warning, she bent her leg, trying to knee him in the groin. Because his leg was positioned between hers, the maneuver only half worked.

"You little bitch," he spat out. "I'll fix you."

He raised his hand and Suzanne ducked her head as she waited for the blow. When it didn't come, she looked back at him. The distant look in his eyes told her he didn't see her.

"I told him I wouldn't hurt you. I promised. I've got to keep my promise."

His eyes suddenly focused on her. "But I can leave my mark on you in other ways."

He smiled and those yellowed teeth repulsed her. She looked away. "I've heard you're real hot, especially with that professor. So I expect you to be hot for me, too." He leaned in, his lips right by her ear. "Be nice to me."

He ran his slimy lips down her neck. That was when she exploded with rage. She pitched him aside and sprinted for the door. And she might have made it but the screen door chose that instant to swing shut in the wind. Fighting with it took a precious second too long. She felt his presence behind her a moment before his fingers closed around her hair, and he jerked her back against him.

Tears of pain and humiliation stung her eyes as he ran his hands down her breasts, holding her back pinned against his front. Images of John Randolph, images she thought she'd buried, were instanteously resurrected. She struggled wildly, but he managed to hold her and finally picked her up and carried her into what at one time must have been the kitchen. A thin clothesline rope was sitting on the counter. Jim looped it around her body several times, pinning her arms at her sides.

When she couldn't move her arms at all, he pushed her down to the dusty floor, sitting on her legs while he tied her ankles together. That accomplished, he turned around and knelt beside her on the floor.

"Now," he whispered, "try to hurt me. I'm a lot smarter an you think I am."

Suzanne tried to control her breathing. She spoke slowly. Look, Jim, if you stop now, there's no harm done." Since e couldn't escape from this situation, she had to use her ain. Maybe logic would appeal to this crazy man. Common sense told her it wouldn't, but she had to try. "I'll for- t this ever happened. I won't press charges and no one will t hurt. *But you have to untie me and let me go.*"

"I promised I wouldn't hurt you."

He was running a finger up and down her cheekbone, and ain the smell of grease nauseated her. She took some deep, adying breaths. She'd glimpsed his hand before it had oved out of her eyesight, and under the nails and in the evices of his skin was grease. He must work as a me- anic somewhere. She knew she would have to remember many details as she could to have him apprehended later. *Logan!* her mind screamed. *Logan, I need you.*

"When I give a promise," Jim was saying, "I keep it."

"Who did you promise, Jim?"

His eyes half-closed and his finger stopped its circular ovement. "I'm not saying. You can't trick me into telling u something I shouldn't."

"Whoever set you up to this isn't going to get in any uble, but you're going to be in a mess, Jim, if you don't rn me loose right now."

"I don't like you thinking that you can scare me. You ed to be taught a lesson." He leaned down, grabbed the llar of her blouse and yanked. Buttons skittered on the oor.

"Stop!" Suzanne knew from the look on his face that he uldn't, but some survival instinct deep in her soul moti- ted her to keep talking. "Please stop."

The cord he'd wrapped around her arms stopped his on- ught after only two more buttons had popped off. With re fingers, he pushed her bra aside, freeing the tops of her le breasts to his hungry stare.

"Jim, stop now. Please!"

But he seemed in a trance and watched his own stain
hand reach out and cover her. She shivered, disgust maki
her want to retch.

"You're beautiful," he said, and then he pinched h
causing her to cry out.

Oblivious to her now, he just stared, fascinated, at h
exposed flesh. She didn't cry out again but lay quietly, b
ing her bottom lip as tears streamed from her eyes and r
down the sides of her face to flow into her hair.

Any minute now she just knew he would snap back to
ality and finish what he'd started. Afraid to move lest s
hasten that eventuality, she tried to detach herself from wk
was happening. She thought of Logan, of his gentle yet fie
kisses, his tender caresses and of the man himself. He h
taught her the things a man and a woman could share a
he had done so in a forceful, masculine way, but he h
never once hurt her.

The evil, hurtful things Jim would do to her soon had
relation to the things Logan had done to her. She had to
member that. But when she felt him move, his hand read
ing for her breast again, she couldn't help it. She screame

He put his lips next to her ear as he seemed to like to
and said softly, "Get out of the drug business. This is t
first and only warning you're going to get. Did you hear m
Get out of the drug business."

Suddenly his weight was off her.

Suzanne closed her eyes tightly and gave in to the te
that flowed. She cried and sobbed and was able to curl h
self into a fetal position.

She didn't know how long she let her emotions take ov
but when the torrent of tears began to ebb, she realized t
Jim was gone.

Cautiously she opened her eyes and looked around. S
was alone, at least for the moment. A wave of relief wash
over her. He had been sent by somebody to warn her aw

rom the drug business. She frowned. Who was behind all his? John Wells? Philip Jones?

She thought about Natalie. Her vow. She closed her eyes nd tried to focus on why she was here, to keep creeps like im from winning. Her inner world became clearer, calmer. t would take more than some creep pawing her to make her give up. In fact, her resolve deepened. She'd catch the whole own if she had to to get the person responsible for Natalie's death.

She wiggled around and managed to sit up. If she could ust get to her feet, she might be able to find something that vould cut the rope imprisoning her. Then she had to get out f this place. Jim might be coming back any minute.

She guessed she'd been here about an hour. Sara wouldn't tart getting worried about her for a while yet. So Suzanne vould just have to be resourceful and get herself out of this ness.

She managed to roll and scoot over to the cabinets and, sing them as a support, she worked her way up to a standng position. Her ankles were bound tightly and didn't leave ny room for her to maneuver. She'd just have to hop out o her van and see if there was something there to help get hese ropes off. But as she tried to hobble out, she lost her alance and went crashing to the floor. Her head hit the ard surface with a thwack, and her last thought before the lackness enveloped her was that Logan might miss her—a ttle.

"Suzanne! Dammit, where are you?"

Logan's voice. He sounded upset, angry. What had she one to make him angry?

"Sweetheart."

Strong arms lifting her. A solid chest supporting her. The teady beat of a heart reassuring her. That endearment cassing her.

"Logan?"

"Yes, it's me, sweetheart. Lord, I'm glad you're alive."

His hands were crushing her against him, but it felt good safe, sheltered.

"I can't move." She could see him then as he drew bac and fished a pocketknife out of his jeans. He looked scare to death and furious at the same time. What was the matte with him? her foggy brain wanted to know.

He slit through the ropes and pushed them away, cursin at the burns they left behind on her pale skin. It was the that he saw her torn blouse and exposed breasts. Framin her face with his hands, he ran his thumb across her lip "Did he hurt you, baby?"

Tears welled in her eyes at the tenderness in his voic "No."

"Thank God," he said as he reached to draw the tattere pieces of her blouse together. Ugly purple bruises caught h eye. He smoothed his hand across her breast.

"Logan, please," she said and tried to cover herself.

He gently but firmly pushed her hands away and contin ued his inspection. When he saw how bad the bruises wer an anguished cry broke from his lips. He looked at her, ar she saw his eyes darken and a muscle begin twitching in h jaw. She touched it with her finger.

He didn't say anything and neither did she, but he gath ered her up and carried her out to his Jeep. "I'll get som one to come with me tomorrow and get the van."

She nodded and they rode in silence back to her hous But she half lay across the seat, snuggled up to his warm because her body shook violently for most of the trip. Whe they got to her place, he carried her up the stairs and straig to her tiny bathroom.

Finally he broke the silence. "Did he rape you?"

"No."

"Strip off and take a hot bath." He faced her ai threaded his fingers through her russet curls as he looked her tenderly. "Do you need my help? I swear I'll only what you tell me to."

Her eyes brimmed with unshed tears and she smiled tremulously. "I need some privacy. I feel safe, though. I know you're here." And she did feel safe. Logan's calm, steady presence did more to wipe out the virulent memory of Jim and of John Randolph than years of therapy could have.

He kissed her softly and said, "I'll be waiting for you when you get out."

He left and closed the door. Suzanne drew a steaming bath and lay soaking in it for a long time. She examined the welts and bruises on her breasts and sudsed them countless times, hoping to erase the smell and feel and touch of Jim from her body forever. She went ahead and washed her hair, too. She had a small goose egg on the back of her head that was tender to the touch, but there was no blood from a gash.

When she was feeling clean again, she finally stepped from the tub, toweled off and slipped into her terry-cloth robe.

After running a comb through her short locks, she opened the door to face Logan.

He was hovering near the door, an endearingly frantic air about him.

"Here." He offered her a cup of hot liquid. "I knew you'd want some herbal tea."

Touched by his thoughtful gesture, she smiled at him. He looked worried. "Lie down on the bed. I have some first-aid cream in the Jeep. It's not much, but it'll help soothe your wounds."

Suzanne didn't consider the bruises wounds, but she crossed to the bed and sat down, sipping some of the steaming brew. It warmed her and made her feel better right away.

Logan returned with the salve and sat gingerly on the edge of the bed, as if he were afraid Suzanne would bolt. His next words confirmed that he was worried about her psychological state. "I figure you might want to talk to the police psychiatrist. She can help you work out what you've been through."

"That's probably a good idea."

He untied the belt of her robe and smoothed the lapels back. "Damn bastard." His eyes were bleak yet stormy as they studied the physical damage Jim had done to her.

With great care, he smoothed the soothing balm on her.

Funny, she thought, but she didn't feel the slightest fear of Logan even after what she'd just been through. She knew he would never hurt her. She also knew she loved him as deeply as a woman can love a man. If anyone else had found her and had tried to do what Logan was doing now, she'd have resisted. But his loving concern and gentle ministrations cleansed her soul of any lasting effects.

She looked up at his face and saw the raw pain etched there. She also saw the fury that he tried to keep banked deep in his eyes. She instinctively tried to defuse his anger.

"Logan, I really am all right. He just wanted to scare me, to warn me. That's what he said."

Logan shut his eyes and said a prayer thanking any and all gods that she was safe. When he'd learned she'd gone on a job alone, he'd been crazy with worry. He had immediately flashed to Carla and her hell-bent recklessness. His guilt had burned the entire trip to the old house. He told himself he was a bastard for using her and putting her in such danger. He'd known she'd never be able to deal with his world, to be distrustful of everyone. But when he'd found her alive, he'd known a relief so sweet he'd almost wept uncontrollably.

He folded her in his embrace then, hauling her up against him. "I thought you were dead, Suzanne. My heart was pounding out of my chest before I found you. If anything had happened to you, I'd have died, too. It would have been my fault."

Suzanne drew away from him, looking into his eyes. "Why?"

"Because I left you all alone, unprotected." Logan eased his forehead onto hers. "Hell, I've botched this entire operation. I'm just grateful you haven't suffered from my incompetence."

Suzanne smiled sadly. "Logan, don't punish yourself. *I* was the one who didn't follow orders. You told me not to leave. I did. I was stupid." Her voice dropped to a whisper. "Just like I was when I gave Natalie money and caused her death."

"What?" Logan cupped her face in his hands. "You caused Natalie's death?"

Suzanne jerked her head, but Logan held firm, making her meet his penetrating stare. "I gave her money, even after everyone told me I shouldn't."

At that instant, Logan understood everything. That was why Suzanne was willing to ruin her reputation, put her life on the line. *She blamed herself for Natalie's death.* Well maybe he couldn't give her the forever she craved, but he could make her see she hadn't killed her sister.

He stroked her hair with one hand, tucking a flyaway curl behind her ear. "Suzanne, Natalie *chose* to buy and take drugs. You had nothing to do with it."

"But I . . ."

He placed his finger over her lips. "You did nothing but love her."

"Maybe too much," Suzanne mumbled.

Logan shook his head. "You can never love someone too much." He kissed her gently on the lips.

"My father . . ." Suzanne's voice died away.

Logan tensed at the word *father.* "What about your father?"

"My father blames me for Natalie's death."

"What on earth would make you say something like that?"

"It's true. After Natalie died he didn't speak to me, and every now and then I would catch him staring at me with

sad, brooding eyes. He and my mother even moved away s
he wouldn't have to see me again.''

''Do you really believe that?'' Logan gave her a leve
look.

''Well, yes.'' The truth was Suzanne didn't know what t
believe anymore.

''Your father is Gram's son, right?''

''Yes.''

''And you really think a man she raised could blame hi
own child for something that just happened.''

''Well . . .''

Logan took her chin in one hand and forced her to loo
right at him. ''Have you and your dad talked this thin
out?'' he asked.

''No, we've never discussed it. I was too ashamed.''

''Tomorrow I want you to write him a long letter and ge
this thing out into the open. I bet he just has trouble ex
pressing his feelings and he doesn't want to lose you, too.'

''I don't know. I *could* have helped Nat—''

''Suzanne, let it go. You've already done more than any
one else would do. Believe me, I know about guilt. Listen t
me.''

''What do you mean, you 'know about guilt'?''

''I let a partner die on the job once.'' There—he'd said it

Suzanne's eyes were filled with compassion. ''You coul
never let a partner die. It must have just happened.''

They looked at each other, realizing they were giving th
same advice.

''You know, maybe you're right.'' Logan held her close
remembering how Carla had always refused to follow th
department rules. She'd been determined to do it on he
own. He'd tried everything, short of tying her up, to kee
her safe. Suzanne was right, he'd protected Carla as muc
as any human being could have.

''Maybe I should write to my dad.'' Suzanne looked int
Logan's golden eyes and found the forgiveness and unde
standing she sought. She waited for the guilt to swamp he

to erase the secure feelings, but it didn't come. Instead, she felt lighter, more whole than she had in a long time. She smiled uncertainly at Logan. "Oh, Logan, thank you."

Logan again folded her in his arms. "You're welcome." They stayed in each other's embrace for several warm, peaceful minutes. Then Suzanne leaned back.

"Maybe what happened to me is a mixed blessing." She loved the strong power of his arms around her, his chest uncompromising under her cheek.

"Even you couldn't believe that?" He stroked her back with circular motions, over and over again, almost as if he had to keep showing himself that she was breathing, that she was alive.

Suzanne raised her head and looked him straight in the eyes. "Without what happened today, you might never have given me the gift you just did."

"What are you talking about?"

"You just gave me a piece of yourself, Logan, and you gave it freely. You shared your emotions with me. You stepped out of your self-imposed emotional prison."

Logan frowned and looked away. This time *she* put her hand under his chin and gently turned *him* back to face her. "This is a breakthrough. The only other time you shared your feelings about anything personal with me was when you told me about Ryan. Don't turn away from your feelings again, Logan. The pain and worry you felt for me might have hurt, but they were honest feelings, so don't shut them out. Build on them."

His eyes searched her face; then he stood up. Suzanne watched him closely, afraid she'd pushed him to see things too quickly. She'd just been released from her guilt. She wanted to help him in the same way.

Instinctively she knew that only if he faced up to whatever, in his past, had scared him from emotional commitment, would he be able to build a solid future. She just hoped that future included her. Right now she wasn't so sure, but she was willing to take the chance.

He looked back at her, his tawny eyes bleak. "I was a total wreck when I thought you were dead."

"How did you know where I was?"

"I got a call from the bastard." She saw his body tense. "He said he'd hurt you bad and it would be even worse next time if I didn't leave you alone and get out of town." He studied her closely. "Would you recognize him again if you saw him, Suzanne?"

She shuddered "Yes, but I'm sure he doesn't live in Gruenville, because that would make it too easy. He does, however, speak with a lisp, and I think he may be a mechanic. He smelled like gasoline and grease and his hands were dirty."

"When I get my hands on him—"

Suzanne sprang from the couch and covered his lips with her fingers, silencing his vow. "I don't want you to stoop to his level. He's little more than an animal. And he was working for someone else. He repeated several times that he'd promised someone he wouldn't hurt me."

Logan cursed again and stroked her arms. "Nothing will hurt you again. *I* promise."

He drew her close again, and she willingly tucked her head under his chin and clung to him. Logan considered what she'd just been through. She was calmer than he was! And thank God she seemed strong enough not to have any lasting problems. When he'd gotten the phone call, his world had shifted crazily. He had known on some gut level that if she had been killed, he would have died, too. Just curled up and not seen another sunrise. She'd become that important to him.

The tears he'd felt inside after seeing her alive had been real. She was right. His father had taught him to lock his feelings away after his mother's betrayal. It was unhealthy and he knew it, but he'd never known how to dig them out. Even the love he thought he'd had for Debby when he married her had been an illusion. And Ryan—

He sighed. If he was honest, then he'd have to admit he was afraid of his son. He wanted to be the kind of father that could throw his arms around his child and tell him he loved him freely. But he was afraid he couldn't nurture him and make him a strong, sensitive man who could respond to love. So instead he'd let his ex-wife take over with Ryan.

But somehow this earth-shattering experience of nearly losing Suzanne had punctured a tiny hole in the dam that held back his emotions. With time and patience maybe the hole would grow larger and larger until he didn't have to hold back.

It dawned on him then, that maybe his mother hadn't betrayed him after all. Perhaps she hadn't known how to tell him she loved him, either. Just like he'd been unable to communicate his need to Debby and even to Ryan. He mentally shrugged, needing more time to sort out his memories. For now it was enough. Maybe he *could* respond with more honesty and emotion to the people around him. Maybe he could even sort out his feelings for Suzanne.

No.

No matter what his feelings, he was all wrong for her. He was too old, too world-worn to inflict himself on someone as fresh as Suzanne.

He'd felt her pain and her guilt when she'd told her story about Natalie. He'd made her see the truth. Why couldn't he admit the truth and let her go to protect her? He had to. He held Suzanne away from him.

"Don't ever do that again. I'm just learning to cope with one partner's death. I couldn't handle something happening to you."

"Logan, I . . ."

"Suzanne, today was the beginning of the end of this operation."

And the beginning of the end for us, he thought.

Chapter 14

Three days later Suzanne was sitting out on her patio recuperating in the early-morning sunshine. Bright rays filtered through her slatted deck roof, creating patterns on the table. An energetic hummingbird zoomed around a feeder she'd hung from the eaves of her house while several bees droned a steady whir in the nearby daylilies as they gathered nectar. In this peaceful setting Logan dominated her thinking. A future with him. A future without him.

Even though this setting was perfect for making wishes come true, right now Suzanne was facing reality. And the reality was that she loved Logan. She'd always known that not much would come of it, but that didn't keep her from fantasizing about what their life could be like together, the beautiful children they could have...

The jangling of the telephone brought her out of the daydream with a start. She jumped and hurried to answer it.

"Hello?"

"Suzanne."

Her heart leapt to hear Logan's deep, rich voice.

"Listen carefully." His voice was strained and excited all at once. "It's coming down this morning."

"Coming down, as in drug bust?" My God, she told herself. She'd known they were close, but she hadn't known they were this close.

"Yes, as in drug bust." There was a trace of humor in his voice.

"Where do you want me to meet you?" Suzanne was terrified of what was to come, but strangely happy, too, because she wanted these people who were stains on society to be put behind bars.

She heard a sigh on the other end of the line. "Suzanne, you can't be a part of the actual bust."

"What? You listen to me, Logan Davis—"

"No, *you* listen to *me*. Civilians are never allowed to go along on these things. Your next job will be identifying who sold to you and testifying at the trials. But you can't come along on the raid." His voice was firm, implacable.

"But I saw the newly elected mayor of one of the major cities in the country going on a drug raid, and *he's* a civilian."

"Yes, and he's also the mayor. That is highly unusual and just a ploy for publicity. This is deadly serious and you can't go."

Suzanne kept silent, knowing that he wasn't going to change his mind.

"What I want you to do now is to stay in your house. Don't go in to work. Just call Sara and tell her you won't be in at noon because you're not feeling well. Will you do that, Suzanne?"

"You never mentioned that I wouldn't be allowed to help make the arrests."

"It never came up, but this is standard police procedure. We want you safe until the deeds are done. Okay?"

It was Suzanne's turn to heave a sigh. "Okay."

"Suzanne, it's important you mean that. I can't do my job if I'm worrying about you. I have to know that you're safe."

"Logan, I'll stay here. I don't like it, but I will."

"Good girl," he said, and Suzanne thought he sounded more relieved than he should have, as if he wasn't so certain she'd cooperate. "I'll call or come by your place in a couple of hours, so stay put until I give you the all clear."

"Logan, be careful." She smiled grimly at the pleading note in her voice. She sounded like Miss Kitty telling Matt Dillon to watch his back as he went to face the Dalton gang.

"Always. Talk to you later."

The phone clicked and the dial tone hummed.

Suzanne stared at it for several seconds, wishing she were a part of the roundup team. Then she hung up and dialed Sara with her message. Why hadn't she asked Logan who was being rounded up? She knew the ones she'd bought drugs from, but she also knew who Logan and Dan really wanted in jail were the main suppliers—the people who made a living off others' weaknesses.

A disturbing thought sprang up. Throughout the whole process, she didn't think she'd ever come in contact with the main dealer. With nothing to do but wait, she began cutting the herbs growing in pots on her kitchen windowsill and setting them out to dry.

An hour or so later she heard the clanging of her doorbell and thinking it was Logan, went to answer it. Pulling open the door, she was surprised to see Mr. Brown standing on the threshold, his face a chalky white.

"Mr. Brown, what is it?" Suzanne closed the door behind the old man after he'd stumbled in.

"Heart pains."

Mr. Brown had never been to her home before, and Suzanne had no idea how he'd found out where she lived, but she knew she needed to get him medical help right away.

She rushed past him to get to the telephone, but the tone of his voice pulled her up short as she started to call for help.

"It's not the usual kind of pain."

Suzanne swung around and raised her eyebrows at his changed appearance. Now his face was a deep red.

"Not the usual kind of pain? What does that mean?" She was uneasy. Mr. Brown was not acting like the kindly old gentleman who visited her store regularly. Instead, he seemed in control yet distant.

"Children can break your heart. Remember that, Suzanne." He watched her with keen eyes.

"Does this have to do with David? Is he in trouble?" What had the little ingrate done now? she wondered.

"David always blamed me for his mother running off and leaving him alone with just me to guide him." Mr. Brown shoved one hand into the pocket of his khaki slacks.

"That's unfair of David and you know it, Mr. Brown." Suzanne wasn't sure what to do with the old man, but she replaced the phone in its cradle.

"Actually, it was my fault. I never made enough money to keep her happy. One day she just up and left and told me to keep David. He cramped her style."

"Well, that's her loss. Money isn't everything."

"Ah, but it is."

"Mr. Brown—"

"David wants money and all it can buy, too. I didn't want to lose him like I lost her." Mr. Brown ran his other hand through his hair, mussing it, giving him an even more disheveled appearance.

"If David wants money, then he needs to work for it." Suzanne was sickened by the leechlike relationship David had with his father.

"That's easy for you to say, but he's all I have left. I want him to be happy. And I was making good money. David had his fancy sports car, fine clothes and whatever else he wanted to buy. But you ruined it."

Suzanne's eyes widened. What was he talking about? "I have nothing to do with your family, Mr. Brown. I like you and enjoy the little visits we have at the shop when you bring your plant in, but that's as far as it's ever gone.''

''I enjoyed our visits, too.'' His eyes narrowed. ''But you've ruined all that.''

''You can always visit me.''

''No. The police won't let me.'' He lifted his hand from his pocket and a revolver gleamed in the morning light.

''Mr. Brown?'' Suzanne's voice was a mere whisper.

''The police came for me today. They want to put me in jail, and I can't get David his money if I'm in jail. He'll leave me just like his mother.''

He gestured with the gun and Suzanne shrank away.

''Why couldn't you just leave well enough alone? Why did you have to be such a little do-gooder? I tried to scare you off, but you wouldn't listen.'' He took a halting step toward her and she backed away again.

Suzanne's mind was racing. Mr. Brown was part of the drug ring and had somehow eluded the roundup of suspects. ''You sent that man to that deserted house to frighten me, didn't you?''

''Yes.'' He looked down for a moment. ''I'm not proud of that.'' He glanced anxiously at her. ''He didn't hurt you, did he? I told him not to hurt you.''

Under other circumstances Suzanne would have laughed at him being worried about her getting hurt while he waved a gun in her face, but she didn't. Mr. Brown wasn't making good sense, and his eyes had a wild, almost insane look in them.

''No, he didn't hurt me and you're not going to, either, are you, Mr. Brown?'' Maybe she could reason with him.

''You've gone to far, Suzanne.'' He shook his head sadly. ''You brought the police in on this. I've got to punish you.''

''No, I haven't brought in the—''

''Your boyfriend, Logan, was leading the police today. I was tipped off by a mole in the local police department just before the raid got to my house.''

"Logan?" Suzanne wondered if she could kick the gun out of Mr. Brown's hand without him squeezing off a shot. Thank goodness Logan had insisted on the self-defense classes.

"Yes. And you've destroyed the central pickup spot for the narcotics." He frowned at her and advanced another step.

"What are you talking about?" She wasn't aware of any central pickup spot.

"The Good Earth."

Suzanne's brows shot up.

"I'd get my supply from Austin, put it in the pot of one of my plants, set it up in your store and one of the dealers would take it out when you and Sara were in another part of the store."

Suzanne reeled as if she had already been shot. *The Good Earth had supplied the drugs for the town of Gruenville!*

What a fool she had been. She'd thought she was in control and helping rid her town of evil when all along *she'd* been the one sitting on top of the supply. "You're the main supplier, then?"

He nodded.

"You have willingly been selling drugs to the people of this community?"

"I didn't sell the drugs to anyone. I just supplied them to others who paid me well."

"John Wells. Is he a dealer?"

"Yes, but not a very good one. He scares too easily." Mr. Brown shook his head but kept the gun trained on her. "He was so suspicious of Logan. I told him not to quiz you about the man. It would just cast suspicion on him, and it did. He's probably under arrest by now."

"Mr. Brown—"

"Shut up."

His eyes glittered now with an unearthly light. Was it rage? Insanity?

"Your boyfriend killed whatever feelings David had for me just as surely as if he'd put a bullet through his head. Now I'm going to kill you, Suzanne."

At Suzanne's horrified gasp, his mouth twisted in a mocking smile. "You see, I believe in an eye for an eye and a tooth for a tooth. Logan Davis will pay for what he did to me and David."

Galvanized by the deadly look in Mr. Brown's eyes as well as his chilling words, Suzanne screamed and blindly kicked, hoping she had knocked the gun from his hand, then made a dash for the door. Unfortunately, Mr. Brown had dodged her foot and was already grabbing her arm as she rushed past. At the same time she heard the door crash open. She and Mr. Brown, his gun pointed at her temple, swung around to look down the barrel of Logan's pistol. Mr. Brown gathered her even closer to him, using her body as a shield.

"Drop your gun, Davis, or she dies."

"Now wait a minute, Brown."

Suzanne could practically see the wheels in Logan's brain turning as he tried to figure out how to get them out of this mess.

"No, *you* wait a minute. How did you know where to find me?"

"I didn't for sure." Logan's eyes were burning with their own light—but this light was as cool as it was deadly. "But when you slipped our net, I got a terrible feeling. Call it instinct or whatever. I knew I had to check on Suzanne. Your van's right outside and that could only spell trouble."

Suzanne felt rather than saw Mr. Brown nod. "I want you to suffer just like I'm going to suffer because of David. I can't let him see that I've gotten caught. I can't go to jail and leave him without anyone to help him."

Mr. Brown's hand on her arm was sweating profusely and Suzanne longed to escape. She went over a catalog of moves she could use to disengage herself, but none were faster than the gun pressing into her forehead.

"Seems to me David needs to be helping *you* at this point, not you still having to help him." As Logan continued to talk to Mr. Brown, he kept his revolver trained on the older man.

"He's a bit spoiled, but I made the mistake of not spoiling his mother, and she left me. I must take care of David so he'll love me."

"Is that right?" Logan looked straight at Suzanne as he spoke to Mr. Brown. "He should be ashamed at being such a squirmy character. He should faint at his behavior."

My goodness, she thought. He's telling me not to try and squirm out of this but to pretend to faint. Mr. Brown, thank God, was too far over the edge to clue into how strange Logan's words actually were. She looked at Logan and blinked rapidly several times, trying to communicate that she understood. Logan gave a barely perceptible nod.

She never thought her escapade into Gruenville's drug world would end like this. Guns and karate had been as foreign to her as Chinese, but now she had to gather her courage and try to help Logan and herself out of this thing alive.

"David's my only child." Mr. Brown's breathing was becoming labored. "He's—"

"Now," Logan shouted.

At almost the same time that Suzanne slumped violently and became a deadweight in Mr. Brown's arm, she twisted her head away. In a blur, she realized that Mr. Brown was swinging the gun crazily on Logan, who had gone down on his knees and was diving at him. And then Mr. Brown's gun exploded with a sickening finality...and Suzanne's world went suddenly black.

Whispers and beeps were the first sounds to pierce the silence as Suzanne opened her eyes. The room was semidark. It took her a few minutes to figure out she was in a hospital room and the whispers were coming from the hallway. Just as she was about to sit up, she heard a movement to her left. Logan appeared next to her.

He took her hand and gently pushed the hair off her forehead. "Ah, sweetheart. You scared us. The bullet barely grazed your head, but I guess you hit the floor pretty hard. It took you longer to wake up than the doctor thought it would."

"I have a doozy of a headache." Her voice was a croak so she swallowed several times.

"I'll bet." Logan smiled at her, but his eyes were bleak.

"Did you put everybody in jail?"

Logan frowned. "You can be sure Mr. Brown is locked up. Attempted murder's been added to his charges."

"Did you get John Wells? Mr. Brown said he was a dealer."

"Yes, but he's already out on bail. Hopefully we can get a guilty verdict when we go to court. We also picked up a fellow who's a mechanic in Austin. Mr. Brown had him shipped in to scare you away from the drug scene. The town was suspicious of me the entire time."

"Who else was involved?"

"Sheila Martin will have to get her nails done in jail for a while."

"Good." She closed her eyes.

"Hopefully, we'll get a conviction on her, too. She was the main supplier at the college. And she also helped keep a meth lab open by getting them the ingredients from the college. We raided the lab this morning and our agents took all the equipment and rounded up their main chemist, a Colombian."

"Oh, Logan." Suzanne opened her eyes, but the pain was still there. "Mr. Brown said there was an informant in the local police department. That's how he knew you were coming out to his house to arrest him."

He smiled tenderly down at her. "Thanks. We'll check it out right away."

"I think I can finally lay to rest the blame I've felt over Natalie's death."

"Then maybe this craziness and trauma has been worthwhile."

She nodded, but quickly stopped as the pain roiled behind her eyes. "Most definitely. I didn't tell you this, but I've written to my parents, asking them to come home on sabbatical this summer so my dad and I can really talk. I think you were right. He just has trouble expressing his feelings, but he doesn't blame me for Natalie's death."

"I *know* he doesn't and when the good people of Gruenville find out they've got a drug buster in their midst, they'll put you on an even higher pedestal than the one you were on before they thought you were dealing drugs."

She smiled. "And Gram and Christine and Brandon will be ever so thankful to find out exactly what I was doing. Brandon might even learn to like you."

He nodded. "I'm glad we can finally tell everyone the truth."

Silence crept between them as they wondered what *was* the truth. Not about the drug bust but about the two of them, their relationship.

Logan broke the quiet. "What you did was very brave. You helped us crack this case, *really* crack it. This is one of the cleanest busts we've had. It stretched out over three counties and down into Colombia. We got the man who sold Natalie the drugs, so you made good on your resolution. We've even managed to get the top man in this sick hierarchy of death."

"Mr. Brown wasn't the top man?"

"Brown was only the main distributor for this part of Texas—his key operatives, Wells and Martin. But we've tied him to Colombia through the man we arrested in the meth lab."

Logan stopped when he saw her wince. "What's the matter? Does your head hurt—should I get the nurse?"

Suzanne sighed. "No, it doesn't hurt." She turned her head away then and he had to lean over to hear what she was saying. "You were right, you know."

"About what?"

"About me living in a fantasy world, about me believing in people. I never had a clue about Mr. Brown. I saw him as a harmless old man."

"Suzanne, he had the whole town fooled."

"Yes, that's what we were. A town of fools." She looked at him. "But there'll be one less fool now."

"What are you talking about?"

"You've taught me well, Logan. I won't be taken in again. As soon as I get out of here, my new world view goes into place."

Suzanne struggled to sit up, even though her head ached unmercifully. Logan plumped the pillows behind her and she settled against them. "Gone is the Suzanne who believes in people and hopes for peace. In her place will be the realistic Suzanne who knows the world is full of deceit and treachery."

She held her hand out to Logan as if she wanted to shake on it. He took it, puzzled.

"Thank you for the new Suzanne, Logan."

Logan stood rooted to the floor, thunderstruck. She was thanking him for turning her into a cynical version of himself. My God, his worst fears were realized. He'd taken everything from her and given nothing in return. He couldn't let her do it.

"Suzanne, you've got it backward. Mr. Brown's the fool in this scenario. He let his fear of losing David drive him to betray you and this entire town." When she turned from him, he took her chin and made her look at him. "*I* should be thanking *you*. You've made me see the value in believing in people, the value in taking an emotional risk. Suzanne, you've changed me with your joy in the world. You brought real laughter back into my life."

Suzanne scoffed. "Logan, you sound like a commercial
or long-distance phone services. Stop lying. It won't work."

"I'm not lying." He searched for some way to convince
er. "I'm going to Seattle to see Debby about getting joint
ustody of Ryan. I'd never dared that until I met you. I was
fraid to make a commitment for fear I'd be even more a
ailure to him. But now I want to—I need to."

"You would've done that eventually." Suzanne smiled
idly. "I didn't do that. But I'm glad you're going."

"Suzanne, please listen to me." Logan wanted to drive the
louds from her green eyes.

"Will you stay in Gruenville?"

Logan increased the pressure on her chin for a moment
efore he let it go. He wanted to stay, but seeing Suzanne
ke this told him he couldn't. He was the one responsible for
er feeling lost and cynical. He was the one who'd brought
er to this grim point in life. Who knows how much more
amage he could cause if he stayed? He couldn't take the
hance of hurting her repeatedly. And he couldn't commit
o a forever because he'd never been successful in his life
ith personal closeness; yet that was what she deserved.

"I can't stay." He winced inwardly at the look in her eyes,
ut was careful not to show it. "My classes will be finished
two weeks and I'll be leaving after that."

He knew she needed healing time, knew instinctively that
ie would regain her optimistic self. But not if he stayed. He
ved her too much to destroy her, and he would destroy her
" he stayed. She deserved someone who could promise her
iagic. He could only promise her maybes. And maybes
eren't good enough, not for this woman, anyway.

Suzanne smiled wanly. "I'm going to spend some time
ith Gram, so you don't have to move out." She closed her
yes for a moment, then opened them and continued.
Please go, Logan. I want to rest now."

Logan slipped from her room and began to walk down the
erile, mint-green corridor that led to his world.

* * *

Three weeks later Logan was in Dan Rider's office. "I'r
not starting on another case right now. I need some down
time, so don't try to convince me."

"Protecting yourself." Dan leaned back in his chair. "I'r
sorry to hear that." He glanced out the window. "We'r
thinking of bringing in a civilian on this case. One with ex
perience."

Logan narrowed his eyes and said, "What did you say?

"You heard me. We're thinking about bringing in a civi
ian. As a matter of fact, you worked with her once—re
member Suzanne Stewart? She did such a good job—"

Logan almost leaped across the desk at his friend. "Don
you dare bring her into this seedy world again." He force
his fingers through his hair. "My God, it almost destroye
her the last time. I can't let you do this." He stopped his t
rade when he saw Rider's smile. "Why, you snake, what a
you trying to pull?" He moved toward the door. "On sec
ond thought, I don't want to know. I'm leaving."

"Go ahead," Rider admonished. "But how will you fee
when you lose that woman because you're still punishin
yourself for another civilian's death?"

Logan stopped in midstride and turned slowly back t
Dan. "You don't know what you're talking about."

"I know more than you think." Dan stood up. "I know
you two love each other, and I know Suzanne Stewart is rar
and well worth any risk." He walked around from behin
the desk. "You've told me before that you can't make a
emotional commitment to anything, but that's not true
You've done just that to your job, and Ryan, and you ca
to Suzanne, too. Didn't you get Debby to agree to let Ryar
fly down here for summers when he's a bit older?" H
grinned at Logan's frown. "I know I don't want you wind
ing up like me, an old, broken-down cop with no woman t
soften my old age." He clasped Logan's shoulders. "Tak
a chance on yourself, Logan."

Logan looked at his friend, but said nothing. After a few seconds, Rider backed away and shook his head. "Logan Davis, you're a fool."

Suzanne sat down on the lightning tree. How she loved this place. The sheltering branches of the tree never failed to make her feel safe, secure, confident in the world. Today was no different. The warmth of the morning was tempered by the canopy of shade offered by the flourishing vegetation. A mockingbird sang a lively solo while the fragrance of honeysuckle floated through the air.

This would be her last chance to relax here for a while. The preceding three weeks had helped restore her; she'd found her center again. She'd come to terms with what had happened, and now it was time to get on with life. There was a terrible ache in her heart, though. Had Logan ever really cared for her? Or had it all been an act, a way to make her a better actress? People had believed they were lovers. *She* had believed they were lovers. But he'd left when his job was finished. She'd been a fool to believe in dreams of forever. She had allowed herself to be used.

She lay down on her tree, closed her eyes and let her mind drift.

Logan found her like that, exactly like the first time he'd seen here there. A princess in her fairyland. He walked toward her but stopped when she opened her eyes to stare at him. She didn't move; she seemed to have stopped breathing. Then Logan noticed that secret, seductive smile she'd used on him before. It lured him to her side. He knelt on the ground and took her hands in his.

"Suzanne, I know you don't want to see me. I don't blame you. But I want you to listen to me."

She tilted her head and waited.

"I know I've given you no reason to trust me. I turned your world into something ugly, made you see the darkness in people. But I . . . I want a chance to change that."

She wasn't sure if her hearing was tuned in correctly to what he was saying, but it sounded like he was asking to come back into her life!

"I'll try to create the same miracle in you that you created in me," he continued. "I thought I couldn't give you a commitment, but these weeks have been hell. You own my heart and my soul."

Her weeks here at Gram's had only reinforced her love for Logan. He was her knight, her world. She had known that she'd never be totally happy without him but had accepted it. And now he'd just rung down the bulwark of his emotional fortress, the one that guarded his heart. Her heart slammed against her ribs and a fire leapt deep inside her. She put her finger over his lips. "Stop. You need to know something."

Logan took her finger away and rushed on. "Don't tell me I'm too late. I won't believe it. You taught me it's never too late. Suzanne..."

This time she kissed him to silence him. She kept her lips close to his. "Listen to me."

When he nodded his agreement, she sat up and pulled him onto the lightning tree with her. "You don't have to go on. I was hurt, yes, but sooner or later I'd have been on my way to Seattle. To convince you to come home."

Logan pulled her into his arms, but she gently pushed him away. "I need to say this."

"Okay."

"I'm not going to change, Logan. In fact, Mr. Brown's betrayal taught me something. It taught me to believe, *really* believe, that I'm the kind of person this world needs." She leaned in and brushed his lips with hers. "You taught me many things. But what I discovered here in the last three weeks is that I can't let others ruin my world."

"You've taught me some things, too. I never told you about my mother's death. She killed herself, and I'd always thought she betrayed me—abandoned me."

"Oh, Logan."

"Let me finish." He took a deep breath. "I've kept my emotions guarded since then—never letting anyone get inside me. But you made me see my life doesn't have to follow that pattern. I *can* commit myself to someone, to *you*, to our future."

Logan looked into her clear green eyes and saw her world of trust and hope, where dreams are real and become fulfilled. He took her in his arms and whispered into her ear, "I love you, Suzanne Stewart, and I want to marry you. I want you to be the mother of my children and a friend to my son, Ryan. Will you create a world of magic with me?"

"Oh, Logan, *yes*. We'll build a beautiful place of love and hope for our children. I love you."

They kissed, sealing their vow of love with a promise of forever.

* * * * *

HE'S AN

AMERICAN HERO

He's a cop, a fire fighter or even just a fearless drifter who gets the job done when ordinary men have given up. And you'll find one American Hero every month, only in Intimate Moments—created by some of your favorite authors. Look at what we've lined up for the last months of 1993:

October: GABLE'S LADY by Linda Turner—With a ranch to save and a teenage sister to protect, Gable Rawlings already has a handful of trouble...until hotheaded Josey O'Brian makes it an armful....

November: NIGHTSHADE by Nora Roberts—Murder and a runaway's disappearance force Colt Nightshade and Lt. Althea Grayson into an uneasy alliance....

December: LOST WARRIORS by Rachel Lee—With one war behind him, Medevac pilot Billy Joe Yuma still has the strength to fight off the affections of the one woman he can never have....

AMERICAN HEROES: Men who give all they've got for their country, their work—the women they love.

Take 4 bestselling love stories FREE

Plus get a FREE surprise gift!

INTIMATE MOMENTS
Silhouette®

If you enjoyed NIGHT SHIFT and NIGHT SHADOW by Nora Roberts, you'll be sure to enjoy this dramatic spin-off.

When the informant Colt Nightshade had been chatting to was shot, Colt hardly blinked—though he did wish he'd gotten more information. But when an overbearing, red-haired lady cop started giving him hell for interfering, Colt sat up and took notice. Lieutenant Althea Grayson wanted answers, but Mr. Nightshade had a few questions of his own to ask....

You first met Althea Grayson as Boyd Fletcher's partner in NIGHT SHIFT (IM #365). Now you can find out the secret lurking in Althea's past while getting your hands on the irresistibly charming Colt Nightshade in NIGHTSHADE (IM #529), available in November at your favorite retail outlet.

NIGHT

INTIMATE MOMENTS®
Silhouette

Southern Alberta—wide open ranching country
marked by rolling rangelands and rolling passions.
That's where the McCall family make their home.
You can meet Tanner, the first of the McCalls, in
BEYOND ALL REASON, (IM #536), the premiere book in

JUDITH DUNCAN's

WIDE
OPEN
SPACES

miniseries beginning in December 1993.

Scarred by a cruel childhood and narrow-minded
neighbors, Tanner McCall had resigned himself to a
lonely life on the Circle S Ranch. But when Kate Quinn,
a woman with two sons and a big secret, hired on,
Tanner discovered newfound needs and a woman
worthy of his trust.

In months to come, join more of the McCalls as
they search for love while working Alberta's
WIDE OPEN SPACES—only in
                    Silhouette Intimate Moments